SEE HOW THEY RUN . . .

The exchange of machine-gun fire built up in intensity, the choppy detonations echoing off in the desert sky. Brannigan ordered the vehicles to the west side of the defensive perimeter to find good fighting positions. Transmissions over the headsets came hot and heavy.

"This is Red One. I can count twenty of the bastards. Out."

"This is Green Three. They are starting to curve around our right flank. Out."

"This is Red Three. Same on our left. Out."

"This is Command One," Brannigan said. "Section leaders, spread your vehicles out to avoid letting the enemy outflank us. Out." Then he turned his attention to the DPVs out on watch. "Hey! You goddamn three blind mice, what're you doing out there? Sitting around with your heads up your asses?"

The first reply came from Mike Assad. "Command One, nobody's slipped through this position." Command Three and Green Two gave the same reports, the dismay evident in their voices even over the radios.

"Alright," Brannigan said. "Get your asses in here and come in shooting!"

SEALS
ROLLING THUNDER

JACK TERRAL

JOVE BOOKS, NEW YORK

THE BERKLEY PUBLISHING GROUP
Published by the Penguin Group
Penguin Group (USA) Inc.
375 Hudson Street, New York, New York 10014, USA

Penguin Group (Canada), 90 Eglinton Avenue East, Suite 700, Toronto, Ontario M4P 2Y3, Canada
(a division of Pearson Penguin Canada Inc.)
Penguin Books Ltd., 80 Strand, London WC2R 0RL, England
Penguin Group Ireland, 25 St. Stephen's Green, Dublin 2, Ireland (a division of Penguin Books Ltd.)
Penguin Group (Australia), 250 Camberwell Road, Camberwell, Victoria 3124, Australia
(a division of Pearson Australia Group Pty. Ltd.)
Penguin Books India Pvt. Ltd., 11 Community Centre, Panchsheel Park, New Delhi—110 017, India
Penguin Group (NZ), 67 Apollo Drive, Mairangi Bay, Auckland 1311, New Zealand
(a division of Pearson New Zealand Ltd.)
Penguin Books (South Africa) (Pty.) Ltd., 24 Sturdee Avenue, Rosebank, Johannesburg 2196,
South Africa

Penguin Books Ltd., Registered Offices: 80 Strand, London WC2R 0RL, England

This is a work of fiction. Names, characters, places, and incidents either are the product of the author's
imagination or are used fictitiously, and any resemblance to actual persons, living or dead, business
establishments, events, or locales is entirely coincidental. The publisher does not have any control over
and does not assume any responsibility for author or third-party websites or their content.

SEALS: ROLLING THUNDER

A Jove Book / published by arrangement with the author

PRINTING HISTORY
Jove mass-market edition / April 2007

Copyright © 2007 by The Berkley Publishing Group.
Cover illustration by Larry Rostant.
Cover design by George Long.
Text design by Kristin del Rosario.

ISBN: 978-0-515-14282-2

JOVE®
Jove Books are published by The Berkley Publishing Group,
a division of Penguin Group (USA) Inc.,
375 Hudson Street, New York, New York 10014.
JOVE is a registered trademark of Penguin Group (USA) Inc.
The "J" design is a trademark belonging to Penguin Group (USA) Inc.

PRINTED IN THE UNITED STATES OF AMERICA

10 9 8 7 6 5 4 3 2 1

This book is dedicated to

Sergeant Major Raul Garcia
U.S. Army Special Forces
Friend and Fellow Soldier

Special Acknowledgment to
Patrick E. Andrews
82nd Airborne Division and 12th Special Forces Group
(Airborne)

NOTE: Enlisted personnel in this book are identified by their ranks (petty officer third class, chief petty officer, master chief petty officer, etc.) rather than their ratings (boatswain's mate, yeoman, etc.) for clarification of status and position within the chain of command. However, when a man's rating is important in the story, he is identified by that designation.

TABLE OF ORGANIZATION
BRANNIGAN'S BRIGANDS

COMMAND SECTION

VEHICLE COMMAND ONE
(Over All Command)

Lieutenant William "Wild Bill" Brannigan
(Commander/Driver)

PO3C Guy Devereaux
(Gunner)

VEHICLE COMMAND TWO
(Reconnaissance)

PO2C Mikael "Mike" Assad
(Scout/Driver/Gunner)

PO2C David "Dave" Leibowitz
(Scout/Driver/Gunner)

VEHICLE COMMAND THREE
(Medical and Communications)

PO2C Francisco "Frank" Gomez
(Commo Chief/Driver/Gunner)

PO3C James "Doc" Bradley
(Hospital Corpsman/Driver/Gunner)

GREEN ASSAULT SECTION

COMBAT VEHICLE GREEN ONE

Lieutenant (JG) James "Jim" Cruiser
(Section Leader/Driver)

PO2C Bruno Puglisi
(Gunner)

COMBAT VEHICLE GREEN TWO

CPO Matthew "Matt" Gunnarson
(Assistant Section Leader/Driver)

PO3C Chadwick "Chad" Murchison
(Gunner)

COMBAT VEHICLE GREEN THREE

PO1C Michael "Connie" Concord
(Driver)

PO2C Garth Redhawk
(Gunner)

RED ASSAULT SECTION

COMBAT VEHICLE RED ONE

SCPO Buford Dawkins
(Section Leader/Driver)

PO2C Josef "Joe" Miskoski
(Gunner)

COMBAT VEHICLE RED TWO

PO1C Guttorm "Gutsy" Olson
(Assistant Section Leader/Driver)

PO3C Peter "Pete" Dawson
(Gunner)

COMBAT VEHICLE RED THREE

PO1C Michael "Milly" Mills
(Driver)

PO2C Andrei "Andy" Malachenko
(Gunner)

Military Maxims dictated by Napoleon Bonaparte as paraphrased by Petty Officer 2nd Class Bruno Puglisi of Brannigan's Brigands:

When you're writing an OPORD, you gotta take into consideration every single thing the enemy can pull on you. Then jot down what you got to do to screw up the rat bastards no matter what kind of crap they try.

CHAPTER 1

FOR the previous several weeks, Brannigan's Brigands had had most of the ship to themselves. Aside from the regular crew, the only other troops aboard were a collection of USMC Force Recon scheduled for deployment to Iraq to support a classified operation in the vicinity of the Syrian border. Additionally, a group of three Osprey helicopters, along with their pilots and crews, were more or less camping out while awaiting reassignment. Because of this dearth of population, the vessel's passageways practically rang hollow from the emptiness.

The SEAL detachment commander, Lieutenant William "Wild Bill" Brannigan, was short a couple of men himself. Petty Officer Arnie Bernardi had been deployed on TDy to an orientation program in Kuwait, while Petty Officer Raynauld Pecheur had to go home on emergency leave to take care of some family problems that resulted from the latest storm in Louisiana. That pair of absences left Brannigan a total of one officer and sixteen petty officers present for duty. All were now growing antsy after the long period of shipboard confinement.

The USS *Dan Daly*, LHX-1, was now a permanent assignment for the Brigands. She was the newest vessel in the United States Navy's amphibious assault inventory, having been designed and built in a concept so new and untried, the Navy couldn't decide whether to put an "A" for general purpose or a "D" for multipurpose on her designation. Thus, a temporary classification of "X" for test and evaluation was still being used even after several months of service.

The USS *Dan Daly*'s length was 390 feet, beam 55 feet, displacement 20,000 tons, and speed thirty knots. She boasted a floodable docking well that could accommodate one LCM-6 landing craft at a time—she carried a pair of these—and had parking space for eighty track and wheeled vehicles. The SEALs' ACV *Battlecraft* was also aboard, but was now only being given PM and taken out for short runs to keep her engine and transmission in tune.

The *Daly* was an aircraft carrier along with her other missions, but because of her petite configuration, she was not designed for fixed-wing takeoff and landing operations. However, her flight deck could accommodate up to a dozen troop-carrying helicopters.

The ship was aptly named after another pint-sized warrior, Gunnery Sergeant Dan Daly. The gunny had been a five-foot, six-inch-tall United States Marine dynamo who won two Medals of Honor. One was awarded in China during the Boxer Rebellion in 1900, and the other was pinned on his chest fifteen years later during counterinsurgency operations in Haiti. He was also known for his bravery in World War I when his unit faced an overwhelming number of Germans in the Battle of Belleau Wood. During a particularly hairy moment, he leaped to his feet and ran toward the enemy, shouting to his men, "Come on, you sons of bitches! Do you want to live forever?"

Evidently, none of them did seek immortality, because they gave lusty cheers and followed him into enemy fire.

FLIGHT DECK
1400 HOURS

THE volleyball game between the Brigand's two assault sections had been the usual violent encounter with elbows and fists being driven into bodies during the hot action close to the net. Normally, Brannigan, his 2IC Lieutenant Junior Grade Jim Cruiser, Senior Chief Petty Officer Buford Dawkins, and Chief Petty Officer Matt Gunnarson would have been among the participants in the bruising competition. But they had been summoned to a special briefing with Commander Tom Carey and Lieutenant Commander Ernest Berringer. Thus, while the rest of the detachment were doing their best to pound and pummel each other into defeat, their leaders were seated in air-conditioned comfort in the company of the staff officers.

Carey and Berringer were not stationed aboard the *Daly*. Although they shared office space on the ship, they were assigned to the USS *Combs*, an unobtrusive DDG that was a floating and very clandestine SPECOPS command post. She maintained almost total anonymity by sailing within the formations of carrier battle groups, seemingly employed on routine duties. Carey served as the N-3, while Berringer took care of the N-2 duties for all special operations that were launched from the *Daly*. Only a scant hour before, they had arrived from a mission briefing aboard the *Combs* that would affect Brannigan and his men.

Upon their landing aboard the *Daly*, Carey and Berringer had immediately sent instructions for the senior members of Brannigan's Brigands to report to their shipboard office. Carey, as soon as the four SEALs arrived, opened the meeting in his usual terse, businesslike style:

"You're going on an operation."

1430 HOURS

BRANNIGAN stepped out on the flight deck with Cruiser, Dawkins, and Gunnarson just behind him. The quartet surveyed the volleyball game, arriving at just the right moment to catch sight of Bruno Puglisi jumping up and hitting Joe Miskoski on top of the head with the edge of a closed fist. At that same exact instant, Miskoski slammed Puglisi in the midsection. Both collapsed to the deck, lying on their backs and staring up into the sky.

Mike Assad, about to serve the ball, yelled out, "Hey! You two guys get on your feet. Nobody called a ten-minute break that I know of."

Puglisi, the breath knocked out of him, managed to roll over on his stomach and get up on his hands and knees. "Uh . . . uh . . . glug . . ."

Miskoski was a bit more articulate. "I . . . got . . . headache . . ."

Senior Chief Petty Officer Buford Dawkins bellowed so loud, the chopper crews on the aft deck turned to look at him. "Secure the game! Up to the isolation area! Move it!"

The SEALs responded immediately. Assad, still holding the ball, headed for the island with his best buddy, Dave Leibowitz, at his side. Meanwhile, Garth Redhawk and Chad Murchison grabbed Puglisi under the arms and hauled him to his feet. Miskoski was as well served by Milly Mills and Pete Dawson. The group left the flight deck under the amused gazes of the officers and chief petty officers.

ISOLATION
1440 HOURS

"TINCH-*HUT!*"

SCPO Buford Dawkins' voice boomed across the compartment as he called the detachment to attention. Everyone immediately slid from their chairs, snapping-to and locking their heels. The two exceptions were Bruno Puglisi and Joe Miskoski. Puglisi, still breathing with some difficulty, slowly got to his feet, while Gutsy Olson grabbed the back of Miskoski's collar and hauled him to a standing position.

Brannigan led the way in, followed by Commanders Carey and Berringer with Jim Cruiser. The SEAL officers continued on to the back of the compartment while the staff officers remained at the front. Carey nodded a greeting to his audience, saying, "Take your seats." As soon as everyone was settled, he went directly into his spiel. "You are going into Afghanistan to participate in Operation Rolling Thunder. The mission statement is as follows: You will conduct security patrols utilizing DPVs in the OA." He paused a moment before continuing. "This is a cut-and-dried routine that is about as complicated as a kitchen match. Maybe even less so. In effect, you are there to 'show the flag,' as the old saying goes. Therefore, there will be no briefback. You are to fly from here to Station Bravo in Bahrain. I believe you launched your first operation from there as a brand-new platoon. You will board a C-One-Thirty at that location for a flight to Shelor Field just outside Kandahar."

Chief Matt Gunnarson raised his hand. "Will them DPVs be going with us, sir?"

"Negative, Chief," Carey replied. "There are nine of the vehicles already waiting for you. They were flown into Shelor three days ago."

"Excuse me, sir," Frank Gomez said. "You said we'd be doing security patrols in an operation called Rolling Thunder. Who else is gonna be in the OA with us?"

"You'll be by your lonesomes," Carey said.

"*Que huevos!*" Gomez said with a laugh. "Rolling Thunder makes it sound like the start of World War Three."

Carey was not amused. "I thought up the name myself."

"And a good name it is, sir," Gomez said. "Real *emprendedor* and *osado!*"

"I'm glad you approve, Petty Officer Gomez," Carey said dryly, not wanting to find out what the Spanish words meant. "To continue then. Your duties, as I said, are quite straightforward. You are going to patrol the area and nose around. There's not much going on, but an outside chance always exists that something interesting might happen."

Berringer added, "But not much of one."

"Commander Berringer is correct," Carey agreed. "But what the hell? It's better than sitting on your asses aboard the *Daly*. You'll be out and about, so to speak."

"How big is our OA, sir?" Doc Bradley asked.

"Approximately 140 by 275 miles," Carey answered. "It's a total of 38,500 square miles. Not really all that large for a motorized operation. Commander Berringer will give you all the details on the terrain." He shuffled through his notes. "Have you all had experience with DPVs?"

Mike Assad stood up. "Only me and Dave Leibowitz, sir. We went on an orientation and familiarization course at the China Lake Naval Weapons Center a little more'n a year ago."

"Okay," Carey said. He pulled some literature from his briefcase. "Here's some photos and data sheets on the vehicles. Pass these around." As the material was distributed through the detachment, he continued his discourse. "The DPV, i.e., desert patrol vehicle, is simply a very aggressive dune buggy, okay? It's one more piece of evidence that the SEALs will not be keeping one foot in the water as is traditional with past operations. They have two-wheel drive and because of their mission have a ground clearance of sixteen inches. Normally, they are manned by three men: a commander, driver, and gunner. But since you guys aren't exactly an armored brigade, Lieutenant Brannigan is going to have to reconfigure crew assignments."

Joe Miskoski's head had now cleared enough for him to ask, "How're they armed, sir?"

"You'll have a single M-Two fifty-caliber heavy machine gun mounted behind and above the front seats," Carey explained. "That's the gunner's position, from which the intrepid lad will fight the enemies of democracy and defend the American way of life."

"Mileage, sir?" Andy Malachenko asked.

"Ten miles to the gallon," Carey said. "The gas tanks hold twenty-one gallons, so you'll be able to go about two hundred ten miles per tankful. And here's some more data for you to digest. It has a wheelbase of one hundred fourteen inches, overall length of one hundred sixty-one inches, height of seventy-nine inches, and can manage a maximum grade of seventy-five degrees and a side grade of fifty degrees. Now hear this: She can go eighty miles an hour if you really have to haul ass."

"Mmm," Guy Devereaux mused. "It's nimble little thing, ain't it?"

"That it is," Carey said. "Now! I have a bit more interesting news for you. You won't be taking the CAR-15s you usually carry along. Instead, there will be a brand-new weapon waiting for each of you at Shelor Field. I'm not familiar with it now, except to say it's a state-of-the-art enhanced carbine designated the Heckler and Koch Four-Sixteen System. Or, as your crowd is going to call it, the HK-Four-Sixteen. Don't ask me any questions about it. I've never even seen one, but the Navy wants written evaluations on all aspects of the weapon's performance submitted by each and every man."

Brannigan, who had been scribbling in his notebook, waved his hand. "What about resupply, sir?"

"Ah, yes," Carey said. "You will need chow and gas, won't you? Everything you need will be at Shelor Field, so you'll have to time your patrols so that there will be enough fuel to get back. You'll fly in with a basic load, then additional goodies will arrive as needed. Both Commander Berringer and I will be aboard the USS *Combs* as usual. You can contact us if anything disturbing pops up." He put everything back into his briefcase. "So, with all that taken care of, I'll turn the meeting over to Commander Berringer."

The N-2 passed out maps of the OA as he spoke to the Brigands. "You are going to be operating in the area already mentioned by Commander Carey. The terrain is flat desert. The eastern limits will be approximately longitude sixty-five degrees east. That is the location of Shelor Field, but you'll be staying well west of there in order to perform effective patrols. But to avoid colliding with other operations, do not go east past that point."

Bruno Puglisi spoke up. "What if we're chasing some assholes?"

Brannigan interjected, "Then we'll keep chasing the bastards even if we go clear across the Asian continent."

"You will remain in Afghanistan," Berringer said. "The sight of mountains will make your northern extreme very obvious. To be safe, make your southern border latitude thirty degrees north. That will keep you well clear of Pakistan. The western edge of the OA will be an impenetrable salt-marsh area, so

Mother Nature will be putting the kibosh on any slapdash wandering around. That is located very close to the Iranian border. Needless to say, stay out of both Pakistan and Iran."

Joe Miskoski piped up. "Unless we're chasing somebody."

Berringer barked, "Don't cross those fucking international borders *period*, goddamn it!"

"Aye, sir!" Miskoski replied.

"The OA is populated by Pashtun people," Berringer continued. "You are very familiar with them from your first operation as a unit in Afghanistan. You know they are a bit cranky—pardon the understatement—so it will be up to Lieutenant Brannigan to establish the sort of rapport with them that the situation dictates."

"Understood, sir," Brannigan acknowledged. "What about opium production in the area?"

"That is indeed going on up in those mountains," Berringer said. "That is not your concern. As of now, we're leaving that problem to the Afghan government. However, there is a UNREO camp that has recently been established some twenty miles north of the Helmand River. They could be handy for information on the local situation."

"Hey, Murchison," Chief Matt Gunnarson called over. "Is that the same outfit your girlfriend is with?"

"Affirmative, Chief," Chad Murchison replied. "I received a letter from her a couple of weeks ago. They've moved down there from that warlord's compound."

"Haw!" Bruno Puglisi laughed. "Romance on the Afghan desert will bloom again."

Everyone chuckled, including Commanders Carey and Berringer, as Murchison slid down a bit in his chair with a red face.

Berringer looked around. "Any questions?"

Brannigan raised his hand. "I need to talk to the men."

Carey stood up. "In that case, Commander Berringer and I will take our leave. We will be aboard the USS *Combs* eagerly awaiting your radio traffic. Good luck, guys, and watch those international borders."

Brannigan went to the head of the room as the two staff officers departed. He had some scribbled notes in his hand.

"Okay. Here's the setup. We'll only have two guys in each vehicle. That means the commander is gonna have to also be the driver. The gunner will be concerned only with his weapon, which, you should recall, is an M-Two fifty-caliber heavy machine gun. The detachment will be broken down into three elements. Command Section, Green Assault Section, and Red Assault Section. I'll be in Command One vehicle with Devereaux. Command Two will be the scout car. That will be the Odd Couple Assad and Leibowitz as usual. Command Three will be Gomez as RTO and Doc Bradley in his usual function as our kindly hospital corpsman."

"What about call signs?" Gomez asked.

"The vehicle designations I've just given you will fill the bill," Brannigan answered. "By the way, everyone will be issued an AN/PRC-One-Twenty-Six radio with LASH headsets. These have a range of three kilometers and will be used for intradetachment yakkety-yakking. Gomez will also have an AN/PSC Shadowfire radio for commo with the *Combs* or any other longer range contacts."

"How are you setting up Green and Red Assault Sections, sir?" Jim Cruiser asked.

"You will be overall commander of the Greens," Brannigan answered. "You'll have Chief Gunnarson, Puglisi, Murchison, Redhawk, and Concord. Break 'em down any way that suits you between your three DPVs." He looked over at Dawkins. "The Reds are yours, Senior Chief. Take the remainder of the detachment and organize things the way you see fit."

"Aye, sir!" the senior chief responded.

"Well," Brannigan said, stuffing his notes into his pocket. "We got some packing to do. Take over, Senior Chief."

"On your feet and move out!"

CHAPTER 2

CAPTAIN Arsalaan Sikes stepped from the tent, pausing to look out over twenty fully armed Brazilian EE-3 Jararaca armored cars properly aligned in parade formation. The combat vehicles looked formidable and deadly in the early morning sun. Sikes was dressed in a desert-camouflage uniform that was bare of markings except for the British three-pip insignia of captain slipped over the epaulets. He sported a black-and-white-checkered keffiyeh on his head and a pistol belt holding a holstered Beretta Model 92 9-millimeter automatic. The crews of the vehicles, dressed similarly to Sikes, also sported UK insignia of rank. They stood dressed right and covered down beside the vehicles they served.

Sikes glanced over to the side where the Iranian brigadier and an elderly Englishman in a safari-style uniform stood ten meters away. They smiled and nodded to the captain as he walked toward them.

"*Sobh be-kheyr,*" Sikes said to the Iranian in Farsi.

"And good morning to you, Captain," Brigadier Shahruz Khohollah replied in English.

The Englishman held out his hand, speaking in a Cockney accent. "Good luck to you, Archie."

"Thank you, Harry," the captain replied in the broad speech of northern England. "Good job on getting ahold o' them EE-3s, hey?"

"I'll admit it took a bit o' doing," Harry Turpin replied. He was an international arms dealer operating out of Singapore and had contacts on every continent on earth. "But enough money and a bit o' tweaked paperwork gets the job done, don't it? Them Spick gen'rals worked their own bit o' magic to get them beauties out o' proving grounds in Camp Maior. This particular model ain't been released to the Brazilian Army yet."

Sikes looked out at the vehicles. "Wot'd you say that word Jararaca means in Portuguese?"

"Me Portuguese ain't wot it should be," Turpin said. "But as it was explained to me, it's a kind o' bad snake. A pit viper to be exact."

"Then it would be called an *afa* in Arabic."

"Ye're right about that, Archie me lad," Turpin said. "I recalls the word from me 'listment in the Foreign Legion. I picked up a bit o' the ol' Arabic lingo during them 'appy days so long ago."

Sikes turned his eyes to gaze appreciatively at the vehicles. "Blimey! Them's real beauties, they are!"

The EE-3 armored car, manufactured in Brazil, was a wheeled vehicle that was thirteen and a half feet long by a bit more than five feet in height. It was highly maneuverable with a fully closable hull manufactured of a double layer of three-quarter-inch steel. The fighting wagon was powered by a 120-horsepower Mercedes-Benz 4-cylinder turbo diesel engine that could push it up to a top speed of sixty miles an hour.

A crew of three served the EE-3. The driver entered through

a hatch in the roof to his seat in the center of the chassis. The gunner was in the turret above and behind him. In these specially configured models, a Russian DShK 12.7-millimeter heavy machine gun—aka Dashika—was mounted on top of the turret. The commander sat to the driver's left. He had his own periscope for use when the hatches were closed and a Russian R-108 tactical radio for commo. Additionally, each of the EE-3s packed an RPG-7 antitank launcher with a dozen projectiles, as well as an American Stinger antiaircraft missile. These were stowed as auxiliary weapons.

The twenty that were now positioned fifty meters from the garrison Quonset huts had arrived through Harry Turpin's efforts. He had legally purchased the vehicles from the Brazilian government using his international weapons export license. But he still had had to grease some palms since the vehicles should have been turned over to regular armored infantry units. When Turpin presented his money for the deal, he showed an end-use certificate that was signed by officials of the Iranian Defense Ministry. The fact that it was genuine impressed the Brazilians, who were shipping them as cargo to an official military warehouse located on the docks in the port city of Bandar-e Abbas. What they didn't know was that Brigadier Khohollah, the receiving officer, was in the Iranian Special Forces. His assignment was the command of a Muslim insurgency group known as Jihad Abadi—Eternal Holy War. However, the mujahideen in the organization were not Iranians. Instead, they were Arabs from several different countries who had been recruited by Iranian intelligence as part of a supersecret program to take over all insurgencies in the Middle East.

The operation was so clandestine that Khohollah had to keep the vehicles out of the army's established intendance system, unlisted and unnoticed. It took him three months of easing them out on commercial transport trucks a few at a time to get them to Chehaar Garrison, where they sat that day.

Captain Arsalaan Sikes's fast-assault company was a brand-new unit of Jihad Abadi. He and his troops were just beginning a campaign out of eastern Iran. The military post, twenty-five kilometers from the Afghan border on the east, was locked in by a near-impassible salt marsh. However, a well-camouflaged solid road had been built through the marshes that offered a way through the treacherous terrain. The Jihad Abadi, under the command and control of Iranian Special Forces, was now ready to conduct a campaign of harassment and intimidation against the infidel invaders of Afghanistan by making surprise attacks out of Iran. Through the use of the secret route, they would be able to strike fast and hard, then retreat back through the salt marshes to the safety of Chehaar Garrison.

Now Captain Sikes shook hands with Turpin and Khohol-lah, then turned to his troops, ordering them inside their vehicles. He walked to his own EE-3 and climbed on top to slip through the hatch and occupy the commander's seat. As soon as he was settled, he grabbed the microphone of his tactical radio. He pressed the transmit button and spoke out the call sign to alert the other nineteen vehicles. *"Ilhakni min karib—*follow at close intervals!"

The convoy quickly formed into a column as he led them toward the road that would carry them through the marshes and into Afghanistan.

IT had been ten years before when Archibald Sikes arrived at the induction depot of the crack Royal Regiment of Dragoons at Ragland Barracks just outside London. Even though he still had that adolescent civilian awkwardness about him, one of the drill sergeants who had been giving the detachment of recruits a critical survey suddenly sighted Archibald. The NCO leaned over to the duty corporal and said, "Now there's a lad that's keen as bluddy mustard."

The sergeant didn't know the half of it.

Archie came from a working-class family—his father was employed in a building materials warehouse as a stockman—and the boy had always hoped for a better life. He disliked school a great deal, being unable to get along with the teachers or his fellow students, who considered him an "odd duck." He had ambitions for money and glory, but lacked the maturity to attain his goals through acquiring superior work skills or an advanced education. Through his illogical and senseless thought processes, he decided that becoming a war hero would be the way to go. He fantasized about leading a division or corps of troops to a great victory, then becoming famous and adored by the British public. Of course, after performing these great deeds, he would be decorated, knighted, and given a peerage and a great estate by a grateful monarch.

Archie used to sit at his desk in the classroom, completely oblivious to what the teacher was saying, writing over and over in his notebook: *Field Marshal Lord Archibald Sikes, VC, DSO, GCB, GCMG.* He would have added more to that abbreviated list of the Victoria Cross, Distinguished Service Order, Knight Grand Cross of the Order of the Bath, and Knight Grand Cross of the Order of Saint Michael and Saint George, but those were the only ones he knew about.

Eventually, as his inattentive moments lengthened in time and frequency, Archie flunked out of school completely, and his exasperated father got him a job as a helper in the warehouse. The young man endured that existence with the same amount of carelessness he had given his studies, and he proved to be a slow, inefficient worker. If it hadn't been for his dad, he would have been given the sack straightaway. When he turned eighteen, he did everybody a favor by announcing his plans to enlist in the Army.

The decision of which regiment to join was something that Archie had already given a great deal of care and attention. In the end, he chose the Royal Regiment of Dragoons for some surprisingly intelligent and mature reasons, and not because of their bearskin busbies and fancy blue uniforms with red facings. While the unit was not a member of the Brigade of Guards, it was a prestigious organization with a long and glorious history in the service of the Empire. The officer cadre were all upper-crust chaps from the right families who could supplement their Army pay to meet the considerable expenses of serving as rankers. These included their privately owned mounts in the regimental stables for polo, individually tailored and fitted uniforms, very high mess dues, correct costly civilian attire, special subscriptions, mandatory social functions, and other outlays required of officers and gentlemen of the Royal Regiment of Dragoons.

Rather than operate as a tank outfit like other cavalry units in the British Army, the regiment closely followed the traditional mission of dragoons, who in bygone days were horsemen who dismounted to do battle. However, in these modern days, armored personnel carriers were used in lieu of mounts. These state-of-the-art dragoons, in fact, were armored infantrymen superbly drilled in the procedures of dismounting APCs to launch well-coordinated attacks against the enemy. These operations were performed while being covered by fusillades from machine guns mounted in turrets on the vehicles.

This was the military environment that Private Archibald Sikes moved into as he began his Army career. And his military goal was to earn an officer's commission in the regiment and eventually become its commander before moving upward into the cadre of general officers to the rank of field marshal.

As it turned out, the daydreaming misfit quickly evolved into a dedicated soldier. Although he developed no close friendships with his fellow dragoons, Archie impressed his superiors enough to earn his way up through the ranks. After five years of service he was a sergeant, efficiently bossing a platoon under the command of an appreciative lieutenant. In fact, it was this approving subaltern who happily signed Archie's application for admittance to officer training.

Unfortunately, this was where Archie's devotion to the Royal Regiment of Dragoons went into the toilet.

When he went before the commissioning board of officers, the aspirant's record was looked on with great approval. His verbal skills in the question-and-answer part of the interview increased the board's collective opinion. After the session went on for a couple of hours, the officers withdrew to consider the application.

Meanwhile, Archie went outside for a smoke, nervous and apprehensive. When the corporal-clerk called him back in, the candidate went back to his chair. A quick look at the faces of the board members showed he had scored big. He fought back a triumphant grin as the chairman, a major who commanded one of the companies of another squadron, looked Archie straight in the eye. "We have approved your application, Sergeant Sikes," he said in the usual clipped, no-nonsense style of the British Army. "You are to be congratulated."

"Thank you, sir," Archie said. "I promise you won't be disappointed in approving me."

"We're certain of that, Sergeant," the major said. "Which regiment have you chosen to be assigned to after you've completed your officers' training?"

Archie frowned in puzzlement. "Why, this one, sir. The Royal Regiment of Dragoons."

The officers looked at each other with amused smiles. The major spoke in a kindly but firm tone. "I'm afraid that is not possible, Sergeant. You must choose another regiment. Actually, it can be either infantry or armored."

"But why can't I choose this regiment, sir?" Archie asked.

"Sergeant Sikes," the major said sternly. "You would hardly fit into our officers' mess, would you? You haven't the background, the education, the money, or the social graces. I fear we would not find you or any other NCO suitable for either professional or social interaction."

"But I know for a fact that Major Brewster was an NCO right here in this same Royal Regiment of Dragoons," Archie argued.

"Major Brewster is the regimental quartermaster," the major explained. "He was given a commission in that capacity because being a quartermaster is not a gentleman's position. It has to do with the handling of supplies much like a shopkeeper. We, because of our stations in society, will not perform such low-class work. He was chosen for the posting because of his experience as the regimental quartermaster sergeant."

Another board member, a slim captain who was considered the regiment's best polo player, spoke up. "He, of course, is not a member of the officers' mess. I suppose the fact he receives a major's pay is compensation enough for being an outsider."

"A *complete* outsider," the major added. "Since accepting the commission, he can neither associate with the officers nor the noncommissioned officers on informal or social occasions."

"Would you be interested in becoming the regimental quartermaster when the position opens again?" the captain asked.

"In the meantime, you would have to transfer from your company to regimental staff as a corporal to learn supply procedures. Then, you must wait for Major Brewster to retire. His place will be taken by the present quartermaster sergeant, of course. Then you could take *his* place when *he* retires."

"All that would take some fifteen to twenty years," the major said. "If you accepted a commission in one of the lesser regiments, you would quite possibly be captain or major by then."

"I'll have to think about it," Archie said.

"Another thing to consider is your manner of speech and deportment, Sergeant Sikes," the captain said. "You will need polish on your grammar and etiquette even for a lesser regimental posting."

Archie was dismissed and told to put in his application within two weeks if he still harbored ambitions to become an officer. That evening Archie, despondent and disappointed, went into town, got roaring drunk, and was arrested for brawling in a local pub. This brought about a reduction to the rank of corporal and a cancellation of his appointment to officer training. Within six months, he was a private after being broken down again for drunken misbehavior, and he ended up in the regimental motor pool as an assistant mechanic. This was a misleading job title given to the poor sods assigned to wash and clean the unit's trucks and APCs.

Then the Royal Regiment of Dragoons was sent to Iraq.

Private Archibald Sikes' standing in his regiment was so low that he worked with civilian Iraqis assigned to the humble tasks of keeping the unit's vehicles cleaned up and topped off with fuel. Although he still had no friends among his fellow dragoons, one of the Iraqis became friendly with him. The Arab's name was Khalil Farouk, a thin, scholarly man who appeared to be in his mid-forties. He seemed to sense a smoldering resentment in the Englishman Sikes, and began engaging him in conversation. Archie at first resisted these overtures of friendship, until one afternoon when both were in the troop compartment of an APC cleaning up a hydraulic leak. They worked on their hands and knees, sopping up the sweet-smelling liquid. Even though all the hatches were open, the smell of the spill was unpleasant. Since the hydraulics were out, Archie couldn't lower the rear hatch to allow more fresh air into the interior.

Farouk, who spoke excellent English, dipped his cleaning rag into the bucket of water they shared for the task. As he wrung it out, he said, "This is not such pleasant work, is it, Mr. Archie?"

"It's the bluddy shit," Archie growled.

"Why do you do this?" Farouk asked. "Are your officers mad at you?"

Archie's first inclination was to tell the Arab to mind his own fucking business, but he said, "Yeah. They're good and mad at me. I told 'em to sod off. That's wot I did."

"Oh, you were defiant to them, were you?"

Archie stopped working and straightened up, still on his knees. "Right. I wanted a fucking commission, yeah? I was a sergeant and a damn good one, let me tell you that straight-away, hey? But they wouldn't let me be an officer in this regi-ment." Suddenly, the words began tumbling out and he voiced all his bitterness at the system in which the enlisted men were not only considered inferior in rank, but also in worth. Every-thing that had gone wrong in his life, from school days to the monotony of the warehouse job, was gone over. The gist of his complaints was that none of this was his fault. He was never properly understood. He was a good man who was not being allowed the opportunity to perform at a superlative level; thus, he was unable to make a name for himself.

Farouk was sympathetic and fed into the other man's dis-contentment. For the next couple of months, he was always at Archie's side during the chores in the motor pool, listening to him and making subtle inquiries and probes to get the man to open up. When the Arab got the chance, he spoke to some of the other Brits, learning that Archie's description of his for-mer status in the regiment was not an empty boast. He had indeed been an outstanding leader and NCO, and the inability to get a commission in the regiment he preferred had turned him into a disrespectful, sullen professional private.

Farouk had a reason to pursue the possibilities he saw in Archie. He finally got the chance he had been waiting for when the soldier's company sergeant major called Archie in and told him he was going to be kicked out of the Army as soon as they returned to England.

Farouk then made his move.

He told Archie he was in the wrong place. An able man like he was would never get the respect he deserved in the Western world. Islam recognized real men and gave them opportunities to go as far as they were able. It didn't matter about their families' status in society. Men were men, by Allah, and women were subordinate in Islam. They were chattel to bear children and keep their homes to please their husbands. If a man so desired, he would be allowed to marry as many as four of them. But Farouk wisely played down the religious side at this point. Instead he spoke of the holy war—jihad—against the unjust. Archie listened intently as Farouk explained that a soldier with Archie's abilities would be welcomed with open arms in the Muslim struggle. He would be a battle leader, eventually leading large units of mujahideen against the infidels.

Archie let the jihad aspects of Farouk's lectures slip past his conscious consideration. But the chance of being a grand field commander stirred those deep emotions he'd had when he first decided to become a soldier. The other matter foremost in his thoughts was that he no longer had a future in the British Army, thus no hope for great accomplishments in the UK.

CHAPTER 3

THE C-130 taxied off the runway onto the airfield proper, following a rather ragtag individual riding a battered Italian Vespa motor scooter. The aircraft's turboprop engines whipped up the thin dust layer on the hard-packed earth as it moved toward a hangar on the far west side of the facility. The weirdo on the scooter suddenly whipped off to the side. He pointed at the hangar, and the pilot took the transport over to a large cement parking area and came to a halt.

The SEALs inside the troop compartment noted the cutting of the engines with a sigh of relief. The eighteen men were crowded in an area packed with various gear, crates, boxes, and three DPVs, all making the flight from Station Bravo both discommoding and uncomfortable. Nevertheless, there was a bright side to the situation. The cargo was for their use only during Operation Rolling Thunder.

The loadmaster appeared from the cockpit, going to the

rear of the aircraft. Within moments, a loud whine broke the silence and the rear ramp slowly opened and lowered to the ground.

"On your feet!" SCPO Buford Dawkins commanded. "Grab your gear and unass the aircraft." The Brigands obediently secured their equipment and other personal belongings and filed down the fuselage to follow the senior chief out into the open. He quickly formed them up into two ranks and had them set their burdens down. "Okay. We had to push those DPVs aboard, so it stands to reason we'll have to push 'em out. Leibowitz! Puglisi! Murchison! Miskoski! Malachenko! Dawson! You six on the vehicles. The rest of you see to the other crap. Do it!"

The men trooped back into the aircraft to find that the load-master was already loosening the strap-downs. They helped him with the job, then the half dozen chosen for the vehicles pushed them down the loading ramp and out onto the parking area. With that done, they returned to help with the rest of the unloading.

Lieutenants Bill Brannigan and Jim Cruiser watched as the work moved into high gear. Now the Vespa rode up sputtering and coughing. The rider got off and walked up to the officers. He was a short, skinny kid in bad need of a haircut and shave, and he wore a blue T-shirt with a wordy announcement in yellow letters that stated:

> *IF GOD MADE*
> *ANYTHING BETTER THAN PUSSY*
> *HE KEPT IT FOR HIMSELF*

He wore shorts obviously made by cutting off the legs of a pair of BDU trousers, and his bare feet were shoved into a pair of leather sandals. A round Afghan *puhtee* cap, tipped like a beret, topped off his garb. Cruiser frowned at the youngster's appearance. "Who the hell are you?"

"I'm Randy Tooley," he cheerfully replied. "You guys must be the SEALs, huh?"

"Yeah," Cruiser said. "What do you do around here, er, Randy?"

"I run the airfield," Randy replied. "I make sure all incoming aircraft get to the proper place here at Shelor. That goes for the cargo and personnel that's brung in. There's all sorts of operations using the facilities. Ever'body's got their own place. This here hangar belongs to you. Put your equipment anyplace you want to."

Brannigan chuckled. "Are you in the military?"

"Yeah. I sure am," Randy said. "I'm in the Air Force."

"Which country's?" Cruiser inquired with a look of puzzlement.

"The United States, o' course," Randy replied. "I'm a senior airman."

"That's an E-Four, is it not, Randy?" Cruiser asked.

Randy grinned. "The last time I seen my pay form it was."

Cruiser said, "Now, I'm a lieutenant junior grade in the Navy. That's the same as a first lieutenant in the Air Force. And my commanding officer here is a lieutenant in the Navy. He ranks with a captain in the Air Force."

"No shit?" Randy remarked.

"No shit," Cruiser said pleasantly. "And I believe it is the practice of all America's armed forces that enlisted personnel utilize the titles 'sir' and 'ma'am' when addressing commissioned officers. And salutes are required when reporting to one."

"Let me tell you something," Randy said. "I got a lot of work to do here. I put in maybe sixteen to eighteen hours a day. And I ain't had any time off for six weeks. I see that everything runs smoothly for the comings, goings, shipments, unloading, and all that shit. I also got to arrange for quarters. An Air Force colonel is the overall commander here. He likes the way I do things 'cause I see that his headaches are kept to a minimum. If you don't like the way I look, speak, or act, you go talk to Colonel Watkins."

"By God!" Cruiser sputtered, "you listen up—"

Brannigan cut off Cruiser by grabbing his arm. He smiled at the senior airman. "We understand, and we appreciate what you're doing, Randy. Let's just let it go at that."

"Sure," Randy said with a smile. "I was told there was eighteen of you and that you don't require separate accommodations for the officers. You'll be in Barracks Two just behind the control tower. The chow hall is a couple of buildings down from there. It's easy to see because of the all the Afghans hanging around the garbage cans."

"Great," Brannigan said. "Anything else we should know?"

"Well," Randy replied, "a half-dozen DPVs arrived about a week ago that's supposed to be for you. I already had 'em put in your hangar."

"Thanks," Brannigan said. "We've just brought three more with us. Where do we top 'em off?"

"Sorry," Randy said. "I don't have a single drop of fuel for you guys. And I can't recall any incoming manifests that list any. I can get you a storage area, chow, and a place to sleep, but that's about all for today."

Cruiser glanced over at the bundles and crates being off-loaded by the SEALs. "Isn't this a hell of a note? We have ammo, MREs, and even extra clothes. But no goddamn fuel."

"Shit happens," Randy remarked. "But if I can help, let me know."

"Okay, Randy," Brannigan said. "Thanks."

"Right," Randy said. "Well, I got another flight coming in and an Army Special Forces team has to turn in their barracks in about an hour. Them guys aren't really into spit and polish, so I got to make sure the place is left decent for my next tenants. See you later." He went to his Vespa, leaped aboard, and sputtered away.

Cruiser frowned. "That little bastard needs some discipline."

"His discipline is the homegrown variety driven by personal pride," Brannigan said. "He does an excellent job because he wants to and he won't let anything else interfere with his performance." He sighed. "Well! I better get Gomez on the Shadowfire and find out about this fuel glitch."

UNREO CAMP

WHEN Penny Brubaker first signed on with the United Nations Relief and Education Organization, she was naïve,

eager, and dedicated to the group's mission of aiding Third
World people to improve their lives. UNREO had multiple
programs of medical examinations and treatment, instruction
in sanitation and hygiene, and provided logistical aid to supplement or replace archaic procedures in the recipients' lifestyles
and environments.

Unfortunately, Penny, a strikingly beautiful young lady
from a background of wealth and privilege, had very little understanding of her fellow Americans, much less these unfortunate people she wanted to help. And now, after two years,
Penny had become a jaded young woman. Her first clash
with cruel reality occurred when her team first arrived in
Afghanistan to help the people who had lived under the auto-
cratic rule of a cruel Pashtun warlord for several years. The
bad guy's reign came to an end when his private army was
defeated by a platoon of U.S. Navy SEALs. During his power
days, he had kidnapped some young girls and women from a
subordinate clan and forced them into prostitution for the
pleasure of his mujahideen. When the SEALs liberated the
sex slaves, they were warned they could not return the females to their homes. According to Islamic traditions, the
women had disgraced their families even though they had
been forced to endure almost continual sexual abuse over a
long period of time. Their male relatives, rather than taking
them back, were planning on murdering them in a ritual
known as honor killings. It was only with help from the
SEALs that an escape could be organized for the doomed
women. They were flown away in a UN transport aircraft to
safety while the Navy men held the male kin back through
the liberal and violent application of punches, kicks, and intense pummeling.

Now Penny was still in Afghanistan, working in yet another rural area as she and her colleagues attempted to en-
lighten the tribal people to improve their lives. But ignorance,
apathy, and distrust stymied the programs. When medical
examinations were made, the women were not allowed to be
seen undressed by the male physicians. A Pashtun man would
bring in his wife, then describe the symptoms to the doctors
in a vague, confusing manner through an interpreter. All that

could be done by the doctors was to make an educated guess on the nature of the illness, then pass out the medicine and hope the doses would be given in a timely and proper manner. Children suffered from illnesses that had disappeared from the civilized world generations before. Yet even when told there was a cure for the ailments, the illiterate parents, constrained by their religious beliefs, hardly ever responded to those offers of help. The foreigners who had come among them were infidels, damned to an eternity in hell by Allah and not to be trusted.

Penny had to admit to herself that she now thought of them as the stupidest, most backward beings on the face of the earth. She sincerely felt sorry for their suffering, but things had reached a point where the efforts to help them just weren't worth it. A cynical American doctor had remarked that the villagers' refusal to accept medical aid was nature's way of "thinning the herd." A proper British orthopedic surgeon had summed it up with the more refined "Survival of the fittest and all that, old chap. Natural selection, what?"

Another, more personal situation also weighed down on her emotions. An old boyfriend of hers had been among the SEALs during the episode with the Pashtun clans. His name was Chad Murchison, and he came from the same wealthy class of Boston aristocrats as Penny. The couple had known each other all their lives, gone to prep school together until Chad, a year older, had gone off to Yale. During her senior year after Chad had left for college, she fell for a member of the prep school varsity football team. This was Cliff Armbrewster, a good-looking muscular guy who had swept her off her feet. She broke up with Chad and became engaged to Cliff. The romance was a disaster. He had the intellect of a fence post and was going to get a position in an insurance firm where his father was chairman of the board. The schmuck didn't have a mind of his own, and his mom was even planning every single detail of the wedding while ignoring Penny and her own mother. At that time, she realized the big mistake she had made. Chad was a skinny, sweet guy who was handsome in a sort of gawky way, but he was very intelligent and had a great future ahead of him either with his banking family or by going off on his own. She hoped to make things up to him, but learned he had dropped out of Yale and joined the Navy.

The next time she saw him was there in Afghanistan when his SEAL detachment showed up at the UN camp after winning a series of battles against Pashtun mujahideen. She hardly recognized her former boyfriend as this rugged, fully armed, capable SEAL whose commanding officer was a fierce fellow called Wild Bill Brannigan. They got back together, even had sex, but something in Chad's attitude rattled her. He looked at her in a different way, and her bold attempt to get them engaged to be married had been met with a marked hesitancy on his part. After he was withdrawn from the area to go back to the States, they stayed in touch by letter, but he had not made any serious attempts to deepen their relationship. This was something she found very difficult to deal with. Penny had always been the belle of the ball, and wasn't used to being treated in such a cavalier manner.

Now, sitting on her bunk in the tent used by the sanitation teachers, Penny held the last letter she had received from Chad Murchison. It had been a nice, polite missive, telling her about a training exercise he had gone through on the island of San Clemente. But there was no outpouring of romantic affection, no expression of desire to see her again. She now seriously considered the very real possibility that she had lost him forever. Penny decided that the next time she saw Chad, she would turn on the charm, the sex, and the tears to bring him back under her power.

"Penny!"

She looked up, startled to see the German dietician, Erika München, standing in the tent flap. "Yes?"

"Have you lost track of time?" Ericka asked in a disapproving tone. "Already we wait for you to present your class on how to be washing the babies. Are you ready for it?"

"Yes," Penny answered.

She slipped Chad's letter in her pocket, then picked up her notes and the videotape. She slipped from the tent and walked over to the instruction area ready to speak to the Pashtun women on a subject in which they had no interest.

SOUTHWESTERN AFGHANISTAN DESERT
1800 HOURS

CAPTAIN Arsalaan Sikes, née Archibald Sikes, stood in the hatch of his EE-3 armored car. He pressed the transmit button of the Russian R-108 tactical radio. It, like the Dashika heavy machine guns, had been gotten by the Jihad Abadi in a roundabout manner. The Iranians obtained the weapons from Afghan mujahideen who had looted them from ambushed Soviet troops during the USSR's invasion of their country. The Iranians eventually passed them on to the Arab insurgents.

"In line—*yamin wa shmal!*" he ordered. The first and third platoons went to his right and the second and fourth to his left, both coming abreast. *"Indak!"* The entire armored car company came to a halt in perfect alignment, facing to the front.

They had just finished two grueling hours of running different battle formations, going from the various echelons along with enveloping and frontal-attack maneuvers. He was pleased with the way the men had performed. They were enthusiastic and eagerly waiting when they could go out on combat patrols to seek out targets of opportunity. But now they were tired. So was the captain. He ordered the engines turned off and gave permission for everyone to prepare the evening meal.

PRIVATE Archibald Sikes deserted the British Army during a routine work assignment he had been given. He was to drive a TM 4–4 vehicle over to the quartermaster depot to pick up a couple of tires for one of the Leyland-DAF four-ton trucks. Instead of following orders, when he left the Royal Regiment of Dragoons compound, he turned in the opposite direction, driving down the main drag of Basra. After going a mile, he turned off onto a side street and drove past startled Iraqis into a poor neighborhood, as he had been directed to do by Khalil Farouk. When he reached the indicated intersection as instructed, a tough-looking guy in an athletic training suit suddenly opened the opposite door and jumped into the left-hand passenger seat. He pointed ahead and said, "That way you go! That way you go!"

"Right, mate," Archie said. "That way I go."

They continued on deeper into the neighborhood, making a couple of turns, then stopped in front of a dilapidated apartment building. Now another man appeared. This one took Archie's place, pulling him out into the street none too gently. The vehicle sped off and the first fellow, having disembarked from the truck, took Archie by the arm, leading him into the building. Archie began growing more nervous every second as he was pulled down a long dark corridor. But when they reached a door and stepped inside a room, Farouk was waiting with warm greetings. He even hugged the reluctant Archie, calling him *sahib*—friend. After completing his salutations with a warm handshake, he pointed to a man sitting at a small table. "That is someone you will know as al-Zaim for the time being."

"How d'you do, sir?" Archie said politely, noting a chair on the opposite side of the table from the stranger.

"I am fine, thank you," the man replied in English. His accent was not Arabian, yet was close. "Will you sit down, please, Mr. Sikes. I wish to make a little test of your military knowledge."

"You blokes don't waste time, do you?" Archie remarked to the man he would eventually learn was Brigadier Shahruz Khohollah of the Iranian Army.

"We certainly do not," al-Zaim replied.

"Fine with me," Archie said agreeably. He took the empty chair. "Fire away when you're ready, sir."

"Let's begin with the subject of ambushes," said Al-Zaim. "Would you describe for me, please, that which is known as a deliberate ambush."

Archie quickly replied, "That's when you're gonna be hitting a specific target at a location you've picked out because it's bluddy handy."

"Mmm. And please tell me two things to consider for a deliberate ambush."

Archie thought a moment. "Well, right off the top of me head, I'd say which direction the enemy is gonna be moving"— he turned thoughtful again—"and what sort o' formation the enemy is and its numbers."

Al-Zaim seemed to be thinking. Then he suddenly asked, "Suppose I were your commanding officer and I wanted you to trail after an enemy unit that had passed through our area. How would you conduct the operation?"

"The first thing is to find the tracks or trails left by the bad blokes," Archie said. "Without that, you ain't gonna find 'em, are you? Then you study the sign and figger out the number o' the blighters, what sort they might be, that sort o' thing. I mean, if it looks like there's a hundred bloody riflemen tramping about the countryside, you don't want to take a dozen o' your mates after 'em, hey? Then, after finding the trail and who they are, I'd go after 'em. O' course, you got to have security all around, since there's always the chance they might figger someone's after 'em and double back or set up an ambush, right?"

Al-Zaim nodded his approval. "And what would you do once you've got them in sight?"

Archie shrugged. "I don't know. You're the commander. You tell me what you want me to do with the wankers."

From that point on, questions were thrown at the Brit regarding numerous subjects, including camouflage, preparation of various types of fighting positions, security during unit movement, handling EPWs, urban operations, use of supporting artillery, first aid, mines, and map reading, among others.

After two hours of intense questioning interspersed with conversation, Al-Zaim suddenly got to his feet and walked over to the door where Khalil Farouk stood. He spoke a few words in Arabic, then left the room. Farouk walked over to Archie with a smile. "You are doing fine, friend Archie. Now you go to the next step. But first we must get rid of your uniform. We have some civilian clothes for you to change into."

Archie began unbuttoning his jacket, knowing that this was the final gesture of his life as a British soldier. He was saying farewell to his Army, his country, and his ethnicity.

CHAPTER 4

THE CHE-53 Super Stallion chopper eased toward the fantail landing deck of the destroyer, gently touching down. Commanders Tom Carey and Ernie Berringer, carrying heavy briefcases, quickly disembarked and headed forward to the ship's superstructure.

Five minutes later, the two officers entered the SPECOPS commo center. They went directly to the message distribution boxes, and each checked the contents of the ones bearing their names. "I don't have a thing," Berringer said. "But I really wasn't expecting much this early in the game."

Carey had one missive and he opened it, scanning the three typed words it contained:

NO FUCKING FUEL

Berringer glanced over Carey's shoulder and read it. He showed a rare grin. "That's one thing about Brannigan," he remarked. "The guy can sum up frustration and rage in just one simple phrase."

Carey was in no mood for flippancy. He stormed out of the center and strode rapidly down the passageway to the logistics office. When he stepped inside, he found a lieutenant junior grade and a yeoman sorting through requisitions. Carey dropped Brannigan's message in front of the officer. "Operation Rolling Thunder has nine DPVs sitting at Shelor Field without a drop of gasoline for them."

The lieutenant looked over at the yeoman. "Check that out, Densmore."

"Aye, sir." The yeoman went to a box marked SUSPENSE and pulled out a set of forms. "The requisition for fuel, gasoline, unleaded in ten fifty-gallon drums, hasn't been filled yet. This includes fifty gallons of motor oil as well."

"Goddamn it!" Carey cursed. "When did you send it in? An hour ago?"

"No, sir," Yeoman Densmore answered. "It's been at Station Bravo for a couple of weeks now."

"Then why hasn't it been filled?"

The lieutenant answered, "It's a matter of priority, sir. Operation Rolling Thunder is way down the list. The operations in Iraq have first call; then a half-dozen missions in Afghanistan come next. Rolling Thunder is at the bottom."

"Priorities be damned!" Carey protested. "Rolling Thunder was officially alerted on four April. That was three days ago."

"I'm sorry, sir," the lieutenant said. "I don't set the schedules." He was used to complaints and screwups, considering them as normal as breathing, eating, and sleeping. "I suppose operations and logistics just aren't on the same page." He shrugged. "The best I can tell you is that Rolling Thunder will get that requisition within ten days or so."

"What about their chow?" Carey demanded to know. "Are the poor bastards going to starve to death?"

"Under the present SOP, the staff at Shelor Field handles that since the guys involved are billeted there."

Yeoman Densmore interrupted. "Even if the mess situation gets screwed up, Rolling Thunder has two weeks' worth of MREs."

"Yeah, okay," Carey said, irritated. He left the supply office and returned to the commo center. When he walked in, he shook his head to show Berringer it was useless. He grabbed a message pad and scribbled a word on it. After ripping out the page, he carried it over to the nearest RTO and dropped it in front of her. "Transmit this to Operation Rolling Thunder."

"Aye, sir." The young woman quickly tapped out the transmission. It contained but one word:

SNAFU.

UNREO CAMP
SOUTHWESTERN AFGHANISTAN
1100 HOURS

DR. Pierre Bouchier was the chief of the UN mission stationed in that area of Afghanistan. Now, after a frustrating morning of nonattendance at all the scheduled classes, he had called his entire staff to a meeting outside his tent. Most had brought camp chairs with them, while others were content with either standing or sitting in the sand. Even a casual observer could have noted that their collective morale was low.

The Belgian MD gazed sadly at the people he supervised in the humanitarian effort. "I know you all feel the same frustration I do. But I ask you to 'keep the faith' as *les américaines* say. I suppose our assignment with Warlord Khamami's people spoiled us with its ease and success."

One of the nurses, a young Spanish woman, spoke up loudly. "That was because those American soldiers were there."

"They weren't soldiers," Penny Brubaker interjected. "They were Navy SEALs."

An Italian dentist laughed. "You should know, *signorina*. One of them was your sweetheart."

"He still is," Penny remarked, while thinking, *I hope he still is*.

"I think we all remember those particular Americans," Dr. Bouchier said. "And I admit it is true that their presence helped us. Especially when one takes into consideration they had defeated the warlord's bandits."

"They helped those poor girls too," Penny reminded him. "The ones that were sex slaves."

"And I am most grateful for that," Dr. Bouchier said. "They saved a dozen lives that memorable day." He lit a cigarette. "But now we have the problem of having to make what we offer in aid appear helpful and attractive to the people of *this* village on *this* day and at *this* time. Frankly, I am unable to figure out exactly what we must do. Surely, some of you ladies have ideas since you're the ones in the closest contact with the native women."

Before any of the females could respond, a shout was heard in the near distance. They all turned to see one of their Afghan security guards gesturing wildly and pointing out into the desert. A quick look showed a cloud of sand swirling near the horizon. After a minute or so, it was obvious it was coming closer. They all stood up, the apprehension on their faces evident by tightened jaws and instinctive frowns of concern.

"It appears we have visitors," Dr. Bouchier said.

"I hear motors," someone announced.

A French surgeon cursed. "*Merde!* It must be some *sacrés américaines!*"

"Everybody be calm," Dr. Bouchier urged them. He glared at the Frenchman. "If they are Americans, we can be grateful. They will have candy for the children. That will bring everybody out from the village and maybe ease the tension here. Perhaps a little levity is what is needed."

Everyone walked around the tent to watch the approaching visitors. As they drew closer and appeared plainer in the desert haze, the UN people could see that three vehicles made up the group. "Look! They are tanks!" a young Polish X-ray technician cried.

"*No seas pandeja,*" a Spanish medical orderly scoffed. "They are armored cars. See? They have tires, not tracks."

Five minutes later, a trio of EE-3s pulled up to a stop. Nine men wearing desert camouflage uniforms and Arab keffiyehs rapidly and efficiently appeared from hatches in the tops of the vehicles. They jumped to the ground and one took the lead, striding toward the UN crowd with the others respectfully following. Dr. Bouchier stepped forward to greet the visitors. He noticed the lead man wore the three-pip insignia of a British captain.

"How do you do, *Monsieur le Capitaine*?" he greeted. "I am Dr. Pierre Bouchier, the chief of this UN mission."

The man stopped. "Good morning, sir. I am Captain Arsalaan Sikes of the Army of Jihad Abadi."

Bouchier, alarmed by the word "jihad," looked closely at the man. He spoke in an English accent and, except for the headgear, looked like a typical Brit with brown hair and blue eyes. But he conducted himself as if he were an Arab officer. "I fear I am confused, *Monsieur le Capitaine*."

Sikes suddenly turned and barked orders in Arabic. Six of his men immediately trotted toward the Pashtun village, and he turned his attention back to Bouchier. "You are in territory controlled by the Jihad Abadi. And I want to know what you're about, yeah?"

"We are a relief mission, *Monsieur le Capitaine*," Bouchier explained. "We offer these people medical care and instruction in sanitation."

"You'll put a halt to your operation straightaway," Sikes said. "Do not have no further contact with the Pashtuns here. Me men are already in the village warning them buggers that they ain't to have nothing to do with foreigners. And that means you, mate!"

"But we are here under an agreement between the United Nations and the Afghan government," Bouchier protested.

"Such agreements don't mean nothing," Sikes said. "You got three days, yeah?" He checked his watch. "It's getting close to noon, so I'll be back here on the tenth. And this place better be bare and empty. Got it? You'll be bluddy sorry if you and these people are still hanging about."

The half-dozen men he had sent into the village now reappeared. On his command, they reboarded the armored cars.

Bouchier's people crowded around him. "What are you going to do, *Docteur*?" the French surgeon asked anxiously.

"I'm going to contact the UN office in Kabul and ask them how we are to respond to the threat," Bouchier said. He shook his head. "I cannot believe what just happened. We are in the middle of a most frustrating situation when an Englishman dressed like an Arab officer appears out of nowhere and orders us to cease our operations and depart."

Out in the desert, Captain Arsalaan Sikes led his three vehicles back to join the rest of his armored car company, waiting some five miles away across the sandy terrain.

WHEN Archie Sikes left Iraq through the courtesy of the Jihad Abadi, he went first to Syria in their E&E net. After a three-day stay in Damascus during which he was given a quick but comprehensive indoctrination on the terrorist group, he was transported to Saudi Arabia in a private civilian airplane. At that point, the deserter was taken to a place where he began classes in the Arabic language as well as the tenets of Islam. Archie, who hadn't attended church much as a youngster, had never received any serious religious schooling whatsoever.

First, an earnest young cleric told him the story of how the angel Gabriel had come to a man called Muhammad to inform him that God, i.e., Allah, had chosen him to be his final prophet. From that point on, Muhammad received divine revelations that made up the Qu'ran, which was the Muslim Bible. At that point, the Qu'ran was brought into Archie's life, and he received intense daily instruction in what it contained. His preliminary response was lukewarm, but as the subject matter deepened, it became all-encompassing to the young Brit. He began to feel a pull toward the religion. His instructor noted this, and put the pressure on.

Meanwhile, between religious classes, his Arabic lessons continued, with a heavy dose of the Muslim side of current world events involving international politics and diplomacy. With no opposing views being expressed, Archie began to feel that the Western nations he came from were indeed decadent and evil, and the United States and Israel were supporting the causes of Satan with the help of Europe. He began to reason that the Royal Regiment of Dragoons had declined to have him commissioned in their ranks because of the ingrained prejudice of the wealthy upper classes who wanted to keep the common man from improving his status in society. In other words, they perceived a serious threat in Archibald Sikes. Even if he had received a commission in another regiment, they would have seen to it that his career went nowhere in the British Army. These were the same people the mullahs accused of conducting Satan's campaigns against Islam.

While the religious and political aspects of the lessons were winning over Archie Sikes, it was the rules about women that brought about his total conversion. He had gotten along even less well with girls than he had with boys when growing up. His first attempts to establish relationships with his feminine classmates during his teen years were rebuffed. This spurning of his artless, clumsy advances made him angry and frustrated, and he found it humiliating that not only did the girls not seem to like him, but they demonstrated a marked disapproval of him as a person. Many seemed to consider him a buffoon. An angry inferiority complex developed out of this, and the lessons of Islam turned that all around to a feeling of superiority and even divine authority where the fair sex was concerned. Those English girls had not been properly subdued and indoctrinated.

Archie happily learned that Middle Eastern nations had an established, legal system of discrimination against human females. They were subordinated to men in every aspect of life. After all, they were not only created from the rib of a man, but from the weakest part, the curved tip. That was written in the Qu'ran.

The laws of Islam demanded that they wear *khimar* head coverings along with burqas that concealed their entire body. Women could never leave their homes unless in the company of a male relative. They had weak morals and needed constant surveillance, or they would become promiscuous with any man they found attractive. Leave it to them, Archie was told by his mullah instructor, and women would give birth to innumerable bastard babies from all their casual love affairs.

Archie also liked the laws of marriage. A Muslim man was allowed to have up to four wives as long as he treated them all equally and could afford to support such a family, which would produce many children. Fantasies of having four humble, compliant women to tend to his every want and desire danced through his head. It would be justified revenge against all the snobby girls he'd had to endure in his schooldays. When the entire world was converted to Islam, they were going to get their comeuppance but good!

With that thought in mind, Archie took the final step one memorable day six months after his desertion from the British Army. He announced to his pleased instructors that he wished to convert to the Islamic faith. And he expressed this desire in fluent Arabic.

Archibald Sikes took the name Arsalaan, which meant "Lion, King of the Jungle." However, in spite of his mentor's insistence, he refused to take an Arabic last name. "The day's coming," he said, "when the name 'Sikes' is gonna ring across England!" As part of his evolution into a Muslim, Archie even submitted to circumcision, though this was done as an outpatient under anesthesia in a doctor's office.

A few weeks later, he was told he would be taken to a special military training camp in Iran. It was there he was to be formerly inducted into the Jihad Abadi—the Eternal Holy War.

SHELOR FIELD
1400 HOURS

WITH nothing much to do, SCPO Buford Dawkins distributed the men among their vehicles and had them get out the manuals. The idea was to get them to perform some maintenance and go through immediate action drills in case of breakdowns. Everyone, including Lieutenant Bill Brannigan and his 2IC Lieutenant Junior Grade Jim Cruiser, joined in the activity. With the hoods up on the patrol vehicles, all the Brigands were either leaning over the motors or beneath the chassis checking out the various mechanical, hydraulic, and electrical functions while referring to the workbooks. Fortunately, the batteries were installed, but the men had to be careful about running them down. Brannigan had Frank Gomez radio in a requisition for a couple of chargers, knowing it would probably be a month before they came in.

As the activity continued among the nine individual groups, Senior Airman Randy Tooley came driving up on his Vespa to see how the SEALs were getting along. On this day, the T-shirt he wore proclaimed:

> SOCCER PLAYERS
> DO IT WITH BIG BALLS!

He rode the motor scooter inside the hangar and braked to a stop. Brannigan noticed the little guy as he came in, and he put down the wrench he had been using to loosen an air filter. The lieutenant walked over with Jim Cruiser at his side, hoping for some good news. The Skipper asked, "How's it going, Randy?"

"Pretty good. I checked on that gasoline you're waiting for, but it ain't in the pipeline yet."

"Bummer," Brannigan grumbled.

"But I may have a way for you to work around that," Randy remarked.

Brannigan was interested. "Yeah?"

"There's an Army transportation company on the other side of the field," Randy said. "They get their supplies from the quartermaster depot in Kandahar. They make regular convoy runs in their gas trucks over there and back. I bet I could talk them into giving some of their fuel to you. When your own comes in, you can pay them back. That would include motor oil and coolant too."

Cruiser was suspicious. "How are you going to manage to talk them into that, Randy?"

"They owe me some favors," Randy replied. "I got them some refrigerators through a contact of mine."

Cruiser looked at Brannigan. "Sounds solid to me, sir."

"Me too," Brannigan said. He gave a Randy a close look. "And what would you want in return?"

Randy glanced past him to the vehicles inside. "I'd be proud to have my very own personal DPV for me alone."

Cruiser sputtered, "Jesus Christ!"

"It will be done, Randy," Wild Bill Brannigan proclaimed.

Randy immediately leaped back aboard his Vespa and roared out of the hangar. Brannigan and Cruiser returned to the vehicles to resume the maintenance work.

1600 HOURS

THE SEALs were cleaning the windshields of the DPVs and wiping down the chassis in the final phases of the PM session. The hours of crawling in and out of the little vehicles had given them all an intimate knowledge of the inner workings. Brannigan noted that the work done that day was beneficial beyond the mechanical aspects. The men had begun developing real affection for the vehicles they would be driving in Operation Rolling Thunder. They were now referring to them in feminine terms, and the names "Ol' Bessie," "Sweet Lil," and others like them could be heard during conversations among the crews.

The squealing of loud tires and a rumbling engine sound interrupted the activity. The detachment looked up to see Randy Tooley on his faithful motor scooter leading an M-35 fuel tanker across the aircraft parking area. They drove straight into the hangar before coming to a halt. Randy got off his Vespa and gestured to Brannigan. "Wheel them DPVs up here. They'll top you off. We got twenty-five gallons of motor oil and enough coolant so's you'll have some left over. We got some lube too, and they're lending you a couple of grease guns."

SCPO Buford Dawkins jumped into the breech as always. "Let's go! We'll load on one at a time. Devereaux! Push Command One up to the tanker."

Jim Cruiser, chuckling, walked over to join Brannigan. "That Randy is one hell of a kid, isn't he?"

"Roger that," Brannigan said. "That's what I mean about the real meaning of discipline. He sees a situation that needs fixing and he sets about putting things right."

"Do you think we could talk him into joining the SEALs?" Cruiser asked.

"Do *you* think he could make it through BUD/S?"

"Not a chance," Cruiser commented.

"Randy's right where God meant him to be," Brannigan said. He turned and motioned Frank Gomez to come over to him. Gomez left Command Three, where he and Doc Bradley had been working all day. "What's going on, sir?"

"Fire up that Shadowfire radio, Gomez," Brannigan said. "Tell 'em we need another DPV ASAP."

"Aye, sir. I suppose having a spare would be a good idea."

"This one isn't for us," Brannigan said, gazing at Randy Tooley sitting on his motor scooter.

CHAPTER 5

EIGHT of the Brigands' DPVs moved in a slightly lop-sided "vee" formation across the desert expanse, kicking up clouds of fine dust. This man-made irritation was dealt with by the use of goggles and head scarves wrapped around noses and mouths.

The ninth vehicle, Commando Two with Mike Assad and Dave Leibowitz—AKA the Odd Couple—was out to the front a couple of kilometers ahead of the pack. As usual, the two buddies were doing recon chores as the detachment continued on a northerly course toward its destination for the day. Mike performed the driving chores, while Dave sat up in the gunner's position keeping an eye on the surrounding terrain through his binoculars. Their AN/PRC-126 radios with the LASH headsets were on frequency and warmed up for intra-detachment commo.

Earlier, Brannigan had called a halt an hour after they left
Shelor Field, and had everyone stand down for familiarization
firing with the HK-416 carbines. The evening before had been
spent learning field-stripping and how the weapons func-
tioned. This class was given by Bruno Puglisi in his role as
the detachment's main weapons man. He had attended both
the light and heavy infantry weapons courses conducted under the Army's USASFC at Fort Bragg, North Carolina.

While out on the desert that next morning, each SEAL shot
up a couple of thirty-round magazines, pumping out short fire
bursts and individual shots into the distance. The weapons
seemed to operate well enough, but there were no suitable targets to test the accuracy. The ever-grumpy Puglisi summed up
everyone's thoughts when he remarked, "I'm glad this ain't a
real hot mission. Them rounds could have been going anywhere." He shrugged. "But at least they seem to head out in
the general direction we're aiming."

"Well," Miskoski replied, "if them HK-Four-Sixteens don't
measure up, we'll just have to throw rocks."

Chad Murchison laughed at the remark. "How pristine,
Joe! It would be much more propitious if we employed bows
and arrows."

"Jesus, Chad!" Miskoski groaned. "Your sense of humor is
as fucked up as the way you talk."

After the small arms were taken care of, attention was
turned to the big M-2 .50-calibers on the vehicles. Everyone
enjoyed firing the powerful weapons, whooping and hollering,
until SCPO Dawkins came unglued at the frivolity. He took
the fun out of the game by having them practice coordinating
their fire bursts to cover a hundred-meter range to their direct
front as they swung the muzzles back and forth across the
width of their overlapping fields of fire. This went on for a
half hour until Brannigan decided it was time to resume the
patrol. The detachment quickly secured from firing, restack-
ing the ammo boxes onto the vehicles.

USS *COMBS*
SPECOPS CENTER
NOON

LIEUTENANT Commander Ernest Berringer stepped from the passageway into the crowded compartment of working people, desks, and computers. He made his way back to the corner, where a small space had been allotted him and Commander Carey. Carey was at their one desk preparing a map of the SEALs' OA to mount on the bulkhead. He raised his eyes as Berringer walked up. "I hope you picked up some positive info down in commo."

Berringer, who had four typed message sheets in his hands, dropped the first one down on the desk. Carey picked the missive up and read it. "What the hell is this all about? Why in hell would Brannigan request an additional DPV from Station Bravo?" He laughed. "Well, he sure isn't going to get it."

Berringer dropped the second sheet down. "As stated here, sir, his audacious request was approved."

"Good God Almighty!" Carey exclaimed.

Now Berringer produced the third sheet. "And it's already on its way to Shelor Field via the next scheduled C-One-Thirty."

"Brannigan never ceases to amaze me. Well! All I can say is that there must not be much of a demand on the inventory. In fact, there must not be any demand at all if they shipped one out so quickly."

"And here's the last and the wordiest. Now get ready for this," Berringer warned him, handing over the fourth message.

Carey, his curiosity boiling, began reading the words. He spoke as much to himself as to Berringer as he made a running commentary. "He's launched active patrolling . . . left Shelor this morning at oh-five-hundred . . . vehicles topped off with fuel and carrying two additional five-gallon jerry cans as contingencies . . . fuel did *not* come through normal supply channels . . . special arrangements—" At this point Carey stopped speaking.

"What sort of special arrangements could he have made, sir?" Berringer asked.

"Oh, God," Carey moaned, "I don't even want to know!"

OPERATIONAL AREA
1400 HOURS

PETTY Officer Third Class Chad Murchison sat in the gunner's seat of Green Two, the wind blowing hard, making the scarf over his lower face flutter rapidly. The DPV bounced across the desert at a bit less than fifty miles an hour, with Chief Petty Officer Matt Gunnarson deftly handling the wheel as he carefully steered to avoid rough patches of terrain.

Chad would have preferred the empty passenger seat on the right side of the vehicle, but he sat at the M-2 .50-caliber machine gun as per Lieutenant Bill Brannigan's SOP. The Skipper wanted the heavy weapons locked, loaded, and manned during transit at all times.

Without exception. Always. Unremittingly. Constantly. Wild Bill had thus spoken, and he was therefore obeyed.

At that particular moment in time, the young SEAL was going through mixed emotions. Their final destination for that day was the UNREO camp. His girlfriend Penny Brubaker was there in her role as an instructor in basic hygiene and sanitation. He hadn't seen her for over a year, and he was not looking forward to this meeting. The thing that was so perplexing for Chad was that he didn't fully understand this hesitancy on his part.

FOR almost his entire life, Chad Murchison had adored Penny Brubaker, who was a year younger than he. Both their families were members of the higher echelons of the Boston financial and banking community, and they had shared the experience of being raised in stunning wealth and privilege among friends and classmates who were their social peers. All the kids went to the best private elementary schools the city offered, then to the prestigious Marchland Preparatory School in New Hampshire. Chad and Jenny began going steady at Marchland and everyone—including the young couple—assumed they would eventually be engaged, then married, and begin procreating to carry on the dynasties of their powerful families. But during her senior year, after Chad had graduated and gone off to Yale, Penny unexpectedly dumped him for a jock. This betrayal caused Chad's world to come apart at the seams.

His grief at losing Penny was so great and pressing, it was nearly unreal. He lay in his dormitory room at Yale unable to get up to go to class, eat, or sleep. Dehydration and exhaustion set in during his mental and physical deterioration until he was looking so bad that the dormitory superintendent was notified by Chad's frantic friends. An ambulance was called immediately and the boy was taken to the nearest ER. Youthful resilience was on his side, and the medical crew determined he could be brought back to physical normalcy if he were immediately admitted to the hospital to get fluids dripped into him. The treatment would include regular doses of Valium to mellow him out.

A week later, he was back in his home in Boston. The family physician recommended that he stay out of school for the rest of the year. If he regained his ability to deal with the real world by the following September, he could reenter Yale and resume his studies. From that point on, Chadwick Murchison's existence consisted of sitting around and moping while barely eating. His days were spent at his bedroom window, sprawled in a recliner and staring out over the broad expanse of the back lawn that flowed down to Lake Saint Michael.

This lethargic style of a miserable existence went on for a bit more than a month before a spark suddenly ignited deep in his psyche. It wasn't a flash of intellect or realization; it was a burst of bald, naked anger. Chad may have been a little skinny guy with two left feet, but one thing he had inside was an instinctive courage and fighting spirit. It took this emotional disaster to fuel that inner self that had been smothered by the good life. It was nine o'clock in the morning when he impetuously got out of the chair and marched down to the kitchen, where the staff was going about their usual routine. Chad announced he wanted three eggs over easy, a half-dozen sausage links, a big pile of fried potatoes, and no less than four croissants with butter and jam.

After stuffing himself, he went back to his room and shucked the pajamas and bathrobe. He put on his jogging duds, went downstairs, out the front door, and began a run through the plush neighborhood. He had to stop once to throw up the enormous breakfast in his stuffed belly; then he continued the circuit.

And thus began a hard-ass, self-imposed program of road-work, lifting weights, swimming laps in the family's Olympic-size indoor pool, and punching a heavy bag. The latter workout was particularly vigorous since he imagined the inoffensive target of his fists as Cliff Armbrewster, the jock who had taken Penny Brubaker away from him.

Then the decision that was to really change his life was made while watching television. The Arts and Entertainment Channel showed an hour-long program on the U.S. Navy SEALs. The next day, Chad presented himself at the recruiting office in Cambridge and signed on for a four-year hitch, volunteering for the SEALs. The petty officer recruiter took one look at the skinny kid and figured he would never make it through much more than about five minutes of Hell Week. But the sailor had a quota to meet, so he signed the young volunteer up.

Chad went to Boot Camp at the Naval Training Center in Great Lakes, Illinois. He came out of those weeks about five pounds heavier, but still skinny. From there, he went to Class A School, where he was given specialized training to qualify him for a disbursement clerk's rating to work in the Navy's financial department. When that was finished, the eager young sailor put in for the SEALs. In order to make it to BUD/S, he had to pass a physical fitness test. In spite of Boot Camp, he barely squeaked by. The pull-ups were particularly tough, and his little arms fairly trembled with the effort before he got out the required number. The run, on the other hand, was a piece of cake. He fairly flew around the course, completing the mandatory distance with time to spare.

When he showed up at the Naval Amphibious Base in Coronado, California, the BUD/S instructors couldn't believe the runt had actually passed the qualifying tests. But eventually, they recognized the big heart in the little guy. He gave it his all, still going when larger, more muscular candidates caved in. His slight frame turned out to be advantageous during underwater free-swimming sessions, since the kid didn't need a lot of oxygen and his eel-like physique allowed him to move rapidly through the water.

Chad continued the training, struggling more with his natural clumsiness than a lack of zeal or courage. One instructor who recognized the inner strength of the Slim Jim gave him encouragement through guidance and compliments where he deserved them. When the BUD/S class curriculum was completed, Chad Murchison had won the eagle and trident of the SEALs. And he now weighed a muscular twenty pounds more than the day he enlisted.

The SEAL and Penny Brubaker were destined to meet again sooner than either expected. It was in Afghanistan during Brannigan's Brigands' first operation as a unit, and she was a UN sanitation and hygiene instructor on the staff of a relief team. The reunion was an emotional whirlwind for them both. Penny happily told him she had broken her engagement with Armbrewster, and returned to Boston to find Chad, only to be told he had enlisted in the Navy.

In the heady days following this unexpected get-together, they became an item once again. But this time, with more maturity and experience, the young couple had sex out in the desert on Chad's poncho. It was primitive and exhilarating for the two sophisticated city kids, and their passion was intense and feral.

Afterward, instead of being thrilled with getting back the girl of his dreams, Chad felt his passion for her begin to wane. It was something that he couldn't understand no matter how much he turned it over in his mind. His experiences in training and combat had turned him into a completely different person, with a life that had no room for conventional romance. The SEALs were everything to him.

1500 HOURS

A blur appeared in the haze on the desert horizon, and Chad Murchison stood up in his position aboard the DPV, steadying himself on the roll bars. He took his binoculars from their case, putting them to his eyes. After a few moments, he could see the white tents with the blue letters UN stenciled on them. Somewhere among those canvas structures was Penny Brubaker. Chad sat back down, wondering how he was going to handle the coming reunion.

Command Two sat at the edge of the camp with several people standing around it. The other two vehicles of the Command Section pulled up to a stop. CPO Matt Gunnarson, driving Green Two with Chad Murchison, slowed down to let Green One go around him. He followed him up to the other vehicles with Green Three just behind his DPV. The Red Assault Section followed, pulling up to the left side of the impromptu vehicle park.

Lieutenant Bill Brannigan and his 2IC Jim Cruiser approached the group of people waiting at the edge of the camp. Dr. Pierre Bouchier stepped forward with his hand extended. *"Bonjour, Monsieur le Lieutenant Brannigan. Je suis charmé de vous revoir encore*—I am pleased to see you again."

"Likewise, Dr. Bouchier," Brannigan said. "How have you been?"

"Quite well, thank you," Bouchier replied. "We finished our work with the Warlord Khamami's people. At least, we accomplished all that was possible under the conditions here in Afghanistan. I have heard he is deep into the farming of opium poppies and smuggling of same."

"No surprise there," Brannigan said. He reintroduced Jim Cruiser, then noticed the attractive young lady standing slightly to the rear. "Hello!" he called over to her. "I remember you quite well."

"I'm pleased that you do," Penny Brubaker replied. "Is Chad Murchison with you, by any chance?"

"He sure is," Brannigan said. He turned toward the Green Assault Section. "Petty Officer Murchison! Front and center!"

Chad slowly dismounted the DPV and walked toward the assembled people, slipping his HK-416 carbine over his shoulder. Penny rushed toward him, her face lit with a smile of pure delight. He felt guilty as he took her in his arms. He responded when she held her face up to be kissed. The SEAL pressed his lips against hers, aware of the growing tightness of her embrace.

Jim Cruiser, suppressing a laugh, called over, "Murchison, you're excused from duty until further notice. Take a break."

"Aye, sir," Chad replied.

The couple walked away with Penny holding onto his arm. She led him over to where three of her girlfriends waited. "Chad, I want you to meet Erika München, Irena Poczinska, and Josefina Vargas. The four of us work together giving classes to the Pashtun ladies."

Josefina glanced over at the SEALs who were sizing up the UN women. The Spanish nurse smiled and gazed boldly back at the sailors. "We hope to meet all your friends while you are here, Chad."

Chad grinned. "Believe me, they hope they can meet you too."

"We'll worry about that later," Penny said. She pulled on him, taking him into the formation of tents until reaching hers. "This is where I live." She gave him what she hoped was a seductive look. "Would you like to see it?"

"Sure," Chad replied.

Penny opened the flap and followed him inside. She embraced him again. "Oh, Chaddie, darling! We won't be bothered in here. My roomies will stay away until we come out."

He was confused. "How did they know I was coming?"

"Those two guys you call the Odd Couple told me you were on your way when they got here earlier," Penny said. "Why didn't you write me and tell me you were in Afghanistan?"

"I didn't find out about this operation until four days ago," Chad said. "I've been out on a ship."

"Chad," Penny said impatiently. "We don't have all day."

He stood there awkwardly, not really happy with a girl who was now an intrusion in his life. But he was a young male with a young willing female. And he was a SEAL.

Duty of a sort had called.

DR. Pierre Bouchier acted as the host as Lieutenant Bill Brannigan, Lieutenant Junior Grade Jim Cruiser, and Senior Chief Petty Officer Buford Dawkins sat around the table in his large tent. Cold bottles of beer had been served, and the doctor also offered snacks of peanuts and pretzels.

"We appreciate your hospitality, Doctor," Brannigan said.

"I wish we could reciprocate, but all we have are MRE field rations."

"*Bien!* Our food here is plain but much better than that," Bouchier said. "However, I have you here for another reason. Yesterday, three armored cars visited us. The men in them wore British-style uniforms with Arab keffiyehs."

SCPO Dawkins took a swallow of beer. "What the hell are keffiyehs?" he asked, reaching for a handful of peanuts.

"Do you remember pictures of Yasser Arafat?" Cruiser asked. "What he had on his head was a keffiyeh."

"The device around it that holds it in place is called an *akal*," Bouchier said. "At any rate, the leader identified himself by an Arabic first name and a last that I think was English or possibly German. And he claimed the rank of *capitaine*. He had a marked European appearance and spoke in an English accent. The fellow told me he was a member of an army called Jihad something-or-other."

SCPO Dawkins showed a crooked grin. "Jesus! A fucking Lawrence of Arabia, huh?"

"I wouldn't say that," Brannigan remarked. "This is a terrorist for sure." He shifted his gaze back to Bouchier. "Did he give you any reason for his visit?"

"*Trés explicitement!*" Bouchier exclaimed. "He ordered us out of this area, giving us three days to leave. That time is up day after tomorrow at noon. He sent some men into the Pashtun village and warned them not to have any contact with us. They are obeying him explicitly."

"I take it you've contacted your superiors," Brannigan said. "What were their instructions?"

"I have received none as of yet, but I am certain I will be ordered to go to Kandahar or perhaps Kabul within twenty-four hours," Bouchier surmised.

"I have a better idea," Brannigan said. "I suggest that you and all your people load aboard some of your vehicles. I'll dispatch one of my DPVs to lead you to Shelor Field, and you can bunk in our hangar. My guy can turn around and come back here, and we'll be ready and waiting for this mysterious Brit with an Arab name."

"But what is going to happen to the tents and all our equipment?"

"Leave everything here except the trucks you'll need to haul your people and necessary personal affects," Brannigan said.

"But *les terroristes* will destroy everything they cannot steal," Bouchier protested. "And if they don't, then those wretched Pashtuns will."

"Not necessarily," Brannigan said. "My detachment will be here to look after your things. And also to meet Captain Jihad and his men at noon day after tommorow."

"I will have to clear it with my superiors," Bouchier said.

"Right now this is the official operational area of a mission the United States Navy is calling Rolling Thunder," Brannigan said. "I'm ordering you to evacuate to Shelor Field. My authority is that I am the commanding officer here. Besides, the UN is not known for any real sense of security."

Bouchier shrugged. "In that case, I will follow your orders, *Monsieur le Lieutenant.*"

CHAD Murchison and Penny Brubaker enjoyed a quick coupling, removing just enough clothing to perform the act. When the two young people rearranged themselves and stepped out of the tent, they immediately noticed near-frantic activity going on in the camp. Her three roomies were hurrying in their direction. *"Ach!"* Erika München said. "We were afraid we would have to break in on you."

"What's going on?" Penny asked, alarmed.

"We are leaving here right away," Josefina Vargas said. "We are to pack one bag and be ready to go when they call us to get on trucks. The Americans are going to take us to their airfield to stay. Then they are coming back here. I think there will be a big battle with the bad soldiers in the armored cars."

Penny turned to speak to Chad, but he was already running over to join the detachment. At that instant, the young woman realized there was only one way she could have him for her own.

She had to get him out of the SEALs.

CHAPTER 6

WASHINGTON, D.C.
STATE DEPARTMENT
9 APRIL
0830 HOURS

CARL Joplin, PhD, impatiently checked his watch, noting he had a half hour minimum to wait. The window to appear for the appointment that morning was 0900 to 0910 hours. Although much of his work was done in the rambling, ambiguous world of diplomatic dealings, he still liked at least a bit of punctuality and predictability. Having a window of even just ten minutes irritated him. Joplin preferred a set time for every bit of business. Now the diplomat sat in the leather office chair behind his desk, tapping his foot impatiently as he waited.

This brilliant African-American Undersecretary's specialty in the State Department was to participate in informal negotiations and agreements between the United States and foreign nations. These unique sessions were clandestine, sensitive, and extremely consequential. They mostly dealt with issues that both sides wished to keep secret from their populations. For example, America might wish to inquire into information another country had gleaned from a "person of interest" through torture. Or perhaps a foreign head of government who had been taking a very loud and public stand against a particular American policy might want to cut a deal with the U.S. regarding another issue. In order to gain on the one, he would have to make concessions on the other. Therefore, he was willing to give in on certain points that would enrage his citizenry if they found out. An example would be guaranteeing no demand on trade imbalances or tariffs in exchange for the release of frozen assets in U.S. banks. Such goings-on required great diplomatic skill. And Dr. Joplin was the best at this game of two-faced diplomacy. All of his polite encounters ended to the USA's advantage, yet also pleased his foreign counterparts on the other side of the table.

One of his most recent assignments had to do with arranging secret military aid to three South American countries because they did not trust their own armed forces to handle a politically hypersensitive mission. The takeover of their entire continent by fascists was the very undesirable alternative. Joplin thought that would be the superlative assignment of his career, but a new state of affairs promised to top this earlier case. While giving only a brief hint of the situation, Joplin's boss, Secretary of State Benjamin Bellingham—who didn't know a hell of a lot himself—warned Joplin that he was about to be tossed into the deep end of a diplomatic pool filled with boiling controversy and peril.

0901 HOURS

JOPLIN stepped from his office, carrying his briefcase, and went down to the end of a hall where a Capitol Police guard stood by the single elevator situated there. The young officer was giving the diplomat's ID badge a studious gaze when another man approached. Joplin turned to see Colonel John Turnbull, U.S. Army, the chief of the Special Operations Liaison Staff. The colonel, also toting the usual briefcase that seemed a fashion accessory in Washington, produced his own ID. As the policeman perused the card, the colonel nodded to Joplin. "I wouldn't be surprised if we were going to the same place."

"Nor would I," Joplin said. "How're you doing, John?"

"Frankly, I'm much too busy to be called away from my office for unstated reasons, Carl."

The policeman approved the IDs, then turned and slid a scanner card into a slot in the wall next to the elevator. The doors buzzed open and the diplomat and officer stepped inside. Turnbull pressed a button that would take them down to the third basement.

When the elevator arrived, there was another armed law enforcement officer present. After yet one more inspection of the ID badges, the two men proceeded a short distance to an unmarked door. Joplin followed as Turnbull stepped into the room. They both came to an abrupt halt, surprised to see Arlene Entienne, the president's Chief of Staff, seated at the head of a large mahogany conference table. A man unknown to them was seated to one side.

Joplin greeted Entienne, saying. "How have you been, Arlene?"

"Fine, thank you, Carl," she answered. "Hello, John." This Cajun-African-American was a beautiful green-eyed woman with dark brown hair. The two ethnicities blended well, giving her an exotic beauty that made her the darling of the media. "Have you had the operation on that ankle yet?"

"I'm putting it off for as long as possible," Turnbull replied. The ex–Green Beret had seriously fractured his ankle on a parachute jump, and the joint was deteriorating to the point that it would have to be fused. He could have gotten a physical disability release from the service, but opted to take a staff job instead. Thus, he ended up as chief of SOLS.

"Sit down, gentlemen," Entienne invited. "I would like to introduce you to Edgar Watson. He's CIA on the Iranian desk."

"Greetings," Watson said. "Ms. Entienne has already told me who you two are."

"You've been called down to this deep inner sanctum for a very special briefing," Entienne said. "As you have surmised, I'm sure, this is a most sensitive situation."

Watson swung his briefcase up from the floor onto the

tabletop. He opened it and pulled some papers out, shoving a separate packet to both Joplin and Turnbull. "Okay. Now hear this. Certain elements of the Iranian Army have initiated a mujahideen movement independent of all others. They have begun operations against the foreign military, i.e., Westerners, in the Middle East. They are calling themselves the Jihad Abadi."

"Wait a minute," Joplin said. "That is Arabic. The Iranians speak Farsi."

"This is because they are using only Arabs in their operations," Watson said. "Unfortunately, this resulted in throwing off our initial intelligence probes. Fact of the matter, we wasted a lot of time before we finally figured out they were operating out of Iran. However, they also have various cells in Iraq, Syria, and Saudi Arabia. Most of their agents are citizens of those countries who have lost faith in the current group of Arab Islamics, suicide bombers in particular."

"I'll be damned," Turnbull said. "They finally figured out that getting their young people to blow themselves up and destroying a generation was not a particularly intelligent thing to do, hey?"

"Evidently," Watson commented. "They want to adopt the more civilized tactic of launching well-planned attacks on their enemy to inflict the most casualties possible while keeping their own losses to a minimum."

Joplin glanced at Entienne. "Are we to assume the President is deeply concerned about this?"

"That would be a correct assumption, Carl," she replied.

"I suppose he's worried about the Israelis getting extra antsy about these latest events," Joplin said. "They are just about a quick breath away from military action against Iran as it is."

"That's been quite apparent," Entienne said. "They think we're soft on Tehran. However, as of now, the Mossad knows nothing of this new development. At least, we don't think they do."

Colonel Turnbull was becoming impatient with the rambling conversation when something important obviously needed to be discussed. He glanced at Watson. "How about giving us one concise but informative statement to describe this situation before we drown ourselves in details."

"Sure," Watson said. "The Iranian military—or certain elements of same—have launched a holy war using foreign, that is, non-Iranian, Muslims to do the fighting. These, of course, would be Shiites, the prevalent branch of Islam in Iran." He paused before speaking again. "Now, with the colonel's permission, I will be a bit wordier. Please permit me to say that we know a force of Arab mujahideen has been built up by Iranian Army officers. This outfit is now beyond the cadre stage. There are fully equipped and manned units. However, we don't know the types, number, personnel strength, or equipment. That goes for their training and garrison centers. All that must be found out."

"Mmm," Joplin mused. "There seems to be no doubt of the existence of this Jihad organization. So what's the CIA's take on this thing?"

"That it's a very real threat and we've got to stay up to date on what's going on," Watson said.

Colonel Turnbull scowled. "Being kept up to date won't get us shit. We got to get one step ahead of the game. If not, we're going to be playing in the dark."

Arlene Entienne spoke up. "Carl, who is your Iranian connection?"

"Saviz Kahnani," Joplin replied. "But don't you think it's a little too early for me to make any contact with him?"

"Agreed," Entienne said. "But the President wants you to drop everything and sit tight until you need to have a tête-à-tête with your Iranian friend."

Turnbull snorted at the French expression as sissified. "What is this? *Bareback Mountain*?"

"It was *Brokeback Mountain*," Entienne said. "And the President has a job for you and your staff, John."

"Please tell me in pure unadulterated English, Arlene."

"You are to instruct all SPECOPS units in the Middle East to keep their eyes and ears open to glean intelligence on the Iranian connection. The President wants every operation out there to have a secondary mission of scoping out the latest on this developing situation."

"Then that's what's going to happen," Turnbull promised. "The word will go out to Station Bravo in Bahrain tonight.

Also, Shelor Field in Afghanistan and the USS *Combs* wherever she might be."

"She's in the Arabian Sea, as a matter of fact," Watson said.
"At any rate, while Colonel Turnbull gets things rolling through
SPECOPS, we in the CIA will be using our own organization
and various personnel, i.e., agents, moles, and informants, to
see what we can dig up."

"Who is the central contact for all of us?" Joplin asked.

"Me," Entienne said. She glanced at Turnbull. "Li'l ol'
me!"

"Well, boil me in gumbo and call me Bubba," Turnbull
said, grinning.

CHEHAAR GARRISON
EASTERN IRAN
1830 HOURS

THE armored cars were aligned for inspection in the
proper company formation with the platoons on line. Each vehicle had been carefully and thoroughly washed and scrubbed
with the insides vacuumed free of dust and dirt. The machine
guns atop the turrets had also been given a complete cleaning
after being field-stripped. Light coats of oil were applied to
each part as the weapons were reassembled.

The uniforms of the crews were also washed and pressed,
and now all stood at parade rest in front of their EE-3s waiting
to be inspected. Warrant Officer Shafaqat Hashiri, the company sergeant major, stood to the front. When he saw Captain
Sikes step from his Quonset hut, the warrant officer snapped-
to, made an about-turn, and called the company to attention.
Boot heels clicked together and hands slapped the sides of
trousers as the men assumed the proper parade-ground position. Hashiri made another about-turn. When Sikes marched
up to him, he saluted sharply. "The company is ready for inspection, sir!" he barked in English.

"Carry on, Mr. Hashiri," Sikes said.

Once more, the warrant officer about-turned, then ordered
the men to parade rest. Then he and Sikes marched down to

the far right of the platoons. The commander of the armored car in that position called his men to attention. Sikes checked the crew's appearance, then made a walk around the vehicle, carefully noting the condition of the steel exterior. He wasn't so concerned about dust since the wind kicked it up constantly, but he wanted to make sure there was no rust. The nearby salt marshes made erosion a constant threat to vehicles, weapons, and equipment.

When he finished with the first vehicle, he marched over to the second. That commander called his men to attention while the first put his crew at parade rest.

Very precise. Very military. Very much "bashing on the square," as the Brits say.

WHEN Arsalaan Sikes, née Archibald Sikes, arrived at Chehaar Garrison, he was put into an intense training program. It was at this time he learned that al-Zaim was actually Brigadier Shahruz Khohollah of the Iranian Army.

After only a few days of the military instruction, it became apparent to Khohollah that this newly converted English Muslim not only knew more than the Iranian cadre, but was better schooled than they in military science. He was promoted to sergeant and turned loose on the mujahideen. Within a couple of weeks, the mob of Arab farm and city boys was disciplined, drilled, and sharp. Brigadier Khohollah was pleased to report to his superiors that the group would be ready for combat two months ahead of schedule.

Sikes's old pal Khalil Farouk, who had enticed him to desert from the British Army, had come along from Saudi Arabia with his protégé. Farouk was not in the military branch of the Jihad Abadi; he was a political officer who conducted propaganda and religious classes to inspire the new soldiers to want to fight for the cause. He emphasized they could serve Islam best by becoming skilled, disciplined soldiers. Allah had blessed the Jihad Abadi, and wanted a logical, pragmatic fighting force able to carry on a prolonged, effective struggle until the final day of holy victory.

Sikes and Farouk roomed together in one end of a hut, and

spent most evenings in talk. Sikes sorely missed his British ale and stout, but enjoyed sipping thick, black *khawe* coffee from tiny cups. That, and smoking an *argili* water pipe during long quiet hours, brought him new comforts and relaxation. Farouk wanted to use those quiet times to impart further encouragement to his English friend, and he decided to tell him about the Arab Legion. Sikes listened with rapt attention as the Arab's narrative enthralled him, feeding his imagination with new fantasies of glory.

The Arab Legion was a large unit of Arab soldiers commanded by British officers. The Legion was first formed in October 1920 by Captain Frederick Peake in Transjordan from the local gendarmerie. At first, they were undisciplined and uncaring after many months without pay. Most did not bother to wear their uniforms. But Peake went to work, shaped them up, and got the right administrative and supply wheels turning to raise morale. When they were ready for active duty, he dubbed this newly reactivated unit the Arab Legion.

Peake was later joined by another Brit ranker, Major John Glubb. This latter officer was an excellent field commander, and further improved the Legion by organizing the Badieh—the Desert Patrol. The fighting force battled rebellious desert tribes and infiltrators from Palestine and Syria. By the time World War II started, Peake Pasha had retired, and Glubb Pasha took over command. The next two leaders were Sidney Cooke Pasha and N.O. Lash Bey. The titles Farouk used confused Sikes, until the Arab explained that officers who held the ranks of second lieutenant and first lieutenant were called "effendi." Captains through brigadiers were addressed as "bey," while "pasha," the highest, was reserved for major general and above.

As Farouk told of the fighting against Germans and further combat in postwar Palestine, Sikes's imagination churned up new fantasies for him. Now his boyhood dreams of becoming a field marshal in the British Army were replaced by those of becoming Sikes Pasha after leading the Jihad Abadi to a smashing victory and throwing the infidels out of the Middle East. Not only would he have high rank and glory, but he would be incredibly rich by owning thousands of acres of oil wells.

When the arms dealer Harry Turpin came on the scene with the EE-3 Jararaca armored cars, Sikes's fortunes took another turn for the better. The Iranians commissioned him in the rank of captain and gave him command of the vehicles with orders to organize them into a fighting force. Sikes and Harry became good friends during the turnover and checkout of the cars. Sikes asked the dealer if he could get him some British rank insignia. He wanted to have it on the uniforms of his men. Getting a few chevrons and pips was child's play for a man who dealt in all sorts of military goods, such as bombs, vehicles, and weaponry that could be as large as heavy artillery. The Iranians thought it would be a good idea. Conspicuous signs of rank would increase discipline and the desire for promotion.

1900 HOURS

NOW the inspection was over, and Captain Sikes stood in front of his men with Warrant Officer Shafaqat at his side. "I compliment you," Sikes said in Arabic to the armored car crews. "Your vehicles and weapons are ready for action. I also wish to make an announcement. Rather than be addressed as Captain Sikes, from this moment on, I will be called Sikes Bey. Do you understand this?"

The well-drilled men replied in unison, loudly shouting, "*Aiwa*, Sikes Bey!"

"Tomorrow we will have reveille an hour earlier than usual," Sikes continued. "After mess call, we will mount the vehicles and go directly into Afghanistan. If the UN camp is still standing, we will attack it without mercy. They have been warned to leave the area. The infidels must learn it is a deadly error to defy the Jihad Abadi!"

"*Aiwa*, Sikes Bey!"

CHAPTER 7

THE Command Two vehicle with Mike Assad and Dave Leibowitz sat some two and a half kilometers southwest of the UNREO camp. Mike straddled the roll bars above the M-2 .50-caliber machine gun, balancing precariously on the steel tubes. He peered through his binoculars in a southern direction, every nerve alert and tingling. Combat was imminent, and his prebattle nerves had kicked into a higher gear.

Dave stood on the hood of the DPV, where the M-60 7.62-millimeter machine gun would have normally been mounted if they were using three-man crews. He was performing the same watch chores as his buddy, and their viewing fields swept back and forth in opposite directions, overlapping on a bearing of 360 degrees from the front of the vehicle.

Over to the north in Command Three, Frank Gomez and Doc Bradley did the same, while Green Two, manned by

Chief Matt Gunnarson and Chad Murchison, was on guard to the east. The side to the direct west of the large perimeter was only given cursory attention because that was where the impassable salt marshes that led into Iran were located. Intelligence analyses indicated that attacks from that direction were impossible.

UNREO CAMP

THE remaining six DPVs were scattered among the tents with all weapons—personal and vehicular—locked and loaded. The dozen SEALs were the only human beings present within the bivouac. Every member of Dr. Pierre Bouchier's UN staff was now in the hangar at Shelor Field, waiting for Brannigan's Brigands to deal with the mysterious Englishman and his trio of armored cars.

The nearby Pashtun village was quiet and subdued, as if the population anticipated some calamitous event to occur at any moment. Although the SEALs kept the place under surveillance, they had not spotted one living creature other than a couple of mangy curs who trotted among the huts, scavenging for scraps of food. Guy Devereaux stood behind the machine gun on Command One, while Brannigan sat in the driver's seat with his legs dangling out the side. The Skipper checked his watch, then pressed the transmit button on the LASH headset. "Watch vehicles, this is Command One. Report. Over."

"This is Command Two," came Dave's voice. "Negative report. Out." Command Three and Green Two made similar transmissions.

"This is Command One. Stay on your toes out there. We don't want Lawrence of Arabia and his bumbling Bedouins to sneak up on us. Out. Green One, this is Command One. What's your situation? Over."

"Nothing but empty country out there to the east," Jim Cruiser reported. "Out."

Guy Devereaux patted his machine gun. "Maybe they ain't coming, sir."

"It's early yet," Brannigan said. "Dr. Bouchier said the guy had given them until noon to get out of the area."

"Oh, well," Guy said, yawning. "I figure the son of a bitch will be anywhere from two to twenty-four hours late. Them fucking camel-jockeys ain't exactly the saints of punctuality."

"This guy's a Brit with an obvious military background," Brannigan said. "He'll be on time. Maybe early."

"How many are they?" Guy asked. "I forgot."

"Three," Brannigan replied.

"Hooray!" Guy exclaimed with just a touch of sarcasm in his voice. "For the first time I can remember, we'll outnumber the bad guys. And at three to one!"

"Yep," Brannigan said, "the gods of war can't shit on us all the time."

1125 HOURS

IT was quiet and still within the UN camp. The calm had lulled the Brigands into a lethargic state of near-dozing. Now and then, someone would yawn widely out of sheer boredom.

BAM-BAM-BAM-BAM!

Heavy automatic fire suddenly erupted from the western side of the camp, sending hundreds of slugs slapping into the tents, shaking the SEALs out of their collective doldrums.

Senior Chief Petty Officer Buford Dawkins yelled into his LASH even though he could have easily been heard if he whispered. "Red Section! Port around starboard! Return fire!"

Red One, Two, and Three's motors were quickly started, and the drivers whipped the DPVs to the right, swinging 180 degrees around to face the incoming rounds. The machine gunners began pumping out spurts of slugs even though they had yet to spot any obvious targets. The idea was to throw out a heavy fusillade to get the unknown attackers to duck down or pull back.

ARMORED CAR COLUMN

SIKES Bey had been standing in his command hatch as
the UN camp's tents first came into view. The sight of the
structures still standing infuriated him. He had brought all
twenty of his EE-3s with him, and they were well positioned
in a line of attack. He grabbed his microphone and pressed the
transmit button.

"*Atlak!*" he yelled. "Open fire!"

The gunners, peering through their periscopes with gun-
sights etched on the lenses, quickly aimed into the center of the
tents. The twenty Dashikas blasted the heavy 12.7-millimeter
slugs straight into the area in combined bursts of 180 rounds a
second.

Now unexpected return fire splattered among the EE-3s,
smacking and clanking on the armored hulls. Sikes Bey and
the other vehicle commanders quickly dropped down into the
interiors, slamming the hatches shut.

UNREO CAMP

THE exchange of machine-gun fire built up in intensity,
the choppy detonations echoing off in the desert sky. Brannigan ordered the vehicles to the west side of the defensive
perimeter to find good fighting positions. At the same time,
transmissions over the headsets came hot and heavy.

"This is Red One. I can count twenty of the bastards. Out."

"This is Green Three. They are starting to curve around our
right flank. Out."

"This is Red Three. Same on our left. Out."

"This is Command One," Brannigan said. "Section leaders spread your vehicles out to avoid letting the enemy outflank us. Out." Then he turned his attention to the DPVs out
on watch. "Hey! You goddamn three blind mice, what're you
doing out there? Sitting around with your heads up your
asses?"

The first reply came from Mike Assad. "Command One,
nobody's slipped through this position." Command Three and

Green Two gave the same reports, the dismay evident in their voices even over the radios.

"Alright," Brannigan said. "Get your asses in here and come in shooting! There's more than six times the number we anticipated. Out."

THE BATTLE

THE fighting opened up as Sikes Bey sent his command into an enveloping maneuver. The SEAL DPVs responded by extending their formation, keeping the armored cars constantly moving in an outward direction.

"COMMAND One! Our bullets is bouncing off the bastards!" Dawkins reported.

Brannigan silently damned the Station Bravo S-4 for not providing them with armor-piercing rounds. He instantly reached the conclusion they were going to have to cut and run. There was no way that patrol vehicles with a single machine gun loaded with ball ammo were going to be able to knock out armored cars. But he couldn't order a retreat until the three watch DPVs had rejoined them. "All units! Fire at their tires!"

"That's what we been doing, sir," Milly Mills said. "But they keep coming."

Brannigan knew that meant the enemy had run-flat tires. "But they're slowed down, aren't they? Over."

"I don't know. Wait," Milly said. A moment passed, then he came back. "By God! They sure as hell are! I don't think they're as fast as we are anyhow. And it looks like they have a tough time steering when the tires on one side are hit."

"All vehicles!" Brannigan said. "Dodge, dart, and shoot! We gotta take advantage of our superior speed. Out."

OVER in his vehicle, Sikes Bey bounced and swung in his seat with each movement of the EE-3. He had now determined his command was impervious to the enemy's fire as he viewed the fight through his periscope. But he also noticed his foes were faster and more nimble, making quick, short turns that the armored cars could not match. And the fact that several tires had been shot up slowed down his vehicles' speed and maneuverability even more.

JIM Cruiser whipped the steering wheel to the left, bringing Green One alongside an armored car some twenty meters away. The guy quickly spotted them and swung his turret and machine gun in their direction, firing long bursts. Bullets cracked and whined around Bruno Puglisi as he lowered the muzzle of his M-2 .50-caliber and made quick pulls on the trigger. Both tires on that side of the enemy vehicle were hit, causing it to lunge violently to the right. That spoiled the bad guy's aim, and Jim went back the other way, breaking clear as Puglisi cut loose with a couple more fire bursts.

Over on the other side of the fight, Red Three, with Milly Mills and Andy Malachenko, managed to come in on the rear of one enemy vehicle. Unfortunately, the ground was uneven in the area, causing the DPV to bounce. This spoiled Andy's aim and his bullets whipped off into empty air. Neither he nor Milly noticed the armored car driving obliquely toward them on the port side. A burst of four heavy rounds slammed into Milly's torso, twisting him violently in the seat belt as he collapsed across the steering wheel. The DPV rolled, tossing Andy out onto the hard-packed desert ground.

Now Command Two and Three arrived on the scene and joined the fight. They had monitored all the transmissions, and the drivers Dave Leibowitz and Doc Bradley moved smoothly into the rolling, circling maneuvering of the battle. It had evolved to the point that the situation was like fighter planes battling it out in dogfights as they sought to gain the advantage over each other. But in this case, there was not the added dimension of height.

The two tardy DPVs immediately opened fire at the exact

moment that Green Two made its appearance. Now all three added to the defensive salvos of the SEALs.

ONE of the armored car platoon leaders reported that additional fire was suddenly coming in. Sikes Bey's mind raced as he made a quick decision. That could mean reinforcements were arriving. He had already determined these were Americans, so there was a very good chance that air strikes had already been called in. It was time for a strategic withdrawal. He reached for his microphone. "*Dauwir*—retreat!"

The fighting broke off with the same abruptness it had begun.

1235 HOURS

BRANNIGAN decided a pursuit was useless. It would only result in a battle of attrition the Brigands would eventually lose even if they were faster than the bad guys. The ammo loaded into the M-2 .50s was not going to penetrate into the armored car interiors. The Skipper also vetoed following after them to see which direction they headed. That could lead to an ambush by a stronger force joining the original attackers. This was one of those maddening situations where a guy was damned if he did and damned if he didn't.

The sad thing was that Milly Mills was dead. He had been one of the original members of the old platoon from which the detachment had evolved in three bloody operations. His vehicle, Red Three, lay on its side as the other SEALs drove up to the site. They quickly unassed their vehicles and rolled the shot-up DPV back upright. Senior Chief Dawkins and Gutsy Olson gently removed Milly's body from the restraints of the seat belt. The corpse was placed in the back of the vehicle under the machine gun. Andy Malachenko, sprawled out on the ground, was badly bruised and dazed, but Doc Bradley said he would be okay within a short time. He was unable to drive, so he would ride shotgun with Dawkins on the trip back to Shelor Field. Pete Dawson would drive Red Three in the convoy.

Now, with the afternoon desert winds picking up, Brannigan and Cruiser stood looking out over the UN camp. All the tents were down and tire tracks had torn up the ground. Valuable medical equipment was smashed, torn up, and scattered across the area. This would bring the camp's humanitarian mission to a sad finish. Cruiser glanced toward the Pashtun village. "They're not even out of their houses."

"All they want is for everybody to leave them alone," Brannigan said He sighed and shoved his hands in his pockets. "It's shitty as hell about Milly, huh?"

"Everybody's really down," Cruiser commented.

"Yeah," Brannigan said. "Well, *c'est la guerre,* as the French say, though that doesn't offer much comfort."

"We stymied the bad guys pretty good by hitting their tires," Cruiser said. "I wonder why they didn't shoot ours up. We don't have run-flats on the DPVs."

"The muzzles on the turret-mounted machine guns don't lower fast enough," Brannigan said. "They had to concentrate on shooting at the guys in the vehicles." He took one more look at the battlefield. "Well, let's mount up and head back to Shelor Field. Everything's about as fucked up around here as it's gonna get."

The two officers walked toward the detachment to get things moving.

SHELOR FIELD
1435 HOURS

THE mood in the hangar was grim. Randy Tooley and his new DPV were present. The enterprising airman had quickly painted the purloined vehicle Air Force blue and stenciled on phony registration and unit numbers to make it appear legal. He had already made arrangements to have Petty Officer First Class Michael Mills flown to Kuwait, where the mortuary center would prepare him for his final trip home. Randy had done this sad duty on numerous occasions as part of his job. He was an emotional little guy, and had seen that the corpse was treated with utmost respect as it was prepared for transport.

"This is an American serviceman," he told the C-130 load-master, "not a piece of equipment."

Now, in the partitioned office in the back of the hangar, the Skipper, Jim Cruiser, and Senior Chief Buford Dawkins sat around a battered desk drinking cold beers. A refrigerator, furnished by Randy as an extra gesture of gratitude for the DPV, sat in the corner of the room. Dawkins lit a cigar, exhaling a thick cloud of smoke. "That UN doctor was fit to be tied, wasn't he?"

"I quieted him down," Brannigan said. "As soon as he started bitching about his camp getting ripped apart, I reminded him that he told us the bad guys had three armored cars, but twenty of the sons of bitches attacked us. If we'd known the enemy was that strong, I would have advised him to haul ass like he was told to do the first place. Then I could have made a report to Berringer."

"I still can't figure out how they snuck up on us," Cruiser commented in irritation. "Not one guy on watch saw them come into the area."

"They had to come from the west," Dawkins said.

"That's an impassable salt marsh," Brannigan retorted. "It would be difficult as hell for men on foot to cross it. It's absolutely impossible for vehicles to negotiate mucky terrain like that."

"I wonder what the S-Three at Station Bravo is going to have us do," Cruiser mused.

"I sent an AAR to Carey," Brannigan said. "I told him we need armor-piercing ammo for the fifties along with some Javelins to give us a solid antiarmor capability. And anything else the headquarters weenies could spare us to help take care of this situation."

Dawkins took a sip of beer, then shoved his stogie back in his face. "They'll need about twenty-four hours to digest that report before they take action. Then we'll either get equipped right and given a definite mission, or they'll pull us the hell out of here."

Brannigan shook his head. "Let me tell you for sure, Senior Chief, they're not going to pull us the hell out of here."

1900 HOURS

EVERYONE else was in the hangar, moping and speaking softly among themselves, as Chad Murchison and Penny Brubaker sat together on a bench outside. They could look out past some parked aircraft to the barren desert beyond. Chad was quiet, and Penny sensed his deep sadness over the loss of his SEAL buddy.

"Did your friend have any family?" she asked.

"He wasn't married," Chad said. "I think his father is dead, but his mother lives in a small town in Iowa. She works in a bank, he said, a teller or something."

"She's going to be heartbroken when she hears the news," Penny said. She glanced over at the dented DPV that he had died in. A large discolored spot caused by his blood was visible. "I want to get out of here."

"I can't blame you," Chad said.

"When is your time in the Navy over with, Chaddie?"

Chad thought a moment. "My hitch is up in about six months."

"Chaddie, you must get out," Penny urged. "You've done your duty now. Most boys don't serve at all. Why, there're thousands of families—maybe more—who don't even have relatives in the armed forces. Nobody is getting drafted like they did in Vietnam."

Chad remained silent.

Penny started to speak again, but sensed it would be better not to say anything. She moved closer to Chad, taking his arm and putting it around her shoulder.

CHAPTER 8

ARSALAAN Sikes—née Archie Sikes—strolled among the armored cars, checking out the crews as they painted over the hundreds of pings and scars caused by enemy machine-gun fire during the previous day's fighting. The Brit had been pleasantly surprised the Yanks had no armor-piercing ammunition. They either had not expected armored cars, or did not know how many there were.

Now, as Sikes Bey continued with his inspection, the men's discipline was evident as they snapped to attention when their commanding officer walked up to them. The senior members of each group reported to him with a sharp salute. The actual supervision of the activity was under the company sergeant major, Warrant Officer Hashiri, but Sikes believed in a hands-on approach as part of his command philosophy. After a quick but observant inspection of each vehicle, he decided everything looked fine, and he left the motor pool to go to headquarters.

Chehaar Garrison was far below the sharp appearance of a typical British Army post, and this irritated Sikes to some extent. But he didn't have enough rank to turn things around to his liking. The Quonset huts were laid out in rows all properly aligned and covered down, but the area between the simple buildings was bare and a bit trashy. Sikes would have laid out walks lined with large whitewashed rocks, and prohibited cigarette butts and other litter to be thrown on the ground. When he earned enough rank in the Jihad Abadi to command his own garrison, it would have an appearance that would meet the approval of even the sternest of British regimental sergeants major.

Sikes walked down the front row of huts bordering the parade field. When he reached the headquarters building, he stepped inside. The Iranian corporal at the reception desk looked up casually from the newspaper he was perusing, then went back to his reading. If he had been a trooper in the Armored Car Company, Sikes would have locked his heels and chewed his ass bloody for this military discourtesy of not jumping to his feet. But this careless bumpkin was on Brigadier Shahruz Khohollah's staff, and the captain had no authority over him.

The brigadier's office was no more than a cubicle at the far end of the building. Sikes went directly to it, finding Khohollah and Khalil Farouk waiting for him. The Brit saluted and took a chair pushed toward him by Farouk. Khohollah flipped the ash off his cigarette into an ashtray at his elbow. "I have reviewed your report on the battle," he said in English, holding up a single sheet of paper. Sikes had scribbled out what had happened on a piece of notebook paper the evening before, then sent it with a sergeant to drop off at headquarters.

"Do you need me to add anything to it, sir?" Sikes asked.

Khohollah shook his head. "It is all plain enough. And I agree with your decision to withdraw. There may well have been an air strike or reinforcements of American tanks nearby."

"Yes, sir," Sikes said. "I didn't have no idea there were

Yanks or anybody else in the area before I got there. I was pretty surprised when we spotted them little cars o' theirs. I ordered my lads to open up on 'em and charge before they saw us."

Farouk smiled. "They were not expecting you to come from the west. The infidels know nothing of the road through the salt marshes."

"Well, you suffered no losses," Khohollah said. "That is what is important."

"We did get our tires bluddy well shot up," Sikes said. "I can't take the comp'ny out till they're replaced."

"Our good friend Harry Turpin has been apprised of the situation," Farouk interjected. "He has promised a delivery of replacements and extras as quickly as he can arrange it. That might take a few weeks."

"That's bad news, ain't it?" Sikes remarked. "It could be a while before we get another crack at the Yanks."

"We shall not be wasting time," Khohollah said. "There is an alternative we have that you do not know about, Captain. But it's about time you were brought up to date. In the mountains north of your battle site is a Pashtun force that is strongly allied with the Jihad Abadi."

"How big a group are them Pashtuns?"

"The number varies," Khohollah answered. "The leader is a very capable fellow named Yama Orakzai. He calls his force the Pawdz de Peshto Baghane. A literal translation is Army of Pashtun Rebels. That is a bit presumptuous on his part since they are not much more than an armed band."

"In actuality, Orakzai is only a warlord," Farouk commented. "However, he is a sophisticated and intelligent man with great potential."

"Yes," Khohollah agreed. "Here in this part of the world, the English acronym of PPB is used when referring to Orakzai's force of mujahideen."

"Why the English initials?" Sikes asked.

"It worked out that way because the main language of Afghanistan is Dari and that of Pakistan is Urdu," Khohollah explained. "A common name is necessary when authorities of the two nations discuss them. The Pakistanis use English for their official administration as much as the Indian government."

"Makes sense then," Sikes said. "Anyway, who the hell are these PPBs rebelling against?"

"The present Afghan government," Khohollah said. "Orakzai wants to establish an independent Pashtun nation in the western part of Afghanistan. He calls it Peshtonkhwa."

"D'you think he can do it?"

"He is a seasoned soldier. He led a band of mujahideen against the Soviets in their invasion of Afghanistan."

"Blimey!" Sikes exclaimed. "He must be an old bloke, hey?"

"Not at all," Khohollah said. "He is in his early forties. He was only sixteen when the troubles over there started. Arrangements are already under way to have him launch a campaign as soon as feasible. His men have very sophisticated weapons looted from the Soviets, as well as what the American CIA gave them during the war."

"Having weapons and using 'em proper is two different things," Sikes said.

"Orakzai is an excellent commander and trainer," Khohollah said. "He is also a proven expert in hit-and-run tactics. He can spring an attack, then immediately withdraw back into his own sanctuary where he and his people enjoy cover and concealment within the mountain caves."

Sikes, pleased, grinned. "Wind him up and turn him loose then."

"Like I said," Khohollah said, smiling back. "Arrangements are already under way for just that."

USS *COMBS*
SPECOPS CENTER
1030 HOURS

BRIGADIER General Greg Leroux, U.S. Army, was the disgruntled commanding officer of the SPECOPS staff aboard the USS *Combs* DDG. He did not opt for a West Point education; take a commission in the infantry branch; go to jump school; qualify for Special Forces; complete Ranger training; serve as a rifle company, infantry battalion, and Green Beret detachment commander in Vietnam; lead a brigade in Operation Desert Storm; then attend the Command and General Staff College at Fort Leavenworth, to be eventually stuck aboard a ship. He was a knock-down, drag-out, ass-kicking ground-pounding, profane-spewing, beer-guzzling, fighting son of a bitch who was a professional soldier with the emphasis on soldier. Leroux was neither a sailor nor a seafarer nor a mariner, nor did he possess skills or interest in any other nautical profession. And he likened being confined within the steel plates of a ship to suffering live burial in a metal coffin.

But somebody had to run the show in this brand-new scheme of having a floating SFOB that moved about with the trickery of a wily con man. So he performed his duties impolitely and rudely, having little patience when problems arose, unless they affected troops in the field. This was when he could use the one big advantage he had in this job that he wouldn't have anywhere else: He had direct access to the powers-that-be and could get things done with the proverbial snap of his fingers.

Now Commander Tom Carey and Lieutenant Commander Ernest Berringer sat in front of him in his little enclosed office, having just delivered an oral report on the unexpected battle that had occurred in the OA of Operation Rolling Thunder. Leroux always had a toothpick stuck in one side of his mouth, rolling it from side to side. It was a habit developed over years of breaking an intense addiction to smoking. He never took notes, but the two SEAL officers' report was etched neatly in his mind. After a couple of silent moments, he spoke.

"Okay. The first thing we do is get those guys an extra machine gun for their DPVs," Leroux announced. "That means they'll have to change their configuration to three swinging dicks per vehicle rather than two. That may cut down the number of them little off-road fuckers, but they'll be better armed. But because of the KIA, somebody is gonna have to work with just one other guy."

"Actually, sir," Carey said, "Brannigan has one man coming in from furlough. That means the detachment strength will stay with eighteen men. So there will be six DPVs with three-man crews."

"That's good," Leroux said. "We'll also see that they get armor-piercing rounds for both the fifties and seven-point-six-twos. That'll give 'em a lot of kick-butt capabilities. And that outfit needs run-flat tires. I figure twenty-four to put on right away and eighteen extras on the first issue."

"We've had trouble with fuel," Berringer interjected. "I'm afraid our commander out there pulled some illegal maneuvering to get his initial allotment."

"Nothing wrong with that," Leroux said. "A good soldier would sell his baby sister to a whorehouse if it would help the mission. They'll have plenty of fuel coming regularly now. And that goes for chow and other items on the TOA." He glanced down at the supply requisitions and issues. "You said they had nine DPVs, but I see another has been sent since they arrived in the OA. What's with that?"

"We don't know, sir," Carey said. "Evidently, the commander worked around us on that one too. He went directly to the Four-Shop at Station Bravo."

Leroux chuckled. "It looks like somebody's baby sister is now a bordello inmate, hey?" He leaned back in his chair. "Okay. Is there anything else before I shove this shit into the pipeline?"

"I just want to remind the general that the situation on Operation Rolling Thunder is fluid and we expect a lot of changes and contingencies to raise their ugly heads."

"So noted," Leroux said. He nodded to Berringer. "Now what's this intel item you want to pass on?"

"Lieutenant Brannigan has sent us information that an Englishman is in command of the enemy armored car unit," Berringer answered.

Leroux frowned. "That's some odd shit. How'd he learn that?"

"He learned about it from the head of the area UN relief group," Berringer replied. "This is a Dr. Pierre Bouchier, a Belgian. He stated the individual who ordered him to vacate the area was obviously English, though he used an Arabic first name. The doctor doesn't recall what it is."

"Well, that's neither here nor there for the three of us right now," Leroux said. "I'll send the info to the Two-Shop at Station Bravo. They'll run with it. Is there anything else? No? Alright then. You gentlemen have a nice day."

With the conference closed, Carey and Berringer made quick exits to get down to the commo center to see if any other messages had come in from Wild Bill Brannigan.

SHELOR FIELD
AIRMEN'S CLUB
2000 HOURS

THE club was filled with young Air Force men and women drinking beer and listening to a self-appointed disc jockey playing CDs over the sound system. Loud conversation and laughter competed with the music amid clinking glasses as a celebration that was a nightly event rolled on.

Chad Murchison and Penny Brubaker walked into the place, going up to the bar. Several nearby celebrants gave them second glances because of Penny's white UN coveralls. Chad's BDU attire was a normal sight on the premises since SPECOPS troops passed through the airfield on a regular basis. After getting a couple of beers each, the couple turned and looked for a place to sit down. A young woman wearing the chevrons of an airman first class waved at them, gesturing to a pair of empty chairs at the table where she sat with several friends. Chad and Penny walked over and settled down.

"Hi!" the young airman said cheerfully. "Welcome to Shelor Field."

"Thanks," Chad responded to her greeting. "I'm Chad and this is Penny."

"I'm Wanda and here we have"—she pointed to another young woman and two men—"Betty, Sam, and Tommy. We all work in the supply warehouse."

"I'm with the SEAL detachment," Chad said. "And Penny belongs to the UN group."

Betty laughed. "It didn't take you two long to get together, did it?"

"We're old friends from school," Penny said. "Actually, we are much more than simply pals." She leaned over and kissed Chad on the cheek.

"Oh, my God!" Wanda said. "What a small world! And you ran into each other here in Afghanistan?"

"This is the *second* time," Penny said.

"Oh, my God!" both Wanda and Betty exclaimed together.

"Y'know," Sam said to Chad, "we see a lot of you special operations guys, but I've never had a chance to talk to any of you." He took a sip of beer. "When I joined the Air Force, I did it 'cause a couple of my buddies had decided to. Now that I'm in and seen a lot that goes on, I wished I'd tried for something like the SEALs." He gestured around the room. "This fucking part of the Air Force is for candy-asses. Hell, even girls can do the jobs here."

"Screw you!" Betty snapped at him.

"Anyhow," Sam continued, "I volunteered for para-rescue and got accepted. I'm being shipping back to the States to go through my training."

"Good riddance," Wanda said with a sneer.

"Oh, yeah?" Sam retorted. "I'll be in a real adventurous outfit. Death-defying shit. Making parachute jumps behind enemy lines to rescue pilots that have been shot down. This is boring here. And will I pick up the chicks between missions! You gals don't like to admit it, but you go for us macho types."

"Not me!" Wanda protested. "I go for guys like Randy Tooley."

Now the other airman, Tommy, jumped into the conversation. "He's a little runty nerd!"

"Maybe so," Wanda said. "But he's a go-getter. He's only an E-Four, but he runs this place. Colonel Watkins trusts him so much he lets him do anything he wants. Have you noticed he doesn't wear a uniform? He looks like a Santa Monica beach bum who hasn't held a steady job in his life."

"So what's that got to do with sex?" Sam asked.

"Nothing," Wanda said. "But when he gets out of the service, he's going to have that same attitude. He's the kind of ninny who ends up rich and powerful. And eventually, I want a rich husband who can get me every single goddamn solitary thing I want."

"Mmm," Tommy said. "You're probably right about Randy."

Sam turned his attention back to Chad. "So I'll be going to Fort Benning for jump school before I go through the rescue course. Is it tough?"

"Not really," Chad said. "The guys that go into the SEALs or Marine Force Recon or Special Forces and Rangers in the Army have a lot tougher training ahead of them. Are you thinking of going to HALO school too?"

"What's that?" Sam asked.

"High altitude, low opening," Chad replied. "You jump and fall a long ways before opening your chute."

"Yeah! I'm gonna do that."

"Jesus! You'll be splattered all over the countryside, you dumb shit!" Tommy exclaimed.

"You'll probably break your ankle before that happens," Chad said.

Penny was growing tired of what she considered boring conversation. She took Chad's arm and stood up. "Let's dance."

They left the table and joined others dancing to the country-western singing of Patty Loveless.

2350 HOURS

BOTH Chad and Penny were drunk as they walked arm in arm back toward the barracks area. She was in a good mood. "That guy Sam is an idiot, isn't he?"

"Why?"

"Oh, for wanting to do all that boyish stuff," Jenny said. "What a moron!"

"He wants to prove something," Chad said, irritated by the way she didn't understand the guy.

"Prove what?"

Chad stopped. "He wants to prove to himself that he can accept a challenge. He wants the discipline that lifestyle will give him. It all points him in a direction he wants to go."

"Well, maybe," Penny allowed. "Anyhow, you've already proved yourself, Chad. In another year, you'll be a civilian."

"Being a SEAL is a complicated thing," Chad said. "It

pulls at you, enfolds you, and makes you feel outside of normal society and its decorum."

"Aw!" Penny said with a light laugh. "You'll get over that shit."

"It's not shit," Chad said. "It's a way of life."

Penny suddenly sobered, glancing at the young man at her side. For the first time, she felt really frightened about her relationship with Chad. Maybe she had lost him already.

PASHTUN STRONGHOLD
GHARAWDARA HIGHLANDS
CENTRAL WESTERN AFGHANISTAN

THE territory occupied by the PPB—Pashto Rebel Army—was dominated by steep peaks that eased down into slanting plateaus broken up by the craggy terrain. Natural caves dominated the region, in some cases honeycombing entire mountaintops. It was in one of these areas, 6,000 feet ASL, that the leader, Yama Orakzai, had established the base camp for his revolutionary movement.

The population of the camp was made up of five thousand men, women, and children scattered across twenty-five square kilometers of the rugged, steep countryside. Approximately nine hundred of the adult males were well-armed and equipped mujahideen. While the younger ones had not participated in actual battles, except for minor raids and ambushes against the Afghan Army and scattered settlements of Taliban fugitives, the older men had fought the Soviets. These elder members of the band saw to it that their nephews, sons, and grandsons were thoroughly trained to conduct combat operations.

Although they seemed a ragtag mob because of a lack of uniforms, they had an organization of sorts made up of various detachments of riflemen, scouts, mortar and machine gun crews, and antiaircraft elements. Most of these men were heavily involved in lucrative opium-smuggling operations that ran from the Afghan mountains through the Gharawdara Highlands and up across northern Iran and into Turkey. There, the European cartels paid hard cash for the raw powder that would be turned into the narcotics for the insatiable appetites of the Western infidels. The men of the PPB not only provided transportation in the operation, but also security. The AK-47s wielded by the fierce and skilled fighters were enough to deter even the most desperate and daring bandits.

The main goal of the PPB, however, was the establishment of a Pashtun state with independent sovereignty. Unfortunately, not only would the Afghan government refuse to give up their western areas, but the Taliban still lurked about. These religious fanatics had their own plan for the nation, and it didn't include having thousands of well-armed Pashtuns living next door. Orakzai had spent several years trying to figure out how to handle the touchy situation when the English arms dealer Harry Turpin approached him as an agent of the Iranians. These Farsis wanted the PPB to join them in an independent jihad to drive Westerners out of the Middle East. Orakzai was not interested so much in the jihad as he was in having a powerful ally that would frighten off even the zealots of the Taliban. At the same time, the Afghans would think twice about resisting his struggle for independence.

Now Orakzai and his people were ready and able to give armed support to the Jihad Abadi in whatever capacity was required. The Pashtuns' main goal was to clear their territory of foreigners and domestic enemies.

CHAPTER 9

THE C-130 stood by the SEALs' hangar, its ramp lowered for unloading. Besides several tons of supplies, ammo, and fuel, it had brought Petty Officer Second Class Reynauld Pecheur back from emergency leave. His wife and two sons lived in San Diego, and he had gathered them up for a trip back to their hometown in Louisiana to check things out after a violent spring storm. The roaring tempest had battered the hell out of Louisiana and Mississippi, and the hurricane season loomed in the near future.

All his SEAL buddies were curious about how Pech's folks had weathered the disaster. His Cajun family lived in boggy country in southeastern Louisiana where a lot of the houses were built on stilts. These residences were scattered through an area called Mouvants Swamp. Like everyone there, they spoke more French than English, and were fiercely self-reliant, fending for themselves in both bad and good times.

Although not flush with cash-money, they were strong and well nourished from hunting, fishing, and growing their own food. By the time FEMA had shown up with help, everyone had already repaired the damage to their homes, docks, and other structures. Any delays in taking care of that necessary mending could result in catastrophic damage during future hurricanes. Pech's last chore before taking Blanche and the kids back to California was to help his father-in-law reshingle his roof. Now, with his family reestablished in their San Diego home, he had returned to duty with Brannigan's Brigands.

THE SEALs had formed a line and were passing the smaller packages and crates off the aircraft into the hangar from man to man. Meanwhile, Randy Tooley, the intrepid little Air Force guy, had arranged for forklifts to come over to handle the heavier stuff. Colonel Leroux, the CO of the SFOB on the USS *Combs*, had made sure the shipment included run-flat tires for the DPVs. He also had arranged for the delivery to include a half-dozen Javelin antitank missile CLUs with trigger mechanisms and four-dozen disposable launch tubes with projectiles to increase the firepower of their arsenal. The other addition of weaponry was six M-60 7.62-millimeter machine guns to be mounted on the hoods in front of the DPVs' passenger seats.

As the unloading progressed, Lieutenant Bill Brannigan was sequestered with Lieutenant Junior Grade Jim Cruiser and Senior Chief Petty Officer Buford Dawkins in the cubicle office at the rear of the hangar. Their concern was the reorganization of the detachment as had been ordered by General Leroux.

"Alright," Brannigan said. "This means we'll now use a total of six DPVs when we go out on an operation."

"That leaves us three surplus," Cruiser said. He grinned. "Of course, they're going to think we have four because of the one we gave to Randy."

Dawkins had some advice. "Skipper, you better write up a report of how it was wrecked. Make that *totaled*."

"You're right, Senior Chief," Brannigan said. "I'll take care of that as quick as I can. At any rate, under this new setup, the way I see it is that each crew will now consist of a commander-driver, an M-Sixty machine gunner, and an M-Two machine gunner."

"What about them Javelins, sir?" Dawkins asked.

"They'll be distributed evenly among all the vehicles," Brannigan replied. "We'll put one CLU and four launch tubes in each one."

"That'll give us a grand total of twenty-four rounds," Cruiser noted. "Wouldn't it be better to put five tubes in each vehicle?"

Brannigan shook his head. "The M-Two gunners would be walking all over 'em. Four can be easily stacked around his seat without crowding him too much."

"How're we gonna break down the vehicle assignments, sir?" Buford asked. "Are you gonna try to keep section integrity as it is now?"

"It'll be impossible," Brannigan said. "With six, we can operate in three teams of two DPVs each as a rather large motorized platoon. We'll have to work out some formations, and practice dry runs in the desert around Shelor. As far as call signs, we'll just use the phonetic alphabet—Alpha One and Two, Bravo One and Two, and Charlie One and Two—for communications." He reached over and grabbed a pad of paper. "You guys be quiet while I figure this out."

The Skipper took the present roster and studied it, then began writing the reorganization. He changed his mind a couple of times, and it took him fifteen minutes. When he finished, he shoved the new roster over for Cruiser and Dawkins to peruse.

Alpha One
Brannigan commander/driver—Devereaux M-60 gunner—Malachenko M-2 gunner.

Alpha Two
Concord commander/driver—Assad M-60 gunner—Leibowitz M-2 gunner.

Bravo One
Cruiser commander/driver—Dawson M-60 gunner—Pecheur M-2 gunner.

Bravo Two
Olson commander/driver—Bradley M-60 gunner—Redhawk M-2 gunner.

Charlie One
Dawkins commander/driver—Miskoski M-60 gunner—Murchison M-2 gunner.

Charlie Two
Gunnarson commander/driver—Puglisi M-60 gunner—Gomez M-2 gunner.

"Looks good to me, sir," Dawkins said. "Who's gonna handle the Javelins?"

"That'll be the M-Sixty gunner," Brannigan said. "You have to keep in mind that the blowback on those babies is terrific. The shooter is gonna have to unass the vehicle to fire it, or the M-Two gunner will be blown from here to Albuquerque. Anyhow, we want to leave the fifties manned at all times." He checked his watch. "We'll do some battle drills as soon as everything is off-loaded and stacked properly in the hangar."

They left the office and walked outside to the C-130. When they approached the rear of the aircraft, they could see Randy Tooley in his DPV leading a couple of forklifts across the airfield toward them.

MANCHESTER, ENGLAND
14 APRIL
2000 HOURS

EVEN though the man wore civilian clothing, he had the look of a soldier about him. He was lean, with a jutting jaw, and his shoulders were squared as if he were on parade at Buckingham Palace. He had parked his car along a street of working-class houses. The triplexes were narrow two-story structures with backyards that were no more than twenty by fifteen feet in size and bordered by tall fences.

He went up to a dingy residence sandwiched between two others, ringing the bell and stepping back. When the door opened, a middle-aged woman wearing a house frock appeared. "Yes, sir?"

"Good evening, ma'am. Are you Missus Sikes?"

"Yes, sir."

"I am Falkes, ma'am," he said displaying a military ID card. "Army Administrative Services."

"Oh, yes. Please come in, Mr. Falkes. I'll let me husband know you've come calling." She stepped back to allow the visitor to enter the house, calling out, "Charlie! A gentleman from the Army is here."

A man carrying a newspaper he had been reading stepped from the parlor into the short hallway with stairs leading to the second floor. The man gave Falkes a quick study, saying, "The Army, is it? Do you have news about our Archie?"

"Actually, I have some questions to put to you," Falkes said. "You are Mr. Sikes, I presume."

"Yes, sir," Charlie Sikes answered. "I'm Archie's father. Won't you come into the parlor then, sir? Make yourself comfortable."

Falkes followed him from the hall and sat down on the small sofa across from an easy chair. Sikes took the latter seat, while his wife settled down on one of the arms next to her husband. Both had worried expressions on their faces, and they waited nervously for the caller to speak.

"Have you heard from your son?"

"Why, no, sir," Sikes said. "Does your asking mean he's alright?"

"There has been no information, as you know, Mr. Sikes," Falkes said. "No insurgent group in Iraq has revealed him as their prisoner. Nor has a corpse been found." He pulled a notebook from his inside coat pocket and looked at it. "According to the records, your son Archibald Sikes was an excellent soldier. Worked his way up to the rank of sergeant in record time."

"Yes," Sikes said. "Archie were a strange lad, I'll not deny it. But when he put his mind to something, he always came out bright as a new penny."

"He was approved for a commission, but was turned down when he applied for it in the Royal Regiment of Dragoons," Falkes said. "Was he angry about that?"

"Yes," Sikes said. "He was quite disappointed, was our Archie. He felt slighted because the officers said he wasn't good enough to be one of 'em."

"Why was he so insistent on serving as an officer in that particular regiment when he could have gone to almost any other?"

Now Mrs. Sikes joined in the conversation. "I suppose 'cause that was the regiment he had enlisted for. He had recruiting papers and folders and such before he joined up. He chose the Royal Regiment of Dragoons after weeks of thinking about it."

"I understand that the very same evening after his interview for officer training, he went into London and got into a drunken brawl," Falkes said. "That started a downward spiral and he ended up being a private once again. And he never straightened up after that."

"That's a sad fact, sir," Sikes said. "Then he went to Iraq."

"Did he mention to you before he disappeared that his conduct was so bad there that he was going to be sacked by the Army when they got back to Blighty?"

Sikes looked at his wife, then back to Falkes. "He never said nothing about that."

"And you've not heard from him? Not a phone call nor letter nor messages from him given you by other persons?"

Sikes shook his head.

"Would you describe his mood as bitter about everything that went wrong?"

"O'course he was bluddy bitter," Sikes said. "He was a noncommissioned officer and recognized for doing a good job; then they same as told him that he wasn't good enough for their officers' mess. I never heard of such a thing! I mean, it's the twenty-first century, ain't it?"

"Right," Falkes said. He stood up and put the notebook back in his pocket, then produced a card, handing it to Sikes. "If you do hear from him, call this number. It's most important, Mr. Sikes."

Mrs. Sikes's voice trembled. "Is Archie in trouble, sir?"

"Believe me," Falkes said, "if he does contact you, it will be to your and his best advantage if you let us know straightaway. And if he's deserted, the best thing he can do is turn himself in. Good evening."

Falkes walked from the room to the hallway and out the front door with Sikes and his wife following. They watched the man get in his car and drive off. Sikes looked at the card. "The bastard! The goddamn rotter! He's an Army copper, that's what that bloke is."

"Then Archie truly is in trouble, ain't he, Charlie?"

"Yeah, Nancy," Sikes said. "Our lad is for it, no doubt." He snorted a sardonic chuckle. "Not that I'm very surprised."

SHELOR FIELD VICINITY
15 APRIL
0700 HOURS

THE Brigands' desert patrol vehicles rolled across the hard-packed terrain at a steady fifty miles an hour on the new run-flat tires. The Skipper had been forced to work out various groupings for attack, defense, and movement. Unfortunately, he had no experience in motorized warfare. After pondering the problem, he decided to apply the same platoon combat formations used on foot.

Now, speeding across the desert, the SEALs were in a platoon line formation that was designed to put all their firepower to the front with the three teams side by side. It was an excellent arrangement to use when attacking a strong enemy in a known location. The commander/drivers all dressed down toward the left, where the Skipper and his Alpha Team rolled along.

"Platoon column!" Brannigan ordered through his LASH headset. The detachment moved over into line with Alpha in the lead, Bravo in the center, and Charlie bringing up the rear. This was actually a basic formation that simplified overall control during long movements from one point to another.

After knocking off a couple of kilometers of distance, the Skipper called for a platoon "vee." Now both Bravo and Charlie teams were side to side to the front, with Alpha centered behind them. This would provide heavy immediate fire in case of enemy contact to the front, but·was hard to control at times. The Alpha Team, however, could move back and forth behind the Bravos and Charlies to lend a hand where needed.

"Platoon wedge!" came over the LASH headsets. Now the Alphas were to the front, with the Bravos to the rear and left and the Charlies to the rear and right. This allowed heavy volumes of fire to the front and both flanks.

The maneuvering continued until the detachment could flow in and out of the various combat formations with ease and speed. The M-2 gunners within their firing positions had a hell of a time, however, as they were up higher than anyone else and caught the blasts of the dust-laden wind straight in their faces as the detachment sped across the expanse of the Afghan desert. Even the goggles and kerchiefs didn't help much at maximum speeds.

At 1030 hours, Brannigan called a halt to the proceedings. The water in their canteens had gotten tepid by then, but felt wonderful to their parched throats. The morning's training was topped off by a lecture from PO2C Bruno Puglisi, who gave a short talk on the proper workings of the Javelin antiarmor missiles. They learned that the CLU was attached to the disposable tube loaded with a HEAT projectile. The whole thing weighed forty-nine and a half pounds. The NVS utilized IR light for the gunner when the weapons were employed during hours of darkness or fog. The missile locked on the target and the on-board processing system guided the projectile where it had to go. With a range of 2000 meters and able to penetrate up to more than twenty-three inches of armor, it was a potent weapon.

When everyone fully understood the workings of the Javelins, they each shot off three missiles for familiarity. The SEALs concentrated on the lesson, knowing that the next time the launchers were fired, it would be done in anger and for real.

USS *COMBS*
SATELLITE PHOTO ANALYSIS
1600 HOURS

THE photographer's mate, Ernie, gazed at the cathode-ray tube that displayed satellite and aerial photos in a three-dimensional mode. The space image he now studied had just arrived aboard from Station Bravo. As he perused the screen, his pal Ned typed the labels to put on manila folders the pictures would be stored in.

"Hey," Ernie said. "What area is this?"

Ned looked at the paperwork that arrived with the package. "Western Afghanistan and eastern Iran. We've had this piece of ground sent to us before."

"Mmm," Ernie said. "Can you pull some of the older ones out of the file for me? I want to check something out."

"Sure." Ned walked over to the file cabinet and thumbed toward the back until he found what he was looking for. He took them over and dropped them at Ernie's elbow, chuckling. "Y'know something? Nobody has ever come down here and asked us for any of these photos. You're the first guy I've had to go to the files for."

"As long as they find me on payday, I don't give a shit," Ernie said. He put an old photo in the scanner, sending it to the computer. Then he looked at the new picture. Now the old one again. Now the new one again.

Ned frowned. "What the fuck are you doing? You look like you're bobbing for apples."

"Come here and check out the Iranian marshes in both photos. Tell me what you see."

Ned walked over and studied them. "There's a shadowy strip across the marshes in the new one. Probably the water in the area sank in deeper. Sinkholes or something."

Ernie shook his head. "That ain't a natural occurrence, pal. Don't you remember your training? Natural objects are irregular and haphazard. This thing is man-made. It's as straight as a frigging arrow."

"You're right!" Ned exclaimed. "There's some kind of facility a few kilometers away. It looks like a military setup."

"Maybe it don't mean shit," Ernie said. "But I'm kicking this one upstairs with a note."

"That's what they're paying us for," Ned said. "I'll fetch you an envelope."

CHAPTER 10

SHELOR FIELD
SEAL HANGAR
16 APRIL
0200 HOURS

DAVE Leibowitz poured the final five gallons of gas from the jerry can into Vehicle Alpha Two, while Mike Assad sat the Javelin CLU in the back with a couple of loaded launch tubes. They looked up from their tasks, surprised to see Chad Murchison stroll into the large building at that early hour. He was dressed for the field, complete with web gear and a locked-and-loaded HK-416 carbine slung on his right shoulder. His boonie cap was pulled low over his eyes.

Dave put the now-empty fuel container on the floor and began to unscrew the pouring spout in the opening. "What the hell are you doing, Chad? Standing watch? I thought the Air Force was in charge of installation security."

Chad shook his head. "I was wondering if I could go along for the ride."

Mike chuckled. "This ain't a drive in the country. We're

going on a recon patrol out in the desert. The Skipper wants to find out how them armored cars snuck up on us from the west the other day. We won't be back till after chow tonight."

"I know," Chad said. "I'd like to go with you."

"Sure," Dave said. "You'll have to ride up in the M-Two gunner's spot."

"Hey, y'know, that's a good idea," Mike said. "Another set of eyes will—" He stopped speaking as a thought leaped into his mind. "Ain't them UN folks pulling out later this morning?"

"I don't know," Chad said.

Dave eyed him closely. "Sure you know. There's an aircraft coming to fly them back to Kabul. We all know about it. Your girl's leaving, ain't she?"

"I suppose."

"Don't you want to say good-bye to her?" Mike asked.

Chad's temper snapped. "No, goddamn it! I don't want to say good-bye to her. I want to get aboard that fucking DPV and go out into the fucking desert. Is that alright with you two guys?"

"Sure," Mike said with a frown. "Don't snap my head off!"

Dave got into the driver's seat. "All right. Let's go, guys."

Mike settled in the passenger seat behind the M-60 while Chad pulled himself up into the M-2 gunner's spot, settling down for what was going to be a rough ride. Dave started the engine, calling out, "Fasten your seat belts."

"What the hell?" Mike growled. "Do you think the CHP is gonna be out there waiting to pull us over like in California?"

"Just going by the old idea of safety first," Dave said, putting the vehicle into gear. It eased out of the hangar, then gained speed as it crossed the runway, heading for open country.

0700 HOURS

SENIOR Chief Petty Officer Buford Dawkins had turned the enlisted men over to Chief Petty Officer Matt

Gunnarson. The idea was for the CPO to take them out to do a morning of firing with the HK-416s at a spot a couple of miles east of the airfield. Lieutenants Brannigan and Cruiser had gone to a meeting called by the Air Force base commander to cover the upcoming comings and goings at Shelor Field.

Dawkins stayed behind by himself in the hangar office to catch up on some of the nagging paperwork that was his responsibility. Most of it was administrative nonsense, such as contrived rosters of who attended mandatory annual classes in sexual harassment, drug abuse, ethnic discrimination, and similar topics. All this was to be sent back to the USS *Dan Daly*, where a staff of yeomen would dutifully enter the information into personnel files as proof of mandatory indoctrination and guidance. This would eventually be pored over by a bunch of incredibly candy-ass headquarters pukes who considered SEALs and Marines one step above Neanderthals.

"Excuse me."

The feminine voice startled the old salt, and he looked up to see a young woman he recognized as Chad Murchison's girlfriend. "Good morning," Dawkins said, displaying his version of a pleasant smile.

"Could you tell me where Chad Murchison is?" Penny asked. "I'd like to see him before I leave for Kabul."

"I'm afraid Petty Officer Murchison is not available," Dawkins said. "He's out on patrol."

"I don't understand," Penny said.

Dawkins had been warned by Cruiser to expect the young lady. The senior chief also knew that for some reason of his own, Murchison wanted to avoid her. Dawkins cleared his throat. "Ahem. Well, now, uh, miss, you see, we got to run patrols. Yep. Got to run 'em. You bet. Normal part of our operations. Routine. But important. Yeah. Patrols are real important."

"But couldn't you have let someone else go in his place?" Penny asked. "I'm leaving the UN when we get to Kabul. I'm going home to Boston."

"Have a nice trip."

"I probably won't see him again for a long time," Penny said. "At least, not until he returns to California." She reached up and wiped at a tear running down her cheek.

"Well, yeah, I guess you won't, huh?" A crying woman was something Dawkins could not deal with.

Now she began sobbing louder. "It was . . . real mean to . . . make him go . . . on a patrol . . . when you knew . . . I was leaving . . . Afghanistan."

"Yeah."

"Why did . . . you send him . . . out there?" Penny asked, sitting down in the chair across from the chief.

"I didn't," Dawkins said. Now he seemed to be stuck with a weeping woman who planned on staying awhile.

She pulled a tissue out of her pocket and dabbed at her eyes. "I was real mean to Chad a long time ago. I threw him over for another guy. Sometimes, I think he's still upset about that."

"He'll get over it sooner or later," Dawkins growled.

"Oh, that's all water under the bridge," Penny said. "I broke up with Cliff, then got back with Chad. It was here in Afghanistan."

The senior chief made a mental note to get hold of Murchison the instant he was back from the patrol and chew his ass bloody for causing this girl to come looking for him. Dawkins considered her presence an extreme annoyance. And, as everyone should know, it's not nice to annoy a senior chief petty officer. He opined to himself that the girl was plainly untutored in certain social graces.

Penny's sobbing became more subdued, and she sighed loudly, saying, "I just want Chad to get out of this awful Navy."

"Look, young lady, I'm really busy right now," Dawkins said.

"Don't let me bother you," Penny said. "Go right on and work."

At that exact moment, Jim Cruiser stepped into the office. The instant he spotted Penny, he whipped around and tried to retreat, but she jumped from her chair and went after him.

Dawkins grinned to himself, then went back to his paper-work.

STATION BRAVO, BAHRAIN
SATELLITE PHOTO ANALYSIS
0945 HOURS

THE operator, a young Army specialist, set the photograph on the scanner, then settled down at the computer. He grabbed the mouse, sliding the arrow to the correct icon. A couple of clicks opened up the program and the image appeared. He took another look at the photograph that had been sent over from the USS *Combs*. The circle drawn over the area of interest was almost in the exact center, and the specialist was able to quickly locate it on the screen. Now, after a few right clicks on the mouse, it had been enlarged ten times.

"Ma'am!" he called out.

The captain in command of the section walked over and took a look at the screen. "What are we supposed to see?"

"According to the request, they want that dark strip analyzed."

"Take it up four times more and print it out," she said.

The specialist followed the instructions and sent it to the Hewlett-Packard color printer on the other side of the office; then, he walked over to wait for the result. It took a full five minutes for the picture paper to come out. He picked it up and took it back to the captain. "What do you think it is, ma'am?" he asked.

She gave it a full five-second study. "It's a road."

"That's what I think."

"What area is this?" she asked.

"It's the salt marshes in southeast Iran," the specialist said. "They border Afghanistan, sort of spilling over into it."

"Well, hell," the captain said, "it doesn't mean shit to me. Package everything up and put it into distribution for the Two-Shop."

"I wonder why somebody would put a road through a salty swamp," the specialist mused to himself.

PASHTUN STRONGHOLD
GHARAWDARA HIGHLANDS
1300 HOURS

YAMA Orakzai, commander in chief of the Pashtun Rebel Army, lounged on the sofa in the roomy cave he used as a combination headquarters and living area. His deputy commander, Khushal Shinwari, was equally relaxed in a nearby recliner.

Orakzai was dressed in a manner he had used for more than a quarter of a century. He wore a *puhtee* cap, an olive-drab slipover woolen military sweater, and green baggy bakesey pants. A pair of American Army boots liberally covered with waterproof dubbing completed his ensemble. His pipe bowl was filled with his favorite *khartumi* tobacco that the opium smugglers always brought him after making a run across Iran and into Turkey. He puffed absentmindedly as he gazed out the small opening of the cave.

Shinwari was a hundred-percent native in his bakesey shirt and trousers. They were in the gray color that the Pashtuns considered the best camouflage when operating in their native mountains. A leather belt with pouches for cartridges was worn across his right shoulder. His feet were shod in chapati sandals with strips of blanket wrapped from ankle up to mid-calf as leggings. All in all, a stranger would not be able to tell these highest rankers of the PPB from their most subordinate mujahideen.

Neither had spoken for the best part of a half hour before Shinwari stretched languidly, saying, "The Iranians have been strangely standoffish lately, *na?*"

"Mmm," Orakzai said. "They need time to complete their preparations."

"They are almost Western," Shinwari complained. "They do things in careful phases, moving like donkeys picking their way through mud."

"We need not worry about how many months or years they take," Orakzai said. "You must keep in mind that we are no longer harassed by their soldiers when we carry the prepared opium powder through the north."

"That is an advantage, I admit, *wror*," Shinwari agreed, addressing him as "brother." "But it takes the excitement out of the journey. There is no chance to kill anybody, and the young men now come back bleary-eyed from boredom." He grinned over at his chief and best friend. "I am surprised by your calmness. You have always thirsted for action."

Orakzai put another match to his tobacco. "I admit some impatience with this waiting around."

YAMA Orakzai was sixteen years old in 1980 when the Soviet Union invaded his native Afghanistan. He had been a schoolboy in Kandahar after being plucked from his native village during a campaign to bring Pashtun youths into the cities for education. The idea was to return them to their people as intellectual superiors who would lead their people to modern civilized ways. Ironically, this was part of a Communist program, and the courses of instruction were heavy with political indoctrination.

The trouble started when the Soviet Union became furious when their handpicked leader of Afghanistan, Mohammed Daoud, began easing out of their sphere of influence toward neutrality. The local Khalq Communist Party was also seriously concerned. They sought Soviet aid and support to organize a coup. The Khalq won the short, vicious rebellion and executed Daoud. The new leader, Nur Mohammad Taraki, took the country back into a Marxist-Leninist-Stalinist way of life. However, because of the now-strong presence of the Soviets in all levels of government, the population, particularly the Pashtuns, became convinced the regime was being run by foreign infidels.

Armed revolt broke out in several provinces, and the Afghan Army responded. However, because of the unpopularity of the government, mass desertions soon plagued the officer cadre as the holy war expanded, making their effectiveness fade at a rapid rate. Within a short time, what the Soviets feared the most began to happen. A Communist government was going down the tubes. They began moving troops into Afghanistan to put a halt to the revolution. From that point on, the situation escalated into an all-out, deadly guerrilla war.

Orakzai, like many of the schoolboys scattered throughout the national education system, ran away and headed for his home village to melt into the craggy mountains. He joined a mujahideen group that was typical of the resistance. Young boys and men from adolescents to graybeards started out with privately owned weapons, gradually building up more state-of-the-art arsenals by looting the dead Soviets who fell victim to their style of fighting. These mujahideen gave battle only when they had the advantage, and withdrew when they were outgunned and outnumbered. The American CIA came on the scene and began giving more weapons, ammunition, clothing, medical supplies, rations, and anything else the mujahideen needed to carry on their insurgency. The CIA also saw to it that these separate groups quickly began affiliating in spite of political and religious differences. The mujahideen united under the single mission to push the Soviet Army out of Afghanistan.

Orakzai proved to be an able fighter and valuable to his commanding officer because of his education. He could do math, work out distances and routes on maps, and thanks to his schooling, he had a working knowledge of the Russian and English languages that gave him the ability to read captured Soviet technical manuals. Within a short time, he went from fighter to small-unit leader, planning and leading raids and ambushes. By 1985, he was twenty-one years old and a senior officer with over two hundred fighters under his direct command. When the UN mediated an agreement that was signed on 14 April 1988, the twenty-four-year-old Yama Orakzai was the overall commander of his mujahideen group.

After the Soviet Army pulled out, fighting between moderates and the fundamental Islamics of the Taliban broke out. Orakzai was a moderate in this civil war, and when the Taliban won control over ninety percent of the country in 1998, he took his band and all his people up into the Gharawdara Highlands.

Orakzai and his people did not stagnate in this self-imposed isolation. They easily got into the opium trade as smugglers, taking the illegal cargo to the markets in rural Turkey for sale to European crime organizations. The money was excellent, providing items of survival, comfort, and war. When the Taliban was beaten down, Orakzai saw it as an opportunity to take over the western part of Afghanistan for the Pashtuns. But the events of 9/11 caused his plans to hit a difficult snag. Armed forces of an international coalition were roaming the country, tracking down Islamic terrorist groups. Their various operations and missions made it difficult for him to organize any sort of revolution. After a couple of years, it began to look impossible.

Then he came into contact with hard-ass Special Forces soldiers of the Iranian Army.

CHAPTER 11

LIEUTENANT William Brannigan planned the ambush carefully. The grid coordinates of the road through the salt marshes where Iran and Afghanistan blended together were clearly marked on the map by Lieutenant Commander Ernest Berringer. The Skipper used his GPS to find the exact location. He would have liked to cross the international border and make a quick recon, or even send Assad and Leibowitz a couple of kilometers down the route for a close look and evaluation of the terrain features. Better yet, he would have preferred loading up the DPVs for bear and charging down the road straight into the frontier post marked on the satellite photo for an old-fashioned ass-kicking raid. But explicit direct orders from the SFOB denied him any chance of entering Iran.

It was the old story: Go into the fight with one hand tied behind your back.

Now Lieutenant Junior Grade Jim Cruiser and his two DPVs were in a carefully selected position close to the salt marshes. The vehicles were a hundred meters from where anyone from the Iranian side would cross into Afghanistan, and Cruiser, with Gutsy Olson, Pete Dawson, Doc Bradley, and Garth Redhawk, were arranged in a formation that allowed them to keep the location under constant surveillance. Their job was to alert the Skipper when and if the armored cars appeared, then run to their vehicles to form up to follow the bad guys. The Bravo vehicles' combat assignment was to hang back out of sight, ready to hem the enemy in when the ambush was sprung. If any enemy "Tail-end Charlies" decided to cut and run, Cruiser and his guys would make short work of them.

The Skipper had the Alpha and Charlie vehicles arranged in a wide "vee." The idea was to let the enemy get in between them while the locations of the individual DPVs would allow the Brigands to fire into the bad guys without having to worry about hitting each other.

As soon as Brannigan felt the armored cars were the most vulnerable, he would order the SEALs to cut loose with Javelins and the armor-piercing rounds from the M-2s with their heavy .50-caliber slugs. Additionally, this ammunition was tracer to help the gunners accurately direct their fire into the targets.

The four M-60 gunners—Devereaux, Assad, Miskoski, and Puglisi—would handle the Javelins. Each had a tube attached to a CLU, with two more loaded and ready to snap on and fire. If one of the eighteen-and-a-half-pound warheads hit an enemy vehicle, it would go through the armor like a lightning bolt through a cardboard box. The resultant explosion would turn anything in the interior—metal, plastic, rubber, or human flesh—into charred, ripped, and melted debris.

The Alpha and Charlie DPVs were camouflaged in a special way. Conventional nets would only work if the vehicles were dug in. That was something Brannigan definitely did not

want to do. It was of utmost importance that they be above-
ground and ready to roll into action in split seconds. Since
they were on flat desert terrain, throwing a net across them
for concealment wasn't any better than having them out in
the open uncovered. A special canvas and frame covering
was thrown over the DPVs to give them the look of boulders.
Outcrops of rocks were commonplace that close to the mountains, and this camouflage would appear natural to the environment.

THE day's mission had been sprung on Brannigan's Brigands two days before on 18 April. It started when an approaching C-130 advised Shelor Field of its arrival less than
an hour before touchdown. The aircraft carried Commander
Tom Carey and Lieutenant Commander Ernest Berringer,
along with the armor-piercing tracer ammo for the M-2 and
M-60 machine guns. The other handy contribution to the detachment's munitions was extra missiles for the Javelins. The
cargo also consisted of the special camouflage coverings, 5.56-
millimeter rounds, and M-67 fragmentation hand grenades.
The latter were necessary since the HK-416 carbines, unlike
M-16 rifles, would be unable to use M-203 grenade launchers.

When the two staff officers unassed the aircraft, they hurried to the SEALs' hangar. Brannigan and Cruiser were waiting for them in the office. Carey didn't bother with the
formalities of a greeting. "Get your guys in here," he snapped.
"We've got some big shit going down."

Cruiser went to the office door and yelled over at the
SEALs, who were once again doing PM on the DPVs because
of the exposure to desert sand and grit. "Senior Chief! Secure
and take the detachment over to the far corner of the building."

"Aye, sir!" Dawkins turned to the men yelling, "You heard
the Lieutenant! Move it!"

Everyone gathered in the indicated part of the hangar,
where Carey and Berringer quickly set up map boards. As the
SEALs either stood or knelt in a semicircle around them,
Carey took the floor. "Nice to see you again," he said. "And I

have an answer to a question that's probably been bothering you. From the AAR sent in by Lieutenant Brannigan, it was obvious you were not sure how those armored cars got to you at the UNREO camp." He turned and pointed to the enlarged satellite photograph mounted on one of the boards. "See that gray narrow rectangle there? It is a road, gentlemen, that's built straight across the salt marshes on the Iranian border. It leads from the garrison shown here"—he used his laser pointer to put a red dot on the exact location of Chehaar Garrison—"into Afghanistan here. On the day of that memorable battle, they entered your OA in that manner, going between your OPs and straight to where your main group was. The result was a surprise attack that was even a surprise to the attackers."

Bruno Puglisi was outraged. "What're them motherfuckers doing in Iran?"

"We don't have that full story down at our level," Berringer, the N-2, interjected. "And frankly, I don't think all the facts are known even at the Pentagon."

Brannigan was more than just a little pissed off himself. "What about that fucking Limey or whatever he was? The UN doctor was positive about that."

"This information was passed on to my counterpart at British Army intelligence," Berringer replied, "and he seems to think they can get to the bottom of that. There's a chance one of their guys deserted or was kidnapped, then defected. For reasons my guy didn't explain, they seem to be thinking that he is an AWOL. Evidently, the guy was a fuckup. They're still looking into it."

"By the way," Carey said. "The Brits said if you could capture the guy, they'd like to talk to him."

"If we capture him?" Joe Miskoski snorted. "How the hell are they gonna talk to a guy that's been bent over double and had his head shoved up his ass? Because that's what'll happen to him if we get our hands on him."

"Now hear this," Carey said sternly. "If you capture that Brit, you keep him healthy and able to respond to questioning. He'll be a walking, talking wealth of intelligence on the Islamic insurgency scene involving Iran. And we don't want to have to wait six months while he heals up from what you fuckers do to him."

"Aye, sir," Miskoski said insincerely.

Jim Cruiser was puzzled. "As I recall, Dr. Bouchier of the UN said the people in the armored cars were definitely Arab and he heard them speaking Arabic among themselves. Iranians speak Farsi. So what's with the Arabs operating out of Iran?"

"Another puzzle," Berringer said. "And it's yet one more we can't solve at our level. But we have gotten the word that this group is calling itself Jihad Abadi. That's Arabic for Eternal Holy War. In Farsi, the words for holy war are *jange maghaddas*. That's a big difference, so these guys are definitely not Iranians."

"Could it be rogue Iranian Army officers pulling some shit on their own?" Brannigan asked.

"We do not know," Berringer said candidly.

"Okay," Brannigan said. "Let's stop wondering about things and get back to the briefing."

"Good idea," Carey agreed. "What we want you guys to do is catch the bad guys coming into Afghanistan from that road. Get EPWs, if possible, but if you end up annihilating that armored car company, then so be it. It will send a strong message to Iran or whoever is back of this operation."

"Sir, do you have any idea when they'll be rolling back into Afghanistan?" Senior Chief Buford Dawkins asked.

"Negative," Carey said. "You'll have to go out there and plan on staying up to a week or a bit more waiting for them to appear. Take enough rations to last no less than ten days, and enough ammo to fight a sustained battle."

"Alright," Brannigan said. "I take it you want me to work out the OPORD. When should we start?"

"Yesterday," Carey responded.

NOW everyone was in position, biding their time in the barren environment of the desert. Off to the north, they could see the Gharawdara Highlands as a long smudge on the horizon. The view on the other three sides was more of the empty terrain without a tree or even a small knoll breaking the monotony of the Afghan vista.

The situation mirrored the old military saying of "Hurry up and wait!"

0645 HOURS
BRAVO TEAM

PETTY Officer Pete Dawson held the binoculars to his eyes with the same intensity he would have used if standing watch aboard a ship. He had been on duty for forty-five minutes since relieving Pech Pecheur at 0600 hours, and his vigil had not relaxed an iota. However, the image in the viewing device showed nothing more than the blending of the brown terrain to the east with the dirty white of the salt marshes on the west.

"This place sucks," Pete murmured to himself, thinking how great it would be if insurgencies broke out in places like the French Riviera or Tahiti. And, of course, there were also the beautiful Italian beaches on the Adriatic Sea. His mind snapped back to the job at hand when a slight purring sound reached his ears. It was very faint at first, but grew louder until he recognized it was motors. "Wake up, sleepyheads," he whispered in the LASH. "We got visitors coming in from the west."

"Everybody into position," Jim Cruiser ordered.

Gutsy Olson's voice came over the commo system. "Bravo Two ready."

Ten minutes later, a column of armored cars some fifty meters away could be seen moving from west to east, heading straight to where the Skipper had set up the Alpha and Charlie vehicles. "Alpha One," Cruiser transmitted, "this is Bravo One. The bad guys are moving toward you. I count five . . . eight . . . twelve . . . seventeen, and now twenty. That's all. Total of twenty. Over."

"This is Alpha One," Brannigan replied. "Let 'em pass well through your position before you head for your vehicles. We don't want 'em to spot you. And remember to hang back while you're following them. It's going to be up to you to stop 'em if they turn and run. Over."

"Roger. Out."

ARMORED CAR COLUMN

CAPTAIN Arsalaan Sikes Bey was in the middle of his company's formation as the unit traveled almost due east at seventy kilometers an hour. He sat up with his head and shoulders outside the hatch, enjoying the morning air. The commanders in the other nineteen Jararacas did the same. All were alert and anxious, remembering the Americans and their fast little vehicles from the sharp battle they had fought ten days before. This time, they would respond with tactics devised by Sikes Bey. Each platoon of four would fight as a single unit, combing the firepower of their Dashika heavy machine guns under the platoon leader's direct command.

Sikes turned to observe his outfit, not liking what he saw. "Platoon leaders, *madd*! Spread your formation! You are too close together!"

THE SEAL "VEE"

GUY Devereaux, Mike Assad, Joe Miskoski, and Bruno Puglisi had moved to individual locations outside the formation. Each of the four carried a Javelin and two extra loaded tubes. The quartet of armor-killers assumed kneeling positions, poised to fire. They had to be careful about where they situated themselves, since the back blast from the weapons was deadly several yards to the rear. Anyone directly behind them would suffer serious injury or even death if the strong burst hit them.

Assad and Puglisi were the farthest out and the farthest apart. Devereaux and Miskoski were situated between the two vehicles of their respective teams. Brannigan had given strict orders that the Javelins were not to be fired until he gave the word. Then, it would be done in turns by individuals.

The commanders and the M-2 gunners stood by, ready to leap onto their DPVs and join the battle as quickly as possible after the Javelins fired their initial missiles. The Skipper listened in the silence that was interrupted from time to time by gusts of wind. But eventually, the unmistakable sounds of diesel engines could be discerned. When they came close enough to be identified by the naked eye, Brannigan issued his first battle commands. "Assad! Puglisi! Stand by!"

Both men strained their eyes until they sighted the approaching column. The range of the AT weapons was 2000 meters maximum. They couldn't be fired from a prone position because if the gunners were too close to the ground, the fins on the missiles wouldn't have the necessary space to unfold before reaching the targets. That meant that during the time for aiming and locking on the target, they would be exposed to the enemy. Now the pair of SEALs peered through the sights, lining up on the two closest armored cars.

"Assad! Puglisi! Fire!"

They were already locked onto the targets by the on-board processing system when they pulled the triggers. The fire-and-forget missiles streaked across the 500 meters and straight into the unlucky vehicles chosen by the gunners. They punched through the armor and exploded inside, the force of the detonation held in for no more than the briefest of milliseconds before violently and instantly expanding with enough force to open up the Jararacas like cheap sardine cans.

"Devereaux! Miskoski! Fire!"

Two more of the armored cars blasted apart.

"Javelin gunners! Fire at will!"

ARMORED CAR COLUMN

SIKES was too shocked and surprised to immediately react to the explosive destruction of the four armored cars. The easy movement across the desert had suddenly been

interrupted by a series of unexpected detonations. From
his position in the middle of the column, he could see the
orange flashes and black smoke. Hunks of armor and debris
flew through the air as six more blasts crashed through the
area.

Now his mind snapped back to the present.

The first thing he thought of was tanks. Surely, the Americans had sent an armored battalion into the area to take on his
vehicles. He forgot Arabic and the smattering of Farsi he had
learned. "Get the fuck out of here!" he yelled in his radio microphone. He dropped back into the interior and viciously
cuffed his driver on the back of the head. "Turn around and go
like hell, you blowsy bastard!"

The man couldn't speak English, but the tone in Sikes
Bey's voice most definitely indicated it would be a good idea
if they got out of the area as quickly as possible.

THE BATTLE

ALPHA and Charlie vehicles were quickly manned as
the men threw the camouflage aside and jumped aboard. They
slowed down only enough to pick up the Javelin team, who
threw the weapons into the backs with the M-2 gunners as
they leaped into their own seats in front. They immediately
took off the safeties of the M-60s and began hosing armor-
piercing rounds at the fleeing armored cars. The four SEALs
were happy campers. Although they hadn't had time to fire all
twelve Javelin rounds, they managed to kick off ten. And
every single one had resulted in a kill.

The Bravo vehicles bounced across the terrain at close to
seventy miles an hour. It was only a matter of a minute before
they sighted what looked like ten of the enemy cars heading
westward as fast as possible. Now the M-2s and M-60s began
spitting out combined fire bursts at the fleeing bad guys.

SIKES had now fully regained his composure. He began
issuing orders calmly in Arabic as he peered through the

command periscopes to check on his force. He counted ten, cursing the fact he had actually taken fifty-percent casualties in a disastrously short period of time. His gunners in their turrets, while shaken up by the pounding they had endured, had now recovered enough to sight in on the enemy patrol vehicles behind them. They squeezed the triggers rhythmically to send fiery spurts of the heavy 12.7-millimeter slugs streaking toward the pursuers.

The First Platoon leader, who had lost all his subordinate vehicles, was now alone. His gunner called on Allah's help as he tried desperately to hit one of the swift, dodging enemy DPVs. Suddenly, a salvo of .50-caliber armor-piercing bullets penetrated the hull from the rear, sweeping across the interior. All three men in the crew were ferociously buffeted by multiple heavy blows as the ammo plowed into them. The armored car veered off to the right, running out into the desert as the trio of ripped corpses rolled back and forth in the interior.

In another Jararaca, there was only the driver alive. The gunner had been the first to die when machine-gun fire ripped the insides of the car. He slumped down, held onto his seat by the belt. His blood ran from a half-dozen gaping wounds, soaking his uniform until it oozed through the material and dripped on the deck. A couple of minutes after his death, the commander was kicked violently by three impacts from an M-60. He didn't die for a few minutes, but had immediately gone into shock. He called for his mother, moaning, *"Umm! Umm! Umm!"* over and over.

Now another fusillade rattled the car as it took more hits. One of the tracers, still spurting fire, hit a spare fuel can strapped to the inside hull. It ignited with a loud swoosh, sending flames over the driver. He screamed and clawed at the fire, both fascinated and horrified by the sight of the flesh on his hands and arms bubbling and turning black.

Back in his vehicle, Sikes was no longer interested in giving battle. The only thing he saw through his periscope was the sight of his force being battered by the speeding enemy that moved in and out of his battle formation like darting, snarling tigers. His gunner's turret rotated as the man returned fire at the determined DPVs.

There was but one thing left for Sikes to do, and that was to keep racing toward the border and safety of Iran. *"Raht qawam!"* he screamed at his driver.

0800 HOURS
THE IRANIAN BORDER

THE detachment had halted and everyone unassed their vehicles. They stood looking into the salt marsh to their direct front. The persistent wind was already eroding the tire tracks of the seven enemy armored cars that had managed to escape back into Iran. A total of thirteen of their number, blown apart or riddled with holes, were scattered between there and the location where the Javelins were first fired.

"Damn the bastards!" Brannigan said.

Jim Cruiser stood next to him. "Yeah. I wish we could have gotten all those Arabs."

"I wasn't talking about the goat-fuckers. I was referring to the headquarters pukes who ordered us not to go into Iran," Brannigan said. "We could've destroyed every single one of those armored cars in another kilometer or two."

Senior Chief Petty Officer Buford Dawkins walked up and saluted, showing a big grin. "No casualties, sir. Not as much as a scratch among those magnificent sons of bitches."

"Victorious and unbloodied," Brannigan said. "That's the way I like it. So let's mount up, Senior Chief. I believe they're having roast beef at the airfield mess hall this evening."

CHAPTER 12

THE President of the United States sat at his desk, looking across its expanse at Dr. Carl Joplin, Edgar Watson, and Colonel John Turnbull. The White House Chief of Staff, Arlene Entienne, stood to the side of the massive piece of furniture, her arms crossed in an unconscious gesture of impatient determination.

The President settled back in his chair, tapping his fingertips together. "We'll go to breakfast just as soon as we hash this situation out." He nodded to Watson. "I think the logical thing to do is commence these proceedings—informal as they are—with the representative from the CIA."

"Of course, Mr. President," Watson said respectfully. He reached in his briefcase and pulled out some papers and a map. He glanced around for an easel to mount the chart, but saw that none was available. "Excuse me, please." He spread the map out on the desk and indicated a specific location. "The armored car column mentioned in yesterday morning's briefing entered Afghanistan via a camouflaged road constructed across the salt marshes on the international border. This man-made route was discovered during satellite photo analyses."

"God bless our space industry," the President said.

"Yes, sir," Watson said. "According to the after-action report submitted by . . . er, I can't remember the Special Forces guy's name."

"Brannigan," Colonel Turnbull said. "Lieutenant William Brannigan, U.S. Navy SEALs."

Carl Joplin grinned with delight. "I know him quite well from the operation down in the Gran Chaco in Bolivia. I enjoyed meeting him and his men. They are very impressive."

"Well, Doc," the colonel said, "you're gonna get some enjoyment again. He's the main player in this OA."

"At any rate," Watson said, a bit miffed at the interruption. "This armored car unit is commanded by an Englishman. MI-5 has informed us he is a deserter from one of their outfits in Iraq. He is, in fact, Private Archibald Sikes of the Royal Regiment of Dragoons."

"Hold on!" Colonel Turnbull snapped. "What the hell is a goddamn buck private doing leading an armored car company?"

Arlene Entienne, who had read the dossier on the deserter, entered the conversation. "Evidently, Sikes was a noncommissioned officer whose feelings were hurt when he wasn't allowed to take a commission in his own regiment. They're a rather posh bunch and didn't think he would fit into their officer cadre."

Turnbull, whose father was a plumber, snorted. "Well, ladee-dah!"

"However, he was okayed to go into any other regiment of his choice," Entienne explained. "Except the Brigade of Guards, of course."

"Of course!" Turnbull said. "One doesn't want the riffraff hobnobbing with upper-class twits, does one?"

"Thank you for your input, John," Entienne said wearily.

"At any rate, his bitterness caused him to misbehave by going out and getting roaring drunk. He was punished and reduced in rank and was assigned to menial duties in their motor pool. His outfit was shipped to Iraq and it was there that he deserted. By the way, the same day this guy disappeared, one of their civilian employees, a Syrian by the name of Khalil Farouk, also went missing."

"So what happened when those armored cars crossed into Afghanistan and met up with this Lieutenant Brannigan?" the President asked.

"He inflicted sixty-five-percent casualties on them," Watson reported. "He and his guys—who call themselves Brannigan's Brigands, by the way—knocked out thirteen of twenty vehicles."

The President raised his eyebrows. "These fellows actually refer to themselves as brigands?"

Turnbull grinned. "I suppose it was that or Brannigan's Bastards or Brannigan's Bird-watchers. When an outfit comes up with a name using the CO's moniker, the letters of both have to be the same." He snorted. "Brannigan's Beer-Belching Bell Ringers."

"No matter what they call themselves," Joplin commented dryly, "Brannigan and his men have demonstrated a marked ferocity. They wrapped up that fascist revolution in South America in a very timely and efficient manner."

Turnbull chuckled. "That's a nice way of saying he kicked butt."

"May I get back to my report?" Watson asked sharply.

"Sure, Edgar," Turnbull said. "Sorry for the digression."

"Anyhow," the CIA man said, "this Farouk character is an agent for the Iranians. Now here's the big item, Mr. President. The government in Tehran wants to take over all the insurgent movements in the Middle East, consolidate them into one - big-ass anti-West army, and get everybody—particularly the Israelis—out of that part of the world. Their goal is to rule over the entire area with its massive oil reserves. They have spent the last ten years organizing a handpicked Special Forces unit to get the ball rolling."

"Good God!" the President exclaimed. "What do they want to do? Start another Persian Empire?"

"That is our assessment, Mr. President," Watson said. "This is a grave threat."

"How far has this Iranian plot developed?" the President inquired.

"We're not sure, sir," Watson replied. "Sorry."

"Mmm," the President murmured pensively. "This nuclear flap they've created could be more for distraction away from this power play than for actual implementation."

Watson shook his head. "The one ties in with the other. These Farsis want to play with the big boys now. Perhaps the situation can be handled diplomatically at this early stage of the game."

"That's my thought exactly," the President said. He looked over at Joplin. "Here's where you come on stage, Carl. Who is your Iranian connection?"

"His name is Saviz Kahnani," Joplin answered. "He is posted as a chargé d'affaires in their embassy here in Washington."

"That's the fellow to see alright," Entienne said. "He's authorized to take their ambassador's place if necessary."

"Alright," the President said. "Arrange a meeting with him. Use those skills of yours to sniff out what Iran is trying to pull off. Then issue a subtle warning that we're onto them and will not—absolutely *will not*—tolerate this sort of political and military adventuring on their part."

"I'll take him to the Bonhomme Richard, Mr. President," Joplin said.

"Excellent," the President said. "Get this done as quickly as possible. When we've enough information, I'll call the cabinet in to have a thorough discussion on this problem." He stood up. "Well, now! Let's go get that breakfast. I'm starving!"

The Chief Executive led the four people out of the office.

CHEHAAR GARRISON
EASTERN IRAN
2200 HOURS

ARSALAAN Sikes was livid. "Fuck this bluddy shit!"

Brigadier Shahruz Khohollah understood the younger man's anger. "You must take time to put things into proper perspective, Captain Sikes."

The two were seated in Khohollah's parlor at one end of his Quonset hut. It was well furnished with ornate plush furniture and thick carpeting. Sikes had come back from the disastrous encounter with the American forces in a roaring rage, and his temper had not improved a bit since then. Khohollah was sincerely sympathetic and empathetic with him. "You must be prepared to deal with reversals and disappointments at this stage of our operations."

"There ain't no preparations of no kind!" Sikes growled. "I got to take me lads out without no reconnaissance, no air support, no artillery support, and no reserves to call in if there's trouble. I ain't got the slightest idea o' what we went up against day before yesterday. We was hit with up-to-date antiarmor rocketry right out o' the blue, we was. In the twinkling of an eye, four of me vehicles was blown apart like they was nothing more than sardine tins, hey? Then six more. I didn't have no choice but to turn and get the hell out o' there. And while that was going on, we lost three more before we got back to that bluddy road through them marshes. And I might add that the Yanks know about it now, so we ain't gonna be using that way into Afghanistan no more, are we?"

"You're absolutely right," Khohollah agreed. "And we're going to have to close down here and pull out. The Americans are going to focus a great of deal attention on this area, so we must disappear."

"Now, ain't that great, hey? Wot's gonna happen to me? Am I supposed to crawl back to Blighty and get meself put up before a fucking firing squad as a fucking deserter then?"

"No, Captain Sikes," the brigadier said. "We have another operation ready to launch. It involves that band of Pashtun fighters in the Afghanistan mountains. They are fully armed and ready to go. You are well versed in infantry tactics, are you not?"

"O' course I am," Sikes said. "Me old regiment was armored infantry."

"Well, you won't be dealing with armor anymore," Khohollah said. "You'll be leading a unit of an insurgent force in hit-and-run tactics."

Sikes calmed down. "Guerrilla warfare, hey?" His old fantasies of being a great battle leader eased back into his conscious mind. "What rank am I gonna be?"

"This group doesn't use ranks," Khohollah explained. "You will be called by your name." He paused, well aware of the Englishman's ego. "If you do well enough and earn glory and respect, you could well end up with a large command. They will call you Sikes Pasha."

"Blimey! When does this start?"

"Arrangements are being made even as we speak," the Iranian said. He got up and went to a liquor cabinet. "Since you're not a devout Muslim in the strictest sense, would you care for a whiskey?"

"Sure!" Archie said. "I didn't know you drank liquor, sir."

"Oh, well," Khohollah said, pouring two glasses of Dewars. "I'm sure there are Jews who enjoy a ham sandwich now and then. And we know that there are Catholic priests who stray into sexual activities, right?"

"Right," Sikes agreed. "And after wot I been through, I needs me a bluddy good jolt."

PASHTUN STRONGHOLD
GHARAWDARA HIGHLANDS
23 APRIL
0445 HOURS

NASER Khadid opened his eyes and stared up at the ceiling of the cave. The Iranian SF captain did not need an alarm clock to break his slumber. Years of soldiering had turned him into a sort of machine when it came to duties that must be attended to. And having to wake up at certain times was paramount; thus, he had an inner clock that sounded a silent alarm. He stretched languidly, glancing over at the fourteen-year-old girl beside him. Her name was Mahzala and she was his second wife.

The marriage between this thirty-two-year-old Iranian and the pubescent Pashtun girl was the sort classified as *muta* in Islam. It is a temporary arrangement in which a carefully negotiated contract details the length of the relationship. This can be from a few hours to up to ninety-nine years. Khadid also had a wife back in his hometown of Shiraz who awaited his return with their two children. However, Khadid's assignment to the Pashtun rebel group was going to keep him away from home for a couple of years. He was a lusty man, and going that long without sex was something he wasn't prepared to deal with. Since he could have as many as four wives, he decided to take a second from among the Pashtun females. He worked out a deal with Mahzala's father after seeing her among the women getting water from the communal well. She was young, slim, and pretty. The girl's father knew the Iranian wanted his daughter for no more than a sexual playmate and housemaid, so he offered no dowry. In fact, he pressed his case until Khadid agreed to give him a donkey and to remain married in the *muta* arrangement for at least two years or pay a penalty. The Iranian captain also had to guarantee he would support any children resulting from the union until adulthood.

Now, at that early hour, he reached over and gently shook the sleeping child bride. She instantly came awake, knowing what was expected of her. She left the covers and went to the fire, stirring up the coals to begin preparing coffee. Khadid then got up and wrapped a blanket around his shoulders to keep off the early morning chill. He went to the long-distance Soviet radio with its wire antenna that was strung along the cave and out the entrance. He turned on the old tube set to warm it up, then slipped the earphones on. He waited for a few moments, then at exactly 0500 hours, the daily scheduled transmission from Chehaar Garrison began sounding its dits and dahs.

The Iranian did not write down the unencoded incoming message verbatim; instead, he jotted just enough to get the gist of the meaning:

serious setback ... heavy losses of armored cars ...
Chehaar deactivated within the week ... troops to join
you ... includes English defector ... prepare to begin active
operations in Afghanistan ... draw attention away from
Iran ...

The transmission came to an end. Khadid glanced over at
Mahzala, kneeling with her back to him as she put the pot on
the fire. He gazed appreciatively at the shape of her rounded
buttocks through the thin *siltirag* undergarments she wore. He
decided he should begin getting into her *kusi* as often as possible in the coming weeks. Once the raiding and ambushes
began, he would be spending a long time away from the base
camp.

BONHOMME RICHARD CLUB
ARLINGTON, VIRGINIA

NOT even the oldest members of the club knew why it
had been named after John Paul Jones's famous Revolutionary
War ship, though it was widely accepted that the first affiliates
were former Naval officers and had probably chosen the name
to honor both the captain and his vessel. In fact, nobody even
knew for sure when the organization was founded. The only
records available, such as minutes of meetings, treasurers' reports, and a few files, showed the earliest date as 1815. However, the Bonhomme Richard Club was referred to in journals
and newspapers as much as a decade or so before that, so the
organization—limited to no more than one hundred gentlemen at one time—was estimated to have been in existence for
some two hundred years.

It was a little-known part of life in old Arlington where
well-to-do merchants, politicians, a few military officers, and
other notables drew off to be among themselves. The original
requirement to have one's name placed on its prestigious roll
was to be a white male, a taxpaying landowner, wealthy, influ-
ential, and with something to contribute to the intellectual and
social characteristics of the organization. It stayed that way
for decades, its quiet stuffy interior a place for harried men of

consequence to retreat for a quiet drink, silent contemplation, and stimulating, but hushed, conversation. Later, as politics and commerce became more complicated, members were allowed to invite in associates for clandestine sessions regarding their various political and commercial concerns.

The club had been at its present location near the Potomac River since 1856. In those days, it took a carriage ride into the country to reach its portals. And, of course, the fratricide of the Civil War from 1861 to 1865 made visiting the place an adventure. The membership was split almost fifty-fifty between Northerners and Southerners, and those from the Confederacy who served in their states' regiments were not much in attendance while North and South were busy slaughtering each other. But at the end of the conflict, everyone was gentlemanly enough to let bygones be bygones, and the ex-Confederates resumed their memberships without resentment from the Unionists. However, until the 1920s, it was considered bad form to discuss the war within the walls. Aside from that, everthing went back to the way it was.

In 1973, because of the changing social environment of the nation, these gentlemen decided that African-Americans who met the criteria for membership should be allowed to join their Bonhomme Richard Club. Although the resolution passed unanimously, only whites were invited when vacancies occurred. Then, in 1995, after a staid "old boy" went off to his reward in that club room in the sky, the ninety-nine survivors each put forth a name for membership. Of that total, seventy-five of the slips carried the name of an African-American; Carl Joplin, PhD, an Undersecretary of State. That broke the race barrier then and forever.

However, even into the twenty-first century, women were not taken into consideration for membership.

24 APRIL
2030 HOURS

ONE entered the premises of the Bonhomme Richard Club through a foyer where a counter similar to a hotel's front desk was located. There were cubbyholes on the wall behind where the concierge stood. Each one was assigned by number to a member, and incoming messages and notices were placed there for his benefit. Farther inside the building was a large library/reading room with the latest newspapers and magazines from all over the world available to the members with special interests. Comfortable, plush leather chairs were scattered helter-skelter across the expanse, each with a small table and ashtray next to it. A single waiter served the readers from the bar located in the next room. Behind all this were a swimming pool, steam baths, and a gymnasium. Upstairs were conference rooms with tables and chairs for meetings when members had business that required the utmost in discretion. Above that, on the third floor, were rooms convenient for overnight stays.

Dr. Carl Joplin with his guest, Mr. Saviz Kahnani from the Iranian embassy, stepped from the taxi and walked across the sidewalk to mount the steps to the club. Jacob, the doorman, lifted the fingers of his right hand to the brim of the top hat he wore and opened the glassed-in portals. The African-American was always on duty from five to ten P.M. six evenings a week. Besides the top hat, he wore a bright red, gold-trimmed jacket (overcoat in cold weather) and navy-blue trousers with a wide red stripe down the outside of each leg. This was the traditional garb for the job, and went back more than a century and a half.

"Good evening, Dr. Joplin."

"Hello, Jacob," Joplin said, allowing Kahnani to precede him.

When they entered the lobby, the desk clerk on duty greeted them politely and informed Dr. Joplin that his reserved conference room on the second floor was waiting for him. Joplin and Kahnani walked side by side up the stairs and down the landing to where a door stood open. When they entered the fourteen-by-fifteen room, they saw a couple of plush leather chairs with a table between them.

Joplin chuckled as they sat down. "I have never figured out why they call these cubbyholes 'conference rooms.' There's barely enough room to swing a cat around in here." He pushed a button on the table to summon a waiter.

"Forgive my rude curiosity, Carl," Kahnani said, "but are the dues high in this club?"

"A bit stiff," Joplin allowed. "But a greater percent of its revenue comes from grants and trusts left behind by deceased members. We're able to make substantial donations to charities."

"I like this ambience," the Iranian said, his accent slightly British from having been educated in the UK. "I feel as if I've stepped back in time."

When the waiter appeared, they ordered drinks and snacks. During the twenty minutes he was gone, Joplin and Kahnani carried on laid-back small talk about mutual acquaintances and interests. The latter included the new Washington Nationals baseball team that both men rooted for. When the waiter returned, he quickly served them, then withdrew and closed the door.

It was time for business.

"Saviz, my friend," Joplin said, sipping his vodka martini, "it's been a while."

"Indeed," Kahnani said, lighting a cigarette. "Are we back to the nuclear situation again?" He picked up his glass of piña colada, made with coconut milk and crushed pineapple but no rum. "For if it is, I fear it will be a repeat of our last session."

"We're beginning to worry a bit less about the Iranian nuclear project," Joplin said. "What concerns us is Tehran's organizational efforts across the Middle East to consolidate all Islamic insurgencies into one army to be under their direct command and control."

"I know nothing of such a thing," Kahnani said.

Joplin was sure he was not lying. "It would be appreciated if you advised the Iranian ambassador of our concern. I am afraid the United States government would be extremely alarmed if this activity continues."

Kahnani now had no doubt that his friend Carl Joplin was speaking the truth. But he still had to remain in his diplomatic mode. "I would hope that an attack on our sovereign territory would not be in the offing, as with our nuclear program."

"The President has stated in the past that we have no intention of attacking Iran," Joplin said, also doing his job.

"But you would abet Israel in such an action."

"We cannot be responsible for Israel," Joplin said.

"But they would refrain from a bombing raid if you insisted."

"We will not accept any accountability for what the Israelis decide to do," Joplin said. "And I cannot stress too much the vital importance of your conveying to your government our concerns about your Special Forces dealing with Arab terrorist groups in the Middle East. If such activities spread to European countries or America, I fear the consequence would be dire enough to cause great harm to Iran."

"Your serious warning has been delivered," Kahnani said calmly. "I will relay the American concerns directly to the ambassador first thing in the morning."

"I appreciate that, Saviz," Joplin said. He drained his martini. "Shall we order another round?"

"An excellent idea, Carl," Kahnani said. "Mmm! And perhaps another small tray of the hors d'oeuvres."

Joplin pressed the button again.

CHAPTER 13

BRANNIGAN'S Brigands were now "stood down" from Operation Rolling Thunder. Everything had been put on hold since intelligence reports of the Iranians deactivating Chehaar Garrison and pulling away from the Afghan border had softened the situation. The brass upstairs wanted to go into a wait-and-see mode.

Lieutenant Bill Brannigan was not going to let down his guard or allow his Brigands to sit around with their thumbs up their asses. Using the clout the victory over the armored car unit had given him, he turned full pressure on the staff at both Station Bravo in Bahrain and the USS *Combs* out in the Arabian Sea. He requested, i.e., *demanded* and received, i.e., was *grudgingly given*, the following items: a set schedule of regular weekly supply and resupply flights into Shelor; the latest issues of all aerial and satellite photographs of the OA to include the highlands to the north; stockpiles of 5.56-milimeter ammo along with 7.62- and .50-caliber armor-piercing rounds; authorization to draw fuel and lubricants from the Army transportation company stationed at Shelor; two AS-50 .50-caliber sniper rifles; and finally, the exchange of the eighteen HK-416 carbines for the same number of M-16 rifles with six M-203 40-millimeter grenade launchers.

The changeover from the HK-416s was not because of any inferior characteristics of those weapons. This was something Brannigan had to do if he wanted to add the half-dozen grenade launchers to his arsenal.

With those logistical issues dealt with, the Brigands turned to keeping tuned up and ready to respond to any combat situation that might arise in the OA. They performed rigorous PT and ten-kilometer runs every morning before chow. After eating, they headed for the desert to conduct combat drill, while every third night was spent in mock war against each other to sharpen their night-fighting skills. Interspersed with this were live-fire exercises and a friendly competition on a hastily laid-out KD range to see which guys were the best shots. This latter activity was always won hands down by Bruno Puglisi and Joe Miskoski. Both were naturally accurate shooters. And that was the main reason they were issued the sniper rifles with scopes. No one else came close to the accuracy they demonstrated with the weapons. Puglisi shrugged it off, saying, "Me and my buddy Joe are natural-born hit men. Guys like us are just blessed with certain talents."

The routine was demanding and exhausting, and Petty Officer Chad Murchison summed up everyone's feelings one evening while the detachment was enjoying some well-deserved cold beers after a long, energy-sapping day. "My mood will be most jocund when we're back in combat and can enjoy a bit of enervation."

"Yeah," Puglisi said. "Me too." Then he leaned over to Miskoski and whispered, "What the fuck did he say?"

"He was telling us how he felt," Miskoski said in a low voice. "Ol' Chad is something-or-other about combat where he'll be something-or-other while he's enjoying himself."

"Oh, yeah," Puglisi said. "That's what I thought he said."

PASHTUN STRONGHOLD
GHARAWDARA HIGHLANDS
1000 HOURS

THE Pashtun lookout on the mountaintop had spotted the small column of men wending their way up the trail toward the natural fortress. He was not alarmed by the sight as he studied them through his Soviet field glasses. The newcomers were expected and, in fact, would be joining the rebel group as permanent residents and fighters. He turned to the Iranian Special Forces officer sitting nearby on a rock. "They are in view, effendi."

Captain Naser Khadid got up and walked over to the man, pulling his own binoculars from the case on his belt to study the sight below. "*Ho,* I can see the Angrez who leads them."

"They are dressed like Arabs," the lookout said, still studying the men moving slowly toward them.

"That is because they *are* Arabs," Khadid said. "Give the signal that they are in sight and all is well."

The lookout picked up a large Soviet banner lying at his feet. The red color was fading with age, but still made a dandy signal flag. He waved it back and forth to catch the attention of another guard farther down on the other side of the mountain. This was a prearranged procedure that would alert the stronghold that the anticipated reinforcements had arrived. Although the Pashtuns had field telephones and radios, they used flags near their home area for security reasons. Telephones required the laying of wires that intruders might discover, and radio transmissions could easily be picked up and the source located by electronic warfare elements of unfriendly intruders, such as the Afghan Army and Coalition forces. For this reason only, the Iranian SF officer Khadid operated a radio, but he neither transmitted nor received long enough to allow vectoring on his exact location.

CAPTAIN Arsalaan Sikes walked directly behind the Pashtun guide who led them upward along the steep, rocky path toward their destination. His twenty Arab mujahideen—the survivors of the two battles with the Americans on the desert—followed, their AK-47s at the ready as the highly disciplined men maintained alertness in their assigned areas of observation. Everyone was loaded down with a heavily laden rucksack, extra ammunition, and web gear. Under those circumstances, the trip was arduous and demanding, but Sikes had always maintained a strong daily PT program for his unit. This activity consisted of demanding calisthenics and punishing five-mile runs. He would have liked to have been able to use weight training as well, but Brigadier Khohollah's TA didn't include barbells and/or dumbbells. At any rate, his men were in as superb physical condition as any unit in the British Army except, perhaps, the SAS.

Sikes glanced back past Warrant Officer Shafaqat Hashiri at the men. He was pleased by their appearance. They showed no signs of suffering under the stress of the march, and they seemed enthused about this new phase in their jihad. The fact that they were going into a new aggressive stage of fighting took a lot of the sting out of the ass-kicking they got earlier from the Americans.

When they reached the top of the hill, Sikes saw both the lookout and Iranian officer. The latter stepped forward with his hand outstretched. "We have been waiting for you, Captain Sikes. I am Captain Khadid, Iranian Special Forces."

"Right," Sikes said. "Brigadier Khohollah told me you was the bloke I was to see when I got here."

"Come on," Khadid said. "I shall take you down to meet the Pashtun leader. You will be pleased to learn that he speaks excellent English. By the way, they are serving Iran, but Pashtuns will always be Pashtuns no matter what. Certain sensitive situations can always arise most unexpectedly. You will find it wise to be diplomatic at all times."

"I understand."

YAMA Orakzai, the Pashtun leader, was on a walking tour of the stronghold, making the usual inspection he did three or four times a week. His deputy, Khusahal Shinwari, walked at his side. They had gone first to the fighting positions to make sure the hand-constructed rock fortifications were still in place and any necessary camouflage was being maintained. They found the mujahideen manning the sites all well armed with extra bandoliers of ammunition along with sets of three Soviet RGD-5 defensive hand grenades. The men on duty were, as always, very diligent in their vigilance. This was not only from a sense of duty, but because their wives and children were nearby.

Now, with the defenses checked out, the two men strolled through the living areas to see how the wives and children were getting along. Besides caves, there were simple, traditional houses skillfully constructed of rock in which families lived along a sunken area below the grottos. At that time of the year, cooking was done outside and now, as was customary in the morning, the women were beginning preparation of midday meals. Orakzai and Shinwari responded to the females' friendly greetings with polite nods and big smiles.

Shinwari leaned toward Orakzai, speaking under his breath. "You must admit our women are indeed beautiful, are they not, *wror*?"

"Ho!" Orakzai agreed enthusiastically. "But I would hate to be a wounded enemy who fell into their hands."

"Surely, Allah has a special place in Paradise for those wretches the women would dispatch into eternity in the slow, painful manner they prefer."

Orakzai laughed. "Perhaps even infidels who die under their knives are also allowed in Paradise, *na*?"

1130 HOURS

ARSALAAN Sikes's men, winded and tired, settled down along the mountainside next to the Pashtuns' main cave. Some unveiled women had brought them hot coffee and *samosas*—fried pastry pies filled with spiced vegetables—for refreshments. The Arabs, as good Muslims, politely kept their eyes from their hostesses' faces while being served, even though the women gazed in curiosity at their keffiyehs and uniforms.

Captains Arsalaan Sikes and Naser Khadid were conducted into the cave's interior by a Pashtun guard. They were taken back to the chamber where Yama Orakzai maintained both his living area and headquarters. He was seated on a carpet-covered chair, and did not get up when Sikes presented himself with a proper British salute and stomping of his boots.

"Cap'n Sikes reporting!"

"We have no ranks, Sikes," Orakzai said while displaying a friendly smile. "We are all *wruna*—brothers here." He nodded to Khadid. "Hello, *wror*."

"Hello, Orakzai Mesher," Khadid said. He turned to Sikes. "This is the Pashtun leader. His name is Yama Orakzai. However, as a sign of respect, his followers refer to him as Orakzai Mesher. It identifies him as the leader."

"Right," Sikes said. "I'm right pleased to make your acquaintance, Orakzai Mesher. Me lads call me Sikes Bey, yeah? I reckon that makes me a leader too."

"I am familiar with the term," Orakzai said. "I shall see to it that my people show you that respect."

"Now, I appreciate that," Sikes said. "I'm hoping the day will come when I got enough men under me command to be called Sikes Pasha."

"You are indeed an ambitious man, Sikes Bey," Orakzai said. "You are obviously not an American. I had many dealings with the CIA and am familiar with their pattern of speech. What would be your nationality?"

"I'm British, but I've converted to Islam and I speak Arabic. I took the name Arsalaan. They tell me it means lionhearted. I kept me family name."

"Why did you not care to switch to one in Arabic?" Orakzai asked.

"I got a score to settle," Sikes said. "I was in the British Army, see? I was a good soldier and they was gonna make me an officer, but not in the regiment I wanted. They said I wasn't the right social type. I want 'em to hear me name and know they made one great big fucking mistake by the snobby way they treated me."

"I understand," the Pashtun said, thinking the Brits were as profane as the Yanks. "My people have a long history of fighting the British. We have tales of long ago when some came over to our side and joined us. They also converted to Islam. Several became great leaders."

"I'm glad to hear that," Sikes said. "But I ain't surprised they changed sides like me, yeah? The old class system is alive and well in some places, hey? It ain't fair to keep good men down."

"I have been informed that you brought twenty fighters with you," Orakzai said. "You understand you will be under my command."

"I got no problem with that, Orakzai Mesher. And me and the lads is ready for action."

"Excellent! Most of our activities involve getting opium poppy powder through Afghanistan and Iran into Turkey," Orakzai said. "But now and then, we ambush Afghan Army motor patrols in the passes through these mountains."

"I'd like to show me stuff if you'd let me have a go," Sikes said.

"I shall do just that, Sikes Bey," Orakzai said. "It is my intention to send my number-one man, Khushahal Shinwari, along with you. He can take you to a good place where the Afghans drive by regularly."

"I shall go along too," Khadid said, then added, "With your permission."

"Of course," Orakzai said. He emitted a loud whistle that brought the guard in. "Go fetch Shinwari. Tell him I want to speak with him." As soon as the man left, Orakzai turned his attention back to Sikes. "Take a seat, if you please. We shall have some refreshments while we discuss your coming battle."

THE SPINDRIFTS, RHODE ISLAND
26 APRIL
0600 HOURS

PENNY Brubaker had been awake for more than two hours, sitting in the east wing guest room as she gazed out over Narragansett Bay, still wrapped in the early morning fog. She was visiting her maiden aunt Beatrice Brubaker, who had the estate in the exclusive neighborhood known locally as the

Spindrifts. Many wealthy New England families had been spending the warmest months of the year in that area for over a century. Each summer since the 1880s, the mothers and children would be taken down to their luxurious summer homes by husbands and fathers. As soon as the spouses and offspring were settled, the males would hie back to Boston to tend to business and mistresses.

Now, with other places beckoning to families for their vacations, only the eldest members of these moneyed dynasties visited the Spindrifts. Aunt Beatrice was one of those who never lost her fondness for the old place. It was five years ago when she decided to leave Boston and make the spot her permanent home. However, she kept the guest facilities available for any Brubaker kin who wished to visit.

Penny, enduring delayed-stress syndrome, was now taking advantage of that standing offer.

WHEN Penny Brubaker returned to the States from Afghanistan, she had resigned from service in the UN, wanting only to let that part of her life drift away into distant memory, and the sooner the better. She immediately went on a shopping spree that covered both Boston and New York City as she revamped her wardrobe and prepared to return to her former life.

She contacted old girlfriends to get back into the party scene, but the young woman found out that her experiences overseas had left her much like a soldier lately returned from war. She had seen too much of the world's worst circumstances not to have it affect her. The young people her age seemed immature and blissfully ignorant of real life. Penny watched her female friends flirt in singles bars as the guys tried to impress them and pick them up. The would-be suitors complimented them, bought them drinks, and did their best to win them over, using gentle persuasion and as much charm as they could muster.

Penny remembered a refugee camp in the Sudan where Arab raiders and plunderers would come into an area looking for women. Their victims had no choice but to carefully lay their infants aside, hoping the children would not be harmed. Then they were forced to submit to gang rape through entire nights before being allowed to return to the miserable shelters awaiting them in the crude bivouacs. No coquetry and sexy teasing as in big-city bars occurred out in that awful desert. Nor were the men's advances refused. Such effrontery would result in a severe beating at the least, and death at the most.

Penny was not favorably impressed with the young men in the dating game either. They seemed shallow, their lives pointless and self-absorbed, as if the world had been created for their enjoyment and benefit. Most were yuppie types working in white-collar jobs with exaggerated feelings about their real worth. When she compared them with Chad Murchison and his SEAL buddies, they came up woefully short. Nor did they measure up to the men working in the UNREO camps who didn't earn much money but made important contributions to the betterment of the world while putting up with crude conditions and extreme danger.

Penny finally became so disgusted with the singles scene that when she wished to go out for an evening's entertainment, she contacted one of the loan officers who worked in her family's bank. He was a very nice fellow by the name of Henry who was gay. He was willing to take her out now and then for dinner and dancing, and she didn't have to worry about him making any moves on her.

NOW Penny turned from the window and went back to the bed, crawling under the covers. Constant thinking about Chad had caused her so much distress and heartache that she had finally escaped the hectic activities of Boston to find some peace and solitude at Aunt Beatrice's place in the Spindrifts. She had written him a letter, but he had not yet answered it.

Because of her return to America, Penny now understood Chad a lot better. There was absolutely no way he would fit back into his former life even if he lived to be a hundred. The old Chad was gone forever, and she realized she loved this new Chad a lot more than the former. Eventually, he would

return to the SEALs' home base in California when his overseas tour was completed.

And Penny Brubaker would be there waiting for him.

GHARAWDARA HIGHLANDS
27 APRIL
0915 HOURS

THE Afghan Army convoy of four Volkswagen 183 Iltis
light utility vehicles rolled along the road that cut through the
mountain pass. The commander was a young junior lieutenant
by the name of Khalili who was riding in the second vehicle.
He was twenty years old, eager, good-humored, and always
volunteered for this assignment on a patrol into the Gharawdara
Highlands. It was good to get out of the garrison, and sometimes the Pashtuns would spring a hasty ambush on them.
There was always lots of shooting, ricochets zinging off into
the air, and yelling as the convoy rushed through the fusillades. But there had never been any casualties on either side,
and it was no more than a very exciting game. He even loved
writing home about it, exaggerating the adventure to make his
parents think he was a real warrior.

The enemy generally made the attacks in the morning, as
if anxious to get them over with before going back to their
hideout higher up in the mountains. Khalili had been making
the run for almost a year now, and they had never been hit on
the way back to the garrison, although sometimes Pashtuns
would be sighted looking down on them. During those instances, his soldiers exchanged shouted insults with the ob-
servers.

Now, on a pleasant morning, the junior lieutenant and his
vehicles entered the fighting zone, and everyone looked eagerly upward to see if they could catch sight of the Pashtuns.
Usually, a silly, grinning face could be spotted peeking over a
boulder, or a flash of sunlight would sparkle for an instant off
someone's weapon.

However, after ten minutes of travel, there was no sign of
ambushers. Khalili sighed, gazing at the lead vehicle ahead,

the dust from the road whipping up into the air from its tires. The young lieutenant spoke to his driver. "It appears we will have a boring trip this time. Nothing is going to happen. *Hech!*"

The soldier laughed. "Perhaps the Pashtuns were *garm* for their women, eh? They didn't want to climb out of their flea-bitten blankets."

Khalili laughed too. "So they stayed in their flea-bitten blankets with their flea-bitten wives. *Khanda dar!*"

Another five minutes passed; then suddenly, the vehicle ahead rocked and the engine came to a stop. Steam and smoke came from under the hood. The sound of firing from above could be heard as the two men bailed out of their now-burning car. They had gone only a half-dozen running steps toward Khalil's vehicle when they buckled and stumbled, falling to the ground in bloody heaps.

Cold fear gripped Khalili. This wasn't the way it was supposed to be. "Speed up! *Zut shodan!* Get us through this area!"

The driver hit the accelerator and the Volkswagen leaped forward. They went only fifteen meters when they began receiving fire, not from above, but from the front. Several mujahideen were alongside the road, using boulders for cover. They had sealed in the front of the ambush site. The last thing Khalili and his driver saw was the windshield smash as dozens of slugs ripped into the interior of the small truck.

The sergeant in the last vehicle saw that the other three were now shot to pieces. He tried to maintain his calm in spite of the terror that gripped him. *"Bar gashtan!"* he said loudly. "Turn around! Let's get out of here!"

His driver had already started the escape maneuver even before the sergeant ordered it. The little vehicle whipped into the opposite direction of travel, but they met the same fate as the junior lieutenant. The rear was sealed in too. A trio of mujahideen stood brazenly in the middle of the road, blasting the doomed car with rapid bursts of full-automatic fire. The driver and sergeant died instantly as their shot-up Volkswagen went off the road and crashed into a stand of large rocks. It rolled over instantly, bursting into flames.

Arsalaan Sikes made his way from the firing site down into the kill zone on the road. Naser Khadid and Khusahal Shinwari followed closely. Shinwari looked in wonder at the killing and destruction that had taken only seconds to be executed. Khadid was also impressed. "Well done, Sikes Bey."

Sikes looked at them and grinned. "Now that, mate," he said, "is wot is called a bluddy ambush."

CHAPTER 14

ARSALAAN Sikes damned the lack of modern equipment as he huddled on the hillside looking down at the village nestled across the valley. He could barely make out the shadowy forms of the stone houses where a population of some 150 people lived. It was estimated that no more than thirty to forty of the Taliban males were of warrior age in the community; perhaps even fewer. At the moment, the desperate villagers were in hiding from the Afghan Army and had only established the primitive hamlet a couple of months earlier.

From his position, Sikes would have to go some twenty-five meters down a steep slope, cross an open space a hundred meters across, then head up another incline to reach the dwellings. Captain Naser Khadid, the Iranian SF officer, was beside him, leaning his elbows on a waist-high boulder while using a pair of French night-vision binoculars to study the target area. After a couple of minutes, he handed the field glasses to Sikes. "You will see better with these, Sikes Bey."

"Thanks, Cap'n Khadid," the Englishman said. He took the devices and sighted through them, the green and black images of the village buildings now easy to discern through the lenses. "That ain't too bad a place to defend if you're in a small-arms fight. But anybody with proper mortars or RPGs could knock the bluddy walls down about their ears."

"Too bad Orakzai Mesher wouldn't lend you any of his," Khadid said.

"He wants to give me a bit of a test, hey? So he says to himself, 'Let's see what this here Inglizi bloke can do. I'll send him out to a fortified village without no heavy weapons and let him have a go at it.'"

"Except he probably referred to you as an Angrez," Khadid pointed out. "That is the Pashtun word for Englishman."

"Bloody shit!" Sikes complained, taking the binoculars from his eyes. "Another fucking language I got to start fretting over."

"I noticed the ten Arabs you sent across the valley all have hand grenades attached to their field-belt suspenders," the Iranian captain remarked. "I hope none of them fall off and detonate. That would betray our presence here in a most emphatic manner."

"Not to worry," Sikes said. "Them grenades is French F-Ones. The pins don't come out with a straight jerk. They got to be twisted, then given a good tug. A bit of a safety feature."

"Are they fragmentation-type?" the Iranian inquired.

"Right," Sikes said. "The F-Ones is plastic with the perforated frags on the inside of the case. And you can count on a good bit of concussion from the bleeders, yeah?" He checked his watch. "I'll give the lads until the sun just starts peeping over that mountain to the east. The minute the first bit o' light gives us a good view, I'll start me plan going, hey?"

He had deployed the remaining ten Arabs with five on each side of where he was now situated. There were also fifty Pashtuns from Orakzai's band spread out along the same area that looked across at the village. The other Arabs, under the command of the ever-faithful Warrant Officer Shafaqat Hashiri, were now making their way across the valley a hundred meters to the east as they headed to their assigned fighting position.

"I am most curious as to how you plan to run this battle, Sikes Bey," Khadid said. "Especially since we are not a group who has fought together before."

"I don't tip me hand to nobody till everything's over and done with," Sikes said. "By the by, Cap'n, the noise discipline o' them bleeding Pashtos is fucking horrible. Wot the hell can I do to fix that and a few other things that need correcting?"

"One must remember they are not soldiers," Khadid said. "The Pashtuns are warriors. Giving advice and explaining things very politely will help you get your way much better than trying to administer brutal discipline."

Sikes chuckled. "So putting me boot up a few bums won't get me shit, hey?"

"Listen to me, Sikes Bey," Khadid said seriously. "Never—never—never—strike one of them whatever you do. That would be something that their culture demands be avenged immediately with the greatest prejudice possible."

"It sounds like they'd kill over getting a punch-up."

"Indeed," Khadid said.

A clack of rocks behind them attracted their attention, and they turned to see Khusahal Shinwari walking up. The field commander of the Pashtun fighters joined them, squatting down. "All my Peshto brothers are in position."

"Thanks, Shinwari Effendi," Sikes said politely. "You made a bit o' noise coming up here, yeah? We should be careful about that. But I don't think nobody in the village heard you."

"I shall inform my men to take great care in that regard," Shinwari said. "It is an excellent suggestion on your part."

"Well, now," Sikes said, "I appreciate that."

Shinwari asked, "Are your Arabs in place now?"

"Half are," Sikes replied. "The ones going to other side of the valley will need another half hour at the most. When they get there, they'll be up on that ridge just above the houses."

Shinwari gazed through the gloom. "*Wabakhsha,* but how can they fire effectively from up there?"

"Not to worry," Sikes said. "They'll be able to do the job I've given 'em."

0551 HOURS

THE sun showed red over to the east even though the fiery orb was still below the mountains. The daylight was slowly encroaching on the night's darkness, meaning that Sikes and Khadid no longer needed the night-vision binoculars. The stone hovels of the Taliban village were becoming easier to see.

Sikes reached down and grabbed his AK-47, looking at Shinwari. "Do your blokes understand when and how to fire?"

"Yes, Sikes Bey," Shinwari replied. "They are not to begin shooting until you go first. And when they do, they will aim carefully and fire on full automatic with short bursts."

"Bluddy good," Sikes said. He aimed his AK-47 toward the center of the village, took a deep breath, then squeezed off two quick five-round squirts of the 7.62-millimeter ammo. Immediately, a loud blast of fusillades flashed out from the firing line of Arabs and Pashtuns. The bullets hit the rock houses, making sparks as they bounced and ricocheted off.

Then a series of detonations began as the ten Arabs situated in their position on the cliff just above the village began dropping the French hand grenades down among the dwellings. All in all, a total of sixty F-1s fell into the village, bouncing and rolling among the houses before detonating. The resultant explosions threw out shards of metal fragments and waves of battering concussion that rocked the poorly constructed rock shelters. These were held together with a minimum of mortar, and the walls began collapsing under the onslaught of the invisible force of the blasts. Roofs caved in on the occupants, exposing the interiors of their domiciles. The final grenades were tossed down to do their damage, and the hand-thrown barrage ended.

Now the attackers had living targets, and they continued to pour in volleys of the short bursts of automatic assault-rifle fire, paying no attention to whether they were shooting at women and children or not. Figures could be seen trying to rise from their blankets, only to collapse back under the hail of steel-jacketed slugs. Some managed to get to their feet, but were unable to go far before being pummeled by the incoming swarms of bullets.

Sikes Bey bellowed his next order in three languages. *"Hujuml! Hamla kawel!* Attack!"

Captain Naser Khadid, fired up by the excitement of the battle, added the Farsi word. *"Hamle!"*

The attackers swept down the steep slope, still firing, but without accuracy until they reached the floor of the valley. At that point, most of them instinctively slowed down to aim and fire off three or four well-aimed bursts. With that precaution taken, they ran onto the farther slope, struggling upward, keeping alert for any resistance. But they received no return fire and they reached the village without a single casualty.

The homes had all collapsed. Those that had not been taken down by the concussion from the detonations were destroyed when others crashed against them in a falling-domino effect. Sikes was at the forefront, carefully and slowly making his way across the jumbled rocks that had once provided shelters for the people.

"Komak!"

The cry for help in the Dari language sounded from a pile of rubble in the center of the village. Khushal Shinwari listened carefully as the plea was repeated several more times. He moved toward the source; then a Taliban in a dusty, bloody robe suddenly stood up and fired his own AK-47. The rounds slammed into Shinwari, who was kicked back by the strike of the bullets an instant before collapsing to the ground. Immediately, a dozen Pashtun attackers blasted the Taliban killer, who took enough hits to fill a thirty-round banana magazine. The man twisted into two pieces from the ripping impacts, both hunks hitting the ground at the same time.

One of the Pashtuns went to Shinwari and knelt down. *"Mer."*

"He says he's dead," Khadid said to Sikes.

"Tell them others to be damn careful while they're poking around then," Sikes said.

As Khadid translated the orders, the ten Arabs who had been up on the ridge emerged from some boulders at the side of the village. Warrant Officer Hashiri walked up to Sikes with the detail and saluted. "Reporting back, Captain Sikes Bey."

"You lads did a *kebir* job with them grenades," the Englishman said.

"We are pleased to be finding that out," Hashiri said. "It was impossible to see below if we were accurate."

Sikes gestured to the destroyed dwellings. "Well, have a look then."

Hashiri studied the fallen structures, then turned his eyes on the bloody, battered remains of Shinwari. "What happened?"

"One of these Taliban yelled for help; then when Shinwari walked up, the bluddy snake shot him," Sikes explained. "Tell the men to begin searching for survivors in the rubble, but be careful. There could be a couple o' more sneaky rotters waiting to start shooting."

Now Arabs and Pashtuns alike carefully probed the village. Sikes, with Khadid at his side, moved slowly through the wreckage looking at the pathetic dead. "God! There was lots o' women and children, wasn't there?"

"Yes," Khadid said, looking at the corpses of a dead woman and baby lying on blankets under a mass of rocks. "I think it is safe now to assume there are no survivors."

"So we didn't get no pris'ners, hey? Well, no matter, Orakzai Mesher said not to worry, they was just a bunch of miserable Taliban hiding out. From the looks of 'em, they wasn't eating too good."

"The Taliban are as much our enemies as the Afghans," Khadid pointed out. "We hate them even more."

"Usama Bin Laden and the al-Qaeda are going to be bluddy upset about this," Sikes said. "But I suppose most of 'em are up in the caves around here somewhere, hey?"

"Eventually, we want to draw them out and deal them a death blow," the Iranian said. He chuckled. "If for no other reason than to embarrass the Americans."

"A lot o' Yank faces will turn red over that," Sikes said. He looked over at the men still combing through the remnants of the now-destroyed community. "We're done here. I'll gather up the lads and we'll head back . . . well, to our new home, right? We're living up here in these fucking mountains now, ain't we?" He whistled loudly to Warrant Officer Hashiri and waved. Hashiri yelled out orders. Although the Pashtuns didn't understand the words, they got the meaning when the Arabs began forming up.

Within ten minutes, the column, with four men bearing Shinwari's corpse on a hastily rigged litter, moved from the area toward the higher country.

PASHTUN STRONGHOLD
ORAKZAI'S CAVE
1400 HOURS

ARSALAAN Sikes Bey and Captain Naser Khadid sat on thick carpets with their host, Yama Orakzai Mesher. They sipped hot thick coffee and slowly consumed the inevitable *samosas* with *paow*—stewed goat's feet. Sikes was not enjoying the latter dish, but followed Khadid's example and forced himself to at least nibble on what the Pashtuns considered a delicacy.

"The death of my old comrade grieves me," Orakzai said. "He and I fought in many battles together against the Soviets."

"He perished answering a plea for help," Khadid said. "Allah, in his benevolence and mercy, will reward his attempt to perform a kind act."

"Waquian," Orakzai agreed, knowing that Shinwari was actually after a prisoner rather than acting out of concern for the Taliban fighter. "But I have not only lost his presence in my life, I am lacking a trusted deputy." He picked up his bowl of stew and put it to his lips, tipping his head back to let the hot thick broth flow into his mouth. He swallowed and set the bowl down. "My mujahideen told me the battle was a very quick one, yet it left the village entirely destroyed."

"I could've made a better job of it with a mortar and heavy machine gun," Sikes said.

"I think it clever the way you had grenades dropped from the cliff above to knock over the houses," Orakzai said.

"When we scouted the place, I noticed they looked like they was about to fall over anyway," Sikes said. "That's when I figured a little push might just make 'em tumble down. O'course, we couldn't go up there and knock 'em over, could we?"

"We tolerated the village because the people were going hungry," Orakzai explained. "We knew they would all eventually perish from sickness and starvation within a couple of months at the most. I wished them slow, miserable deaths to avenge their mistreatment of my people during the time they ruled Afghanistan. When you arrived, I decided the miserable wretches would make an excellent practice target." He smiled. "I suppose, in a way, I was being merciful to them."

Khadid saw a chance to put in a good word for the Iranian-sponsored Englishman. "Sikes Bey's employment of the AK-47s was most effective, Orakzai Mesher. There was not a square millimeter of space in the village that was not shot up. Those Taliban who did not die when their houses collapsed upon them were killed by bullets."

"This is the second time you've demonstrated your skills to great advantage, Sikes Bey," Orakzai said. "I praise your efforts."

"It's always nice to get a compliment for a job," Sikes said. "But I do have a request, Orakzai Mesher. I would appreciate it if the next time I go out to do battle, that I got the proper support with me, yeah? I'm speaking of heavy weapons backup."

"That will be done," Orakzai said. "And I want to speak to you of another thing. With my dear comrade Khusahal now departed to his eternal reward in Allah's Paradise, I no longer have a field commander. I am sorry to say none of my Pashtuns are capable of leading more than just a few men. I would like you to take over those responsibilities."

Sikes could barely believe the words that were just spoken. He stared at Orakzai for a moment before he could respond. "Uh . . . well . . . you mean be in command of your army?"

"That is exactly what I mean."

Captain Khadid smiled discreetly, trying to conceal his enthusiasm. This would make his job as military advisor that much easier. His superiors would also be pleased with the appointment.

Sikes looked over at him, then back to Orakzai. "Yeah. I'd like that. How many men will I have under me command?"

"It varies, Sikes Bey," Orakzai said. "You may be sure of between eight and nine hundred."

"Blimey!" Sikes said. "That's a bluddy battalion, that is!" He thought a moment, then asked, "That ain't enough to be a pasha, is it?"

Khadid spoke quickly, saying, "But you would be leading an entire army no matter its size. Surely you deserve to be called pasha."

Sikes displayed a wide grin of pleasure. "I wouldn't be Sikes Bey no more then, would I? I'd be Sikes Pasha."

"That is an Arab title," Orakzai said. "But if you want to be addressed as such, I shall order it done."

"When do I take command?"

"It will be announced in the morning," Orakzai said. "I will see that a translator is provided for you. I advise you strongly to begin acquiring a good working knowledge of the Pashtun language. My mujahideen are already favorably impressed with you from this morning's battle. Being able to communicate with them in their own language will solidify your stature as their battle leader."

"I know something I could say in Pashtun to you already, Orakzai Mesher," Sikes said. "*Manana*—thank you!"

"Come back this evening," Orakzai said. "We will dine together and discuss the details of this arrangement. That will include a *muta* with one of our young women. That will further consolidate your bond to our group."

The idea of a temporary marriage and having a woman also appealed to Sikes. It had been months since he had last enjoyed the sexual favors of a woman. "Am I gonna get a chance to look around at the birds here?"

"I will pick one for you," Orakzai said. "Do not worry. She will be from a proper family."

"Well, now, Orakzai Mesher, all due respect, hey? But I'd like a looker."

"All our women are beautiful, Sikes Pasha," the Pashtun

leader said. He glanced at Khadid. "The invitation to dine also includes you, my friend. The support of our Iranian brothers is most important do me."

"Yes, Orakzai Mesher," Khadid said. "With your permission, Sikes Pasha and I will withdraw until this evening."

They left the chamber, going through the cave to the opening. When they stepped out into the sunlight, Khadid spoke under his breath. "You must not forget you are in the service of the Iranian government. Your new status with the Pashtuns will meet with much approval at Special Forces Headquarters as long as you maintain yourself under our command."

"Now that sounds like a bit of a threat," Sikes said sullenly.

"Think of it as advice, Sikes Pasha."

"Then do this," Sikes said. "Get a message out to Brigadier Khohollah that I want a commission—a regular bloody commission—in the Iranian Army. Not in the Jihad Abadi like I got now. And in the rank of major. And I want it proper and official. Not just something I'm being called. Understood?"

"I shall take care of that, Sikes Pasha."

"Good," Sikes said. "By the way, how d'you say 'major' in Farsi?"

"Sargord," Khadid answered.

They continued down the narrow trail to the village without further conversation.

CHAPTER 15

UNDERSECRETARY of State Carl Joplin's meeting with the Iranian chargé d'affaires Saviz Kahnani was a follow-up to the session between the two gentlemen at the Bonhomme Richard Club on 24 April. This change of venue was an indication that the situation had become more serious. But it was not yet of such a grave nature that the U.S. Secretary of State, the Foreign Minister of Iran, or the two nations' ambassadors would become overtly involved.

Joplin and Kahnani had settled at a small table in one corner of the former's office for the session. Neither had a briefcase, notes, or any other sort of documents or maps in their possession. Joplin opened the session by reiterating that the President of the United States was now even more concerned about Iranian policies in the Middle East. Particularly where local insurgencies were concerned.

In spite of the increase in tension, Kahnani was relaxed and much at ease. Although not fully briefed, the embassy military attaché had enlightened the diplomat enough to give him a feeling of confidence. "My dear Carl, I am not aware of how the American government has obtained that erroneous information, but let me assure you that the Iranian government is not organizing an army of Arab insurgents in a grand scheme to conquer that part of the world."

"Our intelligence services report to the contrary, Saviz."

"It is true that we are aiding our Shiite brothers in Iraq," Kahnani said. "But only in their struggles against the Sunnis. We do not publicize this, but obviously your intelligence has discovered those activities and arrived at erroneous conclusions concerning the true motives behind them. And if you make mention of it in the media, we will deny the fact for reasons of international sensitivity. But allow me to state emphatically that we will not tolerate atrocities committed by religious rivals against those Muslims who practice their faith in the same manner we do. In other words, we are deeply concerned about the safety and well-being of Shiites in Iraq."

This was one of those candid moments in diplomacy when explicit understandings and previous agreements limit the number of persons who would be informed of the exchanged information. This gave both Joplin and Kahnani more latitude in expressing themselves.

Joplin continued his dissertation, saying, "The United States government is concerned that the Iranians are encouraging a civil war in Iraq. And this could well expand to other Arab nations."

Kahnani shrugged. "This aid program came about from the bombing of the Shiite shrine in Iraq. And Tehran does not have alliances with Shiites in any other country. Such activities are handled by our clergy and involve only religious matters."

"Much, if not most, of Islamic activity involves violence!" Joplin said sharply.

"I resent the implication our faith propagates warfare and murder!" Kahnani shot back.

"The Chehaar Garrison in eastern Iran has been closed," Joplin said. "This coincides with the defeat of an invasion force that came out of Iran and into Afghanistan. It was a unit of armored cars that suffered heavy casualties."

"Chehaar is an abandoned military site that has not been occupied for at least five years," Kahnani insisted. "It is nothing but rusting Quonset huts sitting on the edge of a salt marsh. The idea that a detachment of armored cars has been lately stationed there is absurd. I would even hesitate to pass on your statement to my ambassador."

"That particular unit was commanded by a deserter from the British Army," Joplin said. "His men were all Arabs— Shiites, to be exact, from several Middle Eastern countries— and quite a few of them were killed. The survivors were reorganized into a small infantry unit and left Chehaar. They went to northwestern Afghanistan."

"I cannot accept any of that, Carl. It is data that has been fabricated in a most preposterous manner."

"There are two sorts of insurgents using that particular area for hiding," Joplin continued, unaffected by the denial. "Taliban and disaffected Pashtuns. American intelligence surmises the Arabs from Chehaar joined one of those two groups. Common sense tells us it was the Pashtuns."

Kahnani chuckled. "The idea that a British deserter is commanding a small armored-car unit under the direction of the Iranian government is ludicrous. I stick to my opinion that somebody is making up a story to alarm you Americans."

"The Englishman's name is Archibald Sikes," Joplin said. "British MI-Five has given us a full dossier on him."

"Well, if this mysterious Englishman is working for Iran, why in the world would he and his Arab chums go to Afghanistan to live among Pashtuns?"

"Because this particular group of Pashtuns are being encouraged, bribed, and equipped by the Iranian Army. Obviously, an insurgency in Afghanistan is part of your big picture."

"Conjecture!" Kahnani exclaimed. "And a poor example of it at that!"

"We desire for you to report back to your ambassador and

inform him that the United States is fully aware of the Iranian plot to organize both Arab and Pashtun insurrections in the Middle East," Joplin insisted. "We demand it be brought to an immediate halt."

"What about our nuclear activities that irritate you so much?" Kahnani asked. "Has the United States government grown bored with that old song and dance?"

"That is still very much on our collective minds," Joplin said. "And I can assure you it remains part of our agenda in dealing with the Iranian government. But as of this moment, we will concern ourselves with your nation's contacts among Arab terrorist groups."

"Very well," Kahnani said. "I will pass your message to the ambassador and he will inform Tehran forthwith."

"Excellent!" Joplin said. He looked at his watch. "Where would you like to go for lunch, Saviz?"

"Mmm," the Iranian mused. "I was thinking of that Italian place over on C Street."

"Ah! Mario's, eh?" Joplin said. "Y'know, I just happen to be in the mood for some of his lasagna."

"It's spaghetti and meatballs with a side dish of sausage for me," Kahnani said. "Shall we go?"

"After you, my friend."

The two men got their hats and left the office.

PASHTUN STRONGHOLD
GHARAWDARA HIGHLANDS

THE Pashtuns' reaction to having Arsalaan Sikes Pasha appointed their leader was one of calm acceptance. The men all admired Sikes's leadership skills, and none of them felt capable of taking over the planning and execution of complicated operations involving a lot of men. The leaders among them were in charge of small units, or had specific talents that made them commanders of specific types of missions or weapons—mortars, Stinger AA launchers, etc. There were a few reservations because Sikes was an Englishman and not a Pashtun, but at least he was a Muslim. Nobody stepped forward with any serious objections, and that was pretty much all it took to ratify Sikes's appointment.

Sikes's newly assigned interpreter was a fourteen-year-old boy by the name of Malyar Lodhi. He spoke excellent English, Dari, French, and of course Pashto. He had gone to the same school in Kandahar as his leader, Yama Orakzai. In fact, it had been Orakzai Mesher who chose him out of all the other boys to get an education and return to the mountains an enlightened young man ready to take up a meaningful leadership position within the group. Unfortunately, Malyar's mathematical instructor in the sixth form at the Kandahar school was a bad-tempered New Zealander who ran his classes under his own rules and regulations. This rather large man was prone to spontaneous outbursts of rage that were the worst in the institution's long history. The only reason he wasn't fired was because of the difficulty in attracting teachers to Afghanistan.

One day, he caught Malyar staring out the window during a lecture on algebraic formulae. The boy was gazing to the north toward his home mountains, wishing he were back in the Gharawdara Highlands, minding goats with his pals. When the teacher noted the youngster's inattention, he strode rapidly to his desk and pulled him to his feet. Then he slapped the boy's face.

Pashtuns believe in always being armed, and Malyar was no exception. He was never without the small *qasab* knife in a sheath in the pants waist of his school uniform. This was a tool normally used to strip the last bits of meat off the bones of animals, but Malyar used it on that memorable day to cut into, then across, the New Zealander's ample belly. Fortunately, all that fat protected the victim, but he immediately began bellowing and shrieking like a wounded ox. Eight years of schooling went into the toilet as Malyar made a quick exit through the nearest window despite the fact that he was on the second floor. The young Pashtun hit the ground, rolled, then leaped to his feet and started running north as fast as he could.

Malyar endured six weeks of flight and evasion following the bloody event, with several harrowing close calls during searches conducted by soldiers and police. But he managed to slip through the nets and reached the foothills, where he began a determined climb into the high country. He made it to the stronghold despite a lack of food and rest. When he explained what had happened, Orakzai forgave him and sent him home to his parents. He chose another boy to replace the fugitive at the school, but when the lad reached Kandahar, he was told no more Pashtun boys from Gharawdara would be accepted as students. The New Zealander's wound had required more than a hundred stitches to close it, and other teachers were seriously concerned for their safety if other lads from the same clan came to study at the institution.

Now working for the new leader Sikes Pasha, Malyar accompanied him wherever he went. The first thing Sikes wanted to check out were the defenses. He found them more than adequate in both the protection they afforded as well as the camouflaging techniques to keep them concealed from view. The Pashtuns had learned much during the war with the Soviets.

Every mujahideen was armed with a well-kept AK-47 assault rife with cleaning tools and spare barrels. Everyone was well versed in the care and maintenance of the weapons as well as the need for having a good stock of ammunition on hand. They weren't the most accurate of shooters, but modern warfare consisted mostly of putting out a lot of firepower to keep the enemy pinned down while the attackers maneuvered to close with them.

However, there was a problem with the heavy weapons that the Englishman had not expected. In fact, the difficulty belied all previous information about the stronghold's support capabilities. The mortars and machine guns were all well maintained and operational, but the problem was the different types and calibers. Sikes Pasha discovered there were three different types of mortars: Soviet M-1937 82-millimeters, Soviet M-1943 120-millimeters, and Spanish ECIA 60-millimeters. The machine guns were just as varied, with 5.56-millimeters, 7.62-millimeters, and 12.7-millimeters in models from four different nations. There was also a Soviet ZU 23-millimeter twin antiaircraft gun. Even though this miscellaneous mix was troubling, it was not pressing at the moment, because there was no ammunition available no matter what the type.

Another perplexing situation was that the organization of the mujahideen was inconstant and fluid. If a man had the necessary skills for certain weapons, he generally preferred to serve them. But, for example, Sikes found that many times during past operations, trained mortarmen would tire of the complexities of setting up and sighting in the weapons. There were also the heavy base plates and tubes that had to be lugged around. This was particularly vexing when having to move up and down the steep ridges of the Gharawdara Highlands. When it all got to be too much, the gunners would unilaterally decide to serve as riflemen for a while. Naturally, due to the Pashtuns' instinctively casual attitudes, this was done without informing anyone or seeking permission. Consequently, there had been times when a field commander called for fire support and there were no men or weapons to provide any.

CAPTAIN KHADID'S QUARTERS
1 MAY
1300 HOURS

SIKES Pasha and Malyar Lodhi presented themselves at the entrance of Khadid's cave after an entire morning of inspections, observations, and interviewing among the Pashtun mujahideen. The Iranian SF officer had been waiting for their arrival, and his young wife Mahzala had prepared refreshments for the meeting.

When the two visitors entered the dwelling, they noted the large Iranian flag mounted on the wall. Western-style tables and chairs for dining augmented the traditional Pashtun pillows and *landi mez*—tables where one sat on the floor for snacks and coffee. Khadid's wife had set one with *samosas* and *puri,* a fried bread. She had also included small bags of potato chips and cans of Pepsi.

Sikes thought the choice of food slightly irregular, but the chips intrigued him. "Where'd you get them crisps then?"

"The same place I obtained the Pepsi," Khadid said. "Well, let's settle down and discuss the findings from your tour."

After seating himself on a pillow, Sikes wasted no time in grabbing a bag of potato chips. He ripped it open and reached in to grab a handful. Malyar snapped open a can of Pepsi. Khadid had already eaten, and he waited as his guests took their first bites.

Sikes took a sip of the soda. "It's a bluddy shame we got no ice, hey? Oh, well, there you are then."

Malyar, who had gotten used to cold drinks while at the boarding school, observed Pashtun decorum by making no mention of the warm Pepsi. Sikes set the can down. "The field fortifications here are up to snuff. These Pashtos is real good at setting up a defense."

"They learned well during their war with the Soviets," Khadid remarked.

"And well they should," Sikes said. "And they're right soldierlike with them AK-47s. Got 'em clean as a whistle and shiny as a new penny, yeah? I noticed there's lots o' ammo for 'em and that's good. But I think we should see that all the lads has got pistols. Something like Beretta autos, know what I mean? Nine-millimeter."

"Mmm," Khadid said, nodding.

"But there ain't no bleeding fire support around here," Sikes complained. "I mean, they got machine guns and mortars, but there's too many different types. And there ain't as much as a single bluddy round for any of 'em. Nobody tole me one fucking thing about that."

"Mmm," Khadid said again.

"And there ain't nearly enough Stingers," Sikes continued. "If we go up against the Yanks—and we most certainly will one day—we're gonna need antiaircraft. O'course, there's that great bloody Russian double-barrel job, but that can't be lugged around these mountains, can it?"

"It is actually a trophy from a raid on a Soviet advanced post," Khadid said. "There is quite a story of how they struggled with it up and down mountain ridges before getting it back here."

"Wot a waste o' manpower," Sikes said. He bit into a *samosa*. "Right then. So now we got to get the ol' ball rolling. The first thing is to decide what sort of mortars and machine guns we're gonna have, then get plenty of ammo for 'em, yeah?"

Khadid shook his head. "We are not anywhere near ready to be worrying about such things."

Sikes's temper snapped. "Shit! How the hell are we supposed to carry on a decent war without the proper tools? You explain that to me, hey?"

"We are not going to conduct a 'war,'" Khadid said. "We are going to continue our present activities until further notice."

"I ain't seen no bluddy activities except when we sprung that ambush and hit that village!"

"We are escorting caravans through the Afghanistan mountains and across Iran into Turkey," Khadid explained calmly. "As a matter of fact, they provide the contacts where we get such luxury items as potato chips and Pepsi."

"What are them blokes lugging around?"

"The cargo is the dried powder made from opium poppies."

"So you're telling me we're running drugs," Sikes said.

"Yes," Khadid replied. "And for a very good reason. We are making plenty of money with this activity. The funds are going to be used to buy those weapons we need from your compatriot Harry Turpin. A large down payment has been made to him and he is busy arranging for the weaponry."

"What sort o' weaponry?"

"Let me think," Khadid said. He was pensive for a moment before continuing. "French FA-MAS five-point-six millimeter bullpup rifles . . . Russian seven-point-six-two PK machine guns . . . Spanish sixty-millimeter Model L mortars . . . American Stinger antiaircraft missiles . . . and that is the lot."

"Not bad a'tall," Sikes said. "But how'd you get the Yanks to part with them Stingers?"

"They were left behind in Afghanistan by the American CIA," Khadid explained. "Evidently, the Taliban were short of cash and made arrangements for them to be sold to Mr. Harry Turpin."

Sikes laughed. "That sly old bastard! Now he's delivered 'em back to Afghanistan and made a bluddy big profit on 'em too."

"I wouldn't be surprised," Khadid said. "So you can forget

any active warfare now, Sikes Pasha. You shall escort opium caravans instead."

"Gawd! You mean with bleeding camels?"

Khadid shook his head. "I believe the smugglers prefer modern transport trucks. They also use machine-gun-mounted Toyota pickup trucks for protection."

"Alright then, I'll bide me time," Sikes said. "Say! Could I have another bag o' them crisps?"

CHAPTER 16

ARCHIE Sikes sat cross-legged on the thick carpet with three other men: Captain Naser Khadid, Jandol Kakar, and Ghazan Barakzai. The boy Malyar Lodhi knelt on his knees behind Sikes, acting as translator. Off in one corner, with their *parunay* head scarves held demurely across the lower parts of their faces, were Barakzai's wife and his thirteen-year-old daughter Banafsha, who was the subject of the conversation among the males.

Kakar had been appointed Sikes' personal aide only the day before by the Pashtun leader, Orakzai. He was a thirty-year-old mujahideen whose natural leadership had put him in several positions of authority and responsibility over the years. Sikes had pondered the problem of a title for Kakar. Such things were important to the young Brit in his combination fantasy/pragmatic life. At first, he was going to make him a sergeant major, except he already had one. After turning the matter over in his mind, Sikes decided that, as a pasha, what he needed was an adjutant. And that was the title he bestowed on the young mujahideen.

Now, as the closest thing Sikes had for a Pashtun relative, Jandol Kakar was representing him that day in the negotiations for the Englishman's marriage to Banafsha. She had been picked out by Orakzai and literally assigned as his future bride, depending on what sort of deal could be successfully bartered with her father. At that particular moment, the men were sipping hot tea after munching on *kofte* meatballs.

Sikes, well aware of certain customs regarding women, hadn't given Banafsha a close scrutiny, but the first quick sight of the girl showed a slightly plump youngster with whatever female qualities she had well hidden under her long dress. The glimpse at her face from the side did not give him a complete picture of her features. She looked like one of the many Pakistani schoolgirls in the UK.

As Sikes sat with the men, he noted that his prospective father-in-law, Barakzai, appeared to be in his seventies or eighties, with a snow-white beard and an extremely wrinkled face. Sikes was surprised to learn that the old mujahideen had fought against the Soviets and in reality was only sixty-six years of age. If the marriage in question was a regular one instead of a *muta*—the temporary marriage allowed in Islam— the Brit would have been concerned about the very real possibility that his bride would be an old hag by thirty-five.

Now Malyar whispered his translations into Sikes' ear as the talks between Kakar and Barakzai continued. "Mr. Barakzai says his daughter is young and pretty . . . a virgin . . . if she enters into a *muta* with you, you will leave her someday . . . that will make her less desirable to other men and he will have much difficulty to marry her off again, especially if she is left with children . . . thus, he expects you to pay a generous bridal gift now."

Sikes liked the idea of *muta* mostly because it meant he would have a handy bit of tail, yet be able to end the relationship on friendly and proper terms. Even if he spent the rest of his life with the Pashtuns, he could get rid of the wife in a way that would not dishonor her. Thus, there would be no problems with an oath of vengeance being sworn against him by her male relatives because of any perceived insults.

As the talking went on, he leaned back and spoke under his breath to Malyar. "Do you know the bird then?"

"Yes," Malyar said softly, understanding the English slang for "girl."

"Does she have big tits, hey?"

Malyar shrugged. "Such a thing cannot be determined from the way our women dress." He turned his attention back to the negotiations. "Jandol Kakar is telling Mr. Barakzai what a fine man you are . . . a brave war leader . . . there is a strong possibility you will remain here until the end of your days . . ."

"Listen," Sikes interrupted him softly. "Is the bird a good looker, know wot I mean, hey? Even if you can't see her tits or ass, you've seen her face, ain't you?"

"She seems quite acceptable, Sikes Pasha," Malyar said. "You would not find her unpleasant to gaze upon." He turned his attention back to his interpreting duties. "Mr. Barakzai is wanting two hundred thousand afghanis and three female goats for the bridal gift. . . ."

Archie, not worried about the price since Orakzai would be paying the cost, snickered to himself, thinking, *The old bugger prob'ly wants them goats to fuck 'em.*

Malyar continued. "Now Jandol is making an offer of fifty thousand afghanis and no goats . . . now Mr. Barakzai is wanting one hundred fifty thousand afghanis and two female goats . . . oh, now they are bargaining hard and fast." He was silent for a few moments as the two men continued to talk. Then he said. "It is agreed. Mr. Barakzai is getting one hundred twenty-five thousand afghanis and one female goat."

The session came to an end.

Sikes wondered if he would be introduced to the girl, but at almost the exact instant an agreement was reached, the visitors got to their feet. After making happy and friendly fare-thee-wells with Ghazan Barakzai, Sikes and his companions abruptly left the house and went outside. Khadid took Sikes' arm. "Now we must go to Orakzai Mesher and tell him that the terms for the marriage are successfully completed."

Sikes was curious. "Wot happens now then?"

Khadid explained, "Something you may not understand yet about Islam is that marriage is a contract, not a sacrament as in the Christian world. This agreement will be written up and signed by Mr. Barakzai. You must pay the bridal gift before you can consummate the marriage."

"And how long will that be?" Sikes said. "I've been a while without it, know what I mean then?"

"I understand, Sikes Pasha," Khadid said. "Orakzai Mesher is as anxious as you to get the ceremony over with." He winked at Sikes. "But for obviously different reasons."

"You're right about that, mate!" Sikes said with a laugh.

WASHINGTON, D.C.
STATE DEPARTMENT
LAMP COMMITTEE
3 MAY
0905 HOURS

THIS was the committee's first official meeting since it had been established. It was chaired by Arlene Entienne, the beautiful Cajun-African-American Chief of Staff to the President of the United States. The members were Carl Joplin, PhD, State Department Undersecretary; Colonel John Turnbull, chief of the Special Operation Liaison Staff; and Edgar Watson of the CIA. The reason behind the establishment of the group was the receipt of new intelligence. This information had not yet been provided to the entire panel; only Arlene Entienne had been briefed, but only partially due to the lateness of the data.

Even before Entienne had a chance to call this first meeting to order, Colonel Turnbull spoke up. "Why the hell are they calling this the Lamp Committee, for Chrissake!"

"That will become apparent very quickly, John," Entienne replied. "Now! I declare this first get-together in session and ready to conduct business." She paused to make sure everyone was giving her his full attention. "The President has formed our little group because of unexpected recent developments.

He is going to depend on us for advice and evaluation of intelligence that has literally popped up from somewhere in Afghanistan. Our duties will also include giving him counsel on what covert and overt actions must be taken to turn the situation around to our advantage where the Iranians are concerned. Edgar will bring us up to date on this remarkable incident that has brought about organizing us into a standing committee. And, I might add, we have a lot of official clout. Our decisions will be taken very seriously and reviewed at the Pentagon."

Edgar Watson already had his notes out and prepared for his discourse. "Several weeks ago, our Middle Eastern station began monitoring transmissions that were coming across in the clear, i.e., unencoded, from an unknown person. These messages contained bits and pieces of intelligence that were checked out. This was the source of information I presented to you in this very room on the ninth of April. I also passed on further intelligence from that informant when we met with the President on the twenty-second."

Carl Joplin frowned. "This seems a risky thing to put much trust in."

"I agree," Turnbull said. "I am confused why the transmitter is not worried about being compromised if he uses no code. That also means he is not one of our agents."

"Believe me, gentlemen," Watson said, "we've given this information the most critical of evaluation. That is why it wasn't fully disclosed to you immediately. Further transmissions turned out to contain data that was very timely and accurate, much to the Agency's surprise. It was decided to take advantage of this unexpected source of information, and the sender was contacted and assigned the call sign Aladdin."

"Ha!" Turnbull said. "So that's why we're called the Lamp Committee, huh? Aladdin's lamp!"

Entienne interrupted. "Precisely. And that was my idea, John."

"And a damn good one, Arlene," he replied with a grin.

"At any rate," Watson said, "one of the first things we learned was about this Brit Archibald Sikes who had deserted from his unit in Iraq and subsequently joined the group calling itself the Jihad Abadi. MI-Five confirmed both his existence and status. Aladdin, as I shall refer to him or her, later informed us that the Chehaar Garrison had been closed down and the armored car company deactivated. This information has already been given to Carl Joplin."

"Except I was unaware of the source," Joplin said.

"We figured you needed it for your meeting with the Iranian charge d'affaires," Entienne said. "A little extra ammo, so to speak."

"Precisely," Watson said. "Now this fellow Sikes, who had converted to the Muslim faith and changed his first name from Archibald to Arsalaan—"

"Ha!" Colonel Turnbull interrupted with a laugh. "That's not much of an improvement."

"At any rate," Watson said, irritated by the interjection, "he has taken his Arab force and trekked from Iran up into the Gharawdara Highlands in west Afghanistan to join a Pashtun rebel fighting force. All this is through the command and guidance of Iranian Special Forces in that operation designed to take over all Middle Eastern Islamic insurgence groups. By the way, we don't know what the Iranians are calling this grandiose scheme, but the CIA has dubbed it Operation Persian Empire."

Entienne asked, "And you're sure these Iranian SF guys aren't a bunch of rogue officers running amok?"

"Positively," Watson said. "This is a highly classified military operation under the direct command of the Iranian Government and the Army General Staff. They are determined to dominate the whole of the Middle East." He reached into his briefcase and pulled out a folder, opening it. "This is the latest report from Aladdin. It informs us that the majority of funding for Operation Persian Empire is coming from the smuggling of opium poppy powder out of Afghanistan, through Iran, and into Turkey to the buyers."

Turnbull drummed his fingers on the tabletop. "So this is the latest intel we've received from Aladdin?"

"Affirmative, Colonel," Watson said. "We are waiting to learn the exact route taken by these smugglers from Afghanistan. Without that info, we can't plan any operations. All we know at this point is that it's somewhere in the passes of the Gharawdara Highlands."

"Hell!" Turnbull said. "What about the route across Iran? That would be easier to assess."

"That would be a '*nice*-to-know' item, since we cannot act on it unless we go across the international border," Watson explained. "That is definitely out of the question."

"Shit!" Turnbull said. "If you ask me, the info on where and what they're doing in Iran goes beyond even '*should-*know.' I would classify it as '*must-*know.'"

"Yeah," Watson agreed. "But it's a matter of first things first."

"Alright, folks, let's get to business," Entienne said. "This committee is to advise the President, so let's start concentrating on that. Any comments?"

No one said a word for a few moments as all turned inward to reflect on the information that had just been given them. Carl Joplin was the first to speak out. "I suggest that we wait until we know the smugglers' exact route or routes. Then use extreme prejudice in destroying it."

"The only way that can be done is by putting some of our best people in harm's way," Turnbull said. "But it's obvious we have no choice."

"I agree," Joplin said. "It would seem that the first thing to do is cut off that funding coming from opium smuggling."

"That's a sound suggestion," Turnbull said. "Cut the sons of bitches off from their money, and they're like the proverbial dumb bastard who's up a creek without a paddle."

Entienne nodded. "Yes!"

"That's the Agency's take on things," Watson said. "And I'm bringing that evaluation to this table from the CIA Director himself, folks."

"I move the President's Chief of Staff advise him to launch attacks against the opium smugglers involved in Operation Persian Empire," Carl Joplin said.

"I second the motion," Turnbull said.

"Of course we'll have to wait until we get those exact routes through Afghanistan and into Iran," Watson pointed out.

"Hell," Turnbull said, "we already know it's somewhere in the Gharawdara Highlands. We can at least start getting ready for it." He glanced over at Joplin. "Say, Carl, isn't that where your SEAL friends are?"

"Yes," Joplin replied. "Brannigan's Brigands."

PASHTUN STRONGHOLD
5 MAY
1800 HOURS

THE skinned and gutted goat carcasses had been buried in the ground surrounded by glowing coals for close to twenty-four hours, a procedure that began almost as soon as the marriage contract between Archie Sikes and Banafsha Barakzai was signed. The occasion included the payment of the bridal gift and delivery of the nanny goat to the Englishman's new father-in-law, Ghazan. Archie learned that the 125,000-afghani price for the marriage came out to some £1,434 in UK money or close to 2,000 U.S. dollars.

Now the slow-cooked goats were being dug up by the men in charge of the preparation, while women laid out pots of various foods; *kachumber* salad, *dala* lentil soup, *halva* sweets, *kofte* meatballs, and other goodies that were on the menu for the wedding feast. Although there were no alcoholic beverages, in accordance with the laws of Islam, there was plenty of tea, coffee, fruit juices, and the ever-present Pepsi brought back in cases during the opium-smuggling activities. Tables, bowls, chairs, and stools were contributed for the occasion from just about every household in the camp.

When everything was set up, Sikes, along with his adjutant Jandol Kakar and translator Malyar Lodhi, made an appearance. Sikes responded to the happy greetings shouted at him with nods of his head as he went to his place, where the food was laid out. Normally, the feast would have been held a couple of days after the marriage was consummated, but an opium run was already scheduled and Sikes was expected to participate. The date could not be changed, and Orakzai

Mesher was anxious to get his English field commander fully integrated into his organization.

When Sikes settled down on the cushions provided for sitting, he was served some *sur chai* tea with milk. He sipped slowly, continuing to nod to the many Pashtuns who shouted their congratulations at him. The noise of talking, shouting people looking forward to the banquet was loud with babbling and laughter. It increased even more when Orakzai and his entourage of bodyguards appeared. He waved to the people, then smiled at Sikes as he took his reserved place where he would be able to get a full view of the event.

The people turned back to their loud celebrating as they waited for the festivities to move into a higher gear. Suddenly, the noise began subsiding, and within a quarter of a minute, silence reigned over the scene.

Ghazan Barakzai and other male relatives of the bride appeared with her. Sikes looked at Banafsha, disappointed she was completely covered by a *chadari* over her face and a long burka that concealed her body. The girl looked a bit like a midget as she made her way to her own place at the feast. This was the first time he had seen her standing, and he noted she wasn't quite five feet tall. As soon as she sat down, the noise started up again and the people turned to the joyful task of consuming the food.

SIKES' QUARTERS
2000 HOURS

SIKES lived in a small cave within the complex where the senior mujahideen maintained their dwellings. It was only fifteen meters from the main entrance to Orakzai's residence. Sikes' bed had been made up by a group of women especially for the wedding night. The usual blankets and the chador he used for a pillow had been taken off, carefully folded, and placed in a corner. Some flannel sheets, a quilt, and thick pillows and cushions had replaced the coverings.

The groom had left the feast as per instructions a half hour before and gone to his quarters. He now waited for his bride as the flames in the cooking hearth provided the only illumination. Banafsha was to be brought to him to be deflowered and made a woman. Normally, as in a whorehouse, he was anxious for a coupling, but there was something almost foreboding about the Islamic arrangements. They lacked passion and excitement. It was as cold as if he were about to change the oil in an APC. Jandol Kakar had given Sikes explicit instructions as to what he was to do, and the procedure drained all the randy feelings out of him. This was not going to be an experience replete with sexual desire and romantic affection. It was almost antiseptic and clinical.

A new spate of yelling occurred, and began to grow louder. He turned his eyes toward the entrance to the cave and waited. Within minutes, the crowd had arrived, still hollering and laughing. The blanket over the door was brushed aside and a Pashtun with Banafsha stepped inside. The man, one of her uncles, led the girl to where Sikes sat on the edge of the bed. Then he abruptly turned and left the cave.

Sikes looked up at her face, able to see only the young bride's eyes. They were downcast and without expression or emotion. He stood up, reaching over and removing the *chadari*. He was now able to see her face quite plainly in the firelight. He gazed at her, noting she had a childlike quality with dark brown hair, black eyes, and smooth skin. Sikes felt like a pedophile; she was obviously not fully a woman, even though she would have to be experiencing menstrual cycles or she would not have been permitted to marry.

Kakar had explained she would be silent and docile through the consummation. Sikes took a deep breath and pulled her toward the bed. She lay down on it, now with her face turned toward the wall. Sikes lifted the hem of her burqa, revealing her nudity. She didn't have the curves or thighs of a woman, but he ignored her immature body. After a deep breath of resignation, he did what he was supposed to do.

Banafsha gasped with a subdued groan, then the job was done.

Now Sikes picked up a piece of white flannel and wiped at her bleeding crotch. After arranging his own clothing back to decency, he walked to the entrance of the cave and stepped out. The crowd, all male, cheered as he showed them the bloody material.

This was irrefutable proof that the bride, a proper Islamic woman, had gone to her marriage bed a virgin.

CHAPTER 17

PASHTUN STRONGHOLD
GHARAWDARA HIGHLANDS

ARSALAAN Sikes Pasha's appointment as the Pashtuns' field commander, in addition to his marriage, assimilated him deeper into the stronghold society, its mores and lifestyle. His first concern was to sharpen up his new command, hopefully at least to a condition that was close to the discipline and skills of the twenty Arabs he had brought with him from Chehaar Garrison. He knew he had a hell of a tough job ahead, but at least he could count on the Iranian SF officer Naser Khadid, his adjutant Jandol Kakar, and his interpreter Malyar Lodhi for guidance if and when he hit any rough spots.

Sikes had no illusions about being able to instill a "bashing on the square" discipline into the Pashtun mujahideen's collective psyches. This was against their nature, and in their culture such a thing would be seen as unnecessary and peculiar as putting *puhtee* caps on their goats. They considered the saluting, standing at attention, and stomping of boots as some weird ritual the foreigners felt they must do. However, Sikes knew there was one kind of systemic method he could apply to the Pashtuns, and that was crew drill.

He started with the mortarmen, using the Soviet M-1937 mortars. These 82-millimeter heavy weapons were perfect for developing the teamwork necessary for their effective application. There were four of them available, and Sikes was happy to learn all the Pashtun mortarmen knew how to use the sights and aiming stakes to properly align the tubes on the same azimuth at spaced intervals. This was the means of assuring that battery fire on a target or area would be accurate and effective. The problem was that when it came to firing, as far as the weapons crews were concerned, it was a matter of first come, first served for the different jobs in manning the mortars. The Pashtuns would run with their best friends toward the same weapons and grab the sights and bipods. The slower guys ended up with the least desirable jobs of handling tubes and weighty base plates.

Sikes began his training with a strict organization. He broke down the twenty-one mortarmen available into crews of four for each weapon. That meant he had five left over as supernumeraries to handle the donkeys that carried the boxes of shells. Each crew would consist of a gunner, who would carry the sight and use it to align on the aiming stakes; an assistant gunner, who would be the one to drop the shell down into the mortar during firing, and carry the tube and bipods; and two ammo men, who would carry the base plate as well a set of aiming stakes each. They would also be the ones to prepare the shells for firing and pass them off to the assistant gunner during fire missions.

The way Sikes got the Pashtuns to carry on crew drill was to have them run to an indicated spot to set up the mortars. The two ammo men would lug the heavy base plate into position, and immediately, the assistant gunner would attach the tube and bipod. At that point, the gunner attached the sight to the weapon, while the ammo men ran out to set up the aiming stakes. The gunner would then sight in on the stakes, telling the ammo men which direction to move until both sets were aligned one behind the other. When that was done, the gunner would leap up and yell, *"Chamtu,"* the Pashto word for "Ready."

When everyone understood the procedures, Sikes had them rotate the jobs until all had several opportunities to perform at each crew position. Then he began timing them, making a contest of the drills. Before long, the Pashtuns worked hard to have their mortar properly laid and ready, and the competition became so hot and heavy that any member of a crew who stumbled or made a mistake was loudly but good-naturedly jeered by his buddies. Even Jandol Kakar and Malyar Lodhi joined a couple of the crews to participate in the practice drills. Everyone was having a good time, yet they all were still being shaped up into damn good heavy-weapons teams.

Naser Khadid, who had carefully observed the drill, complimented Sikes. "You have these fellows keen to be the best. Well done, Sikes Pasha. I do believe you are going to be quite successful in this endeavor."

"Right," Sikes said. "Wot about that bluddy commission for me as major in the Iranian Army?"

"I have put in the request," Khadid assured him, "along with my strongest personal recommendation."

"We'll have to see," Sikes said. He decided to spring an impromptu drill on the men. Turning from the Iranian officer, he suddenly hollered, "Fire mission!"

The crews flew into action, each man keenly aware of his duties within his team.

WITH the mortarmen evolved into an efficient and standardized organization, Sikes turned his attention to the machine gunners. He had them perform the same applicable drills on the Dashika 12.7-millimeter machine guns with gunners, assistant gunners, and ammo bearers. Shaping this bunch up was a much easier task than with the mortars since the machine gunners had watched the mortarmen acquire their different skills. When their English field commander got around to them, the Pashtuns were more than ready to get with the program. Contests in speed also encouraged them to try to be the best of their group.

BOTH the machine guns and the mortars had some problems with parts that were either missing or broken, and it was at this time that Sikes became acquainted with the most important logistical and maintenance members of the Pashtun communities: the blacksmiths.

These craftsmen were traditionalists, passing the skills of their trade down from father to son through countless generations. The *peshane*, although using only the most basic of tools such as hammers, tongs, anvils, and hand bellows, manufactured cutting tools, pots, ladles, and other items necessary for the day-to-day life of the community. This also included such implements as crescent wrenches and pliers. This work was done using smoldering charcoal arranged within fire rings on the floors of their small shops.

They could also turn out gun parts through the use of sand molds. Although bolts were a bit too much for them, these *peshane* could manufacture operating slides with handles, flash suppressers, iron sights, butt plates, and other simple parts. After items were cast and cooled, hand files were used to further shape them for proper fit. The craftsmen could also turn out crude, albeit efficient, smoothbore single-shot rifles and pistols. All the metal needed for these operations was melted down in homemade furnaces, which, though slow and cumbersome, could produce the molten steel for pouring into the molds.

Sikes had the machine gunners and mortarmen check all their weapons and see if any missing or broken parts could be taken care of by the smithies. Since the weapons had not been fired in months, most all were in good shape; thus, the only things needing attention were a broken carrying handle on one of the Dashikas and a couple of adjustment knobs for the heavy mortars.

HOWEVER, Arsalaan Sikes Pasha had more to worry about than his military responsibilities. There was also his marriage to deal with. At times, he wondered what his parents back in Manchester would think if they knew he had married a thirteen-year-old girl.

Banafsha was a complete enigma to Sikes. Although she looked her age now, he knew that within a couple of years she

would be like the rest of the *shedze*, women, and begin to age
fast. He had taken notice of the females he knew to be in their
early twenties, and all had lines around their eyes and hard-set
mouths that resulted from their lives of hard work and many
births. The hair of a few was streaked with the first signs of
graying. Banafsha's hands were already calloused, with the fin-
gernails short and worn down from the grasping, handling, lifting, and other activities of her daily chores. The Englishman
had to admit she was more than a satisfactory wife. She was always up before he awoke, having the cook fire going and the
cave interior warm and lit. The food she prepared, while still a
bit exotic and strange to Sikes, was tasty and filling.

He had begun to feel an affection toward the girl, and wanted
her to enjoy their sex life as much as possible. Some passion on
her part would increase his own pleasure. Sikes was no great
lover by any stretch of the imagination; he had never had a
steady girlfriend and all his sexual experiences had been with
prostitutes. But he had read manuals on marriage, and knew that
women liked what is called foreplay with all its show of affection, tenderness, and a slow approach to sexual intercourse. He
did his best, cooing to her in English, since he didn't know any
love phrases in Pashtun and wasn't about to ask any of the men
what he should be saying to his woman. He realized she didn't
understand the words, but he hoped the tone of his voice would
please her. Sikes also caressed her gently, in his campaign of
arousing her passions, but it was useless. No matter what he did,
she was the same as on their wedding night: submissive, quiet,
and cold as she waited for him to have his way with her.

It was strange, but Arsalaan Sikes was beginning to have
more of a sense of loneliness than before he had taken a wife.
The lack of real affection in the relationship was hard to bear
for this living product of Western society.

12 MAY
1430 HOURS

A signal from the lookout post was passed down to
Orakzai's headquarters. Those people in the stronghold who

saw the waving of the old Soviet flag by the guard on duty burst out in loud shouts of happiness, running around the area to inform others of the good news.

The men on the latest opium run were only a short distance away and rapidly approaching the stronghold.

Sikes, using his twenty Arabs as assistant instructors, was in the middle of having his infantry mujahideen run through squad formations with their AK-47s when the call reached the mountain meadow where the drill was taking place. The men immediately abandoned the activity and hurried up toward the village beneath the caves, leaving the Arabs confused and dismayed at this unauthorized departure. Warrant Officer Shafaqat Hashiri looked over at Sikes, raising his hands in a gesture of perplexity.

"Wot the bluddy hell!" Sikes shouted in rage as the mujahideen made a rapid disappearance.

Captain Naser Khadid, beside him, laid a hand on his shoulder. "Calm yourself, Sikes Pasha. The smugglers have returned from their latest expedition."

"Yes, Sikes Pasha!" Jandol Kakar said. "It is a time of great excitement and joy among the people."

The young translator Malyar Lodhi was also excited. "Let us go see their arrival. *Tadi kawa*—hurry up!"

Sikes signaled Hashiri to form up the Arabs, then reluctantly allowed his three companions to lead him from the meadow, back up into the higher country where the village and caves were located. "I swear to God!" he grumbled. "There's gonna be some discipline applied around here before much more time passes. And I don't give a thundering fuck who I offend!"

When the men reached the village, it seemed that every single man, woman, and child of the community was present, and all were yelling and talking at the same time. Even Orakzai and his attendants stood with the throng, gazing upward at the trail that led down from the lookout post. After a couple of minutes, loud shots erupted and the women's shrill trilling sang out over the scene.

The first man, leading a heavily laden donkey, appeared from the boulders. He waved down at his people as he continued toward them. Then another man appeared with a burdened donkey, then two more, another, and yet another, until a total of twenty could be counted.

Sikes leaned toward Kahnani. "Wot's on them donkeys then?"

"Many things, Sikes Pasha," the Iranian replied. "There are gifts, tools, food, and other items prized by these Pashtuns. That is how the Pepsi and potato chips are brought in here. Also—" He pointed to a couple of donkeys. "See those cubes of metal? That is scrap for the blacksmiths to melt down for their work."

Now Sikes became excited. "Look at them ammo boxes, hey?"

"That would be the ammunition you wanted for the machine guns and mortars," Kahnani said. "The smugglers do a double duty. There are sellers of many wares awaiting them in Turkey at the place where they turn the opium powders over to the buyers. That includes Harry Turpin when he has things for us."

Now physical pandemonium broke out as the people surged forward. Several blacksmiths took the reins of the donkeys with the metal and led them away. The smugglers were hugged by their male relatives with smiles and more shouts of greeting. Sikes noticed the women stayed off to one side, looking happy but demure, though they made no rush to welcome any of the men as husbands or relatives.

One of the smugglers went up and shook hands with Yama Orakzai. Malyar tugged at Sikes' sleeve. "That is Husay Bangash, the chief of the smugglers. A very important man."

Orakzai and Bangash spoke for a few moments, then left the location to go up to the Pashtun leader's cave. Sikes watched them for a moment, then turned his attention back to the activity at hand. "I want that bluddy ammunition," he said.

"We can get it now, Sikes Pasha," Malyar said. "There are the donkeys with the crates. Call to four of your Arabs and we shall fetch them."

Sikes bellowed at Hashiri to send a quartet of the men to him. When they arrived, Malyar took them to the animals. After the boy spoke some rapid Pashtun to the smugglers, the animals were turned over to the Arabs. Sikes gestured to his warrant officer, Hashiri. "Take them bluddy little beasts up to the bivouac with the men. I'll be there shortly."

Hashiri saluted and barked orders at the Arabs to get them moving. As the group headed up the far slope to where they had established their camp, Sikes went over to the smugglers and began circulating around, seeing what had been brought in. Khadid walked with him as Kakar explained who the stranger was to the opium runners, who had never seen Sikes before. They were slightly leery of the Englishman, but greeted him with respect when they learned he was the new field commander.

Sikes noted bolts of cloth, canned food, sugar, salt, flour, sandals, clothing, and other items to meet the basic requirements of a simple life. The potato chips and Pepsi were also being picked up, every family representative getting a certain amount. Sikes pointed to the activity, asking Khadid, "How come they don't get Coca-Cola or maybe some fruit juice, hey? And why crisps all the time? Ain't they heard o' pretzels or crackers?"

Khadid shrugged. "They can only obtain what the trader with the opium buyer has to offer. He, on the other hand, must take what his own supplier can produce for him to sell. Right now it is Pepsi and potato chips, and has been for more than a year. Who knows when something else will be available. At any rate, the Pashtuns consider them delicacies."

"I'd like to see them poor bleeding blighters in a proper supermarket," Sikes remarked. "They'd think they died and went to heaven." He grinned. "Right, then, let's get to the bivouac and see what sort o' ammo ol' Harry sent us, hey?"

They had to follow a steep path up to the Arabs' bivouac. The area was a small plateau between craggy outcrops of boulders that offered good cover and concealment. The Arabs had set up two-man lean-tos made from extra ponchos and shelter halves arranged in convenient spots among the big rocks. When Sikes and Khadid, along with Malyar and Kakar, arrived, they found the donkeys had been unloaded and the crates were stacked neatly beside Warrant Officer Hashiri's bucolic quarters.

Sikes immediately inspected the crates and had them pried open. He liked what he found inside. "Here then!" he exclaimed.

"Look wot we got in this'un, hey? Sixty-millimeter shells for them Spanish mortars!" He laughed. "Them Pashtuns is gonna be glad to learn they won't have them heavy Soviet M-Thirty-Sevens to lug around, hey?"

"The sixties will be much better for mountain operations," Khadid remarked. "It looks like the second crate has more of the same."

"Let's have a look at them other two," Sikes said. The third and fourth crates contained 7.62-millimeter ball ammo that could be used in both the AK-47s and the Soviet PK machine guns. "This is a good start, but we'll need more."

"There will be three additional deliveries of the same thing," Khadid said.

"Well!" Sikes said. "You're real sure of yourself, ain't you?"

"I'm the one that put in the supply requisitions, Sikes Pasha."

"And you made a damn good job of it, Cap'n Khadid," Sikes said in good humor.

Further inspection of the ammo boxes was interrupted when one of the mujahideen in Orakzai's headquarters guard came up the hill. He went straight to Sikes and babbled some words at him.

Malyar stepped into the breech. "Sikes Pasha, Orakzai Mesher commands you to dine with him and Husay Bangash at sunset."

"I'll be there o'course," Sikes said. As soon as his reply was given, he turned to Warrant Officer Hashiri. "Get some tarpaulins to cover this ammo. And I want at least two bluddy guards on it twenty-four hours a day, yeah?"

"Yes, Sikes Pasha!" Hashiri replied, snapping to attention.

ORAKZAI'S QUARTERS
1900 HOURS

THE three men—Archie Sikes, Yama Orakzai, and Husay Bangash—sat in a circle on the thick carpet in the firelit cave. Bowls and plates of food were spread between them, consisting of *samosas*, fried bread, and the contents of some of the vegetable and fruit cans brought in by the smugglers. Several women had been honored with invitations to prepare the meal. The trio of diners ate by dipping their right hands into the dishes to pick out what they wanted.

Sikes had been surprised to learn that Bangash had lived for several years in Chicago in the United States. He had gone there on a student visa to study at DePaul University, overstaying his time. As an illegal alien, he began living and working in the city's Muslim neighborhood. His English was excellent, and he spoke with an accent that was almost American. Sikes had been surprised by the informality the man used when talking to someone the other Pashtuns addressed as Orakzai Mesher.

Bangash took a handful of green beans and, after studying them for a moment, shoved them into his mouth. He chewed and grinned. "I'd much rather have a fork, y'know what I mean? And these are supposed to be eaten hot." He winked at Orakzai. "Not that I'm complaining, Yama."

Orakzai laughed. "I have been up in these cursed mountains so long I have forgotten the comforts and conveniences of civilization, not to mention the proper preparation of foods."

"Too bad you never had the chance to get a taste of Western culture," Bangash said. "There's nothing better'n that in the whole world."

Sikes gave him a direct look. "So wot brought you back to this place, hey?"

Bangash grinned. "A little trouble in America. It had to do with a lapsed visa and dealing drugs to some undercover narc. I jumped bail and got the hell out of there. The cops knew I'd make a run for it, but they didn't care. It was cheaper letting me flee the country than locking me up. You gotta think of the taxpayers, y'know."

"At any rate," Orakzai said, taking a sip of tea. "He is back here running our opium operation. And that is why I invited you to dine with us, Sikes Pasha."

"What?" Bangash exclaimed with a laugh. "What's this 'Pasha' shit? Are you the great British raj commanding your faithful little wogs?"

"Me responsibilities with Orakzai Mesher give me the right

to that title, mate," Sikes said testily. "Besides commanding the field forces for him, I got me twenty Arab fighters that I brung with me, hey? And let me tell you something for nothing, yeah? Them blokes is disciplined fighting men, thanks to me. I sharpened them up almost as good as UK soljers, and they're me elite troops."

"Hey, chill out, Sikes!" Bangash said. "Whatever you do is cool, okay? It doesn't matter a damn to me if you want to be called Your Royal Highness. I run the dope from Afghanistan and across Iran into Turkey. And that's all I do. If you want to play soldier boy, go right ahead. But I'm not going to call you 'Pasha.' "

"I was in the Royal Regiment of Dragoons," Sikes said coldly. "I left them and my country 'cause they didn't give me the respect I deserved."

"Believe me," Bangash said. "I don't want any trouble."

"Let us all calm down now," Orakzai said. He looked at Sikes. "You are going on the next opium run with Husay. It will be a good experience for you, and you will meet the man who supplies us with arms and ammunition."

"That wouldn't be a Mr. Harry Turpin, would it?" Sikes asked. "I already know him from Iran."

Bangash laughed. "You know Harry, huh? Hey, he's a cool old dude. I hope to hell I got his moxie when I'm his age. He's still a bad-ass. The old guy still likes to get out and into the middle of things."

Orakzai smiled at Sikes. "I am sure you will be pleased to see your old friend when you get to Turkey."

"Right," Sikes said. "Pass me one of them *samosas*, will you—Bangash?"

"I'd be glad to," Bangash said, reaching for the bowl. "Here you go—Sikes."

CHAPTER 18

"I apologize to everyone for summoning you at this late hour," Arlene Entienne, the President's Chief of Staff, said. Unperturbed by the time of the meeting, the members of the Lamp Committee had taken seats in the hastily arranged semi-circle of chairs facing the large desk. As soon as everyone was settled and attentive, Entienne turned to the Chief Executive. "And I beg your pardon in particular, Mr. President. But when Edgar called me with this latest intelligence, I felt it required immediate assessment, then a quick decision."

The President smiled good-naturedly. "That's perfectly alright, Arlene. All I was going to do this weekend was unwind at Camp David after this previous two weeks of banging heads with Congress over immigration reform."

Edgar Watson of the CIA was not a man with a sense of humor, nor was he tuned in much on the art of repartee; thus, he failed to note the lightness in the exchange between the Chief Executive and Entienne. "I assure you, Mr. President, that this intelligence is the sort that merits instantaneous reaction."

Carl Joplin and Colonel John Turnbull looked at each other with mutual grins, noting Watson's lack of social graces. Like most people in the intelligence community, his thought processes were coldly logical, almost plodding in the analysis of what went on around him. Turnbull always got a kick out of putting in a dig at the somber CIA man. "Relax, Watson, nobody's upset with you," said the colonel.

Watson frowned at Turnbull, who he didn't like very much. He leaned back in his chair and crossed his arms. "At any rate, earlier today we received word of another transmission from Aladdin to our Middle East monitoring station. He has sent the exact coordinates of the route taken by the opium smugglers who are engaged in Operation Persian Empire."

Turnbull, clad in the civvies he was wearing when summoned to the White House, sat with his legs extended, his bad ankle crossed over the uninjured one. "Has this info been properly evaluated, Watson?"

"Of course it has!" Watson snapped. "Do you think I'm going to contact the President's Chief of Staff and recommend a meeting over some iffy data? The Agency's best minds have studied this latest transmission as well as all others, and they have judged the whole group to be worthy of consideration."

"I don't hear the word 'trust' in there," Turnbull said.

Before Watson could talk back, Joplin displayed his diplomatic skills. "Listen, everybody, this is not the time for nitpicking and fault-finding. At some point, we must have enough confidence in each other's ability and opinions to move forward. Nay-saying in a case like this can only bring about delays that may cause irreparable harm. And that goes double for intentional sarcasm."

"Listen, Carl," Turnbull said, "I've been on the ground as a grunt, see? And I want to make sure that—"

Entienne quickly interrupted. "The CIA recommends this intelligence be taken seriously. That is all we need to consider."

"And it will be taken seriously," the President said, irritated. "Please continue, Edgar."

"Thank you, Mr. President," the CIA man said. "This opium-smuggling route is financing the Iranians big-time in their efforts to take over all insurgencies in the Middle East. Every single, solitary run brings more funds into their coffers. That means weaponry, ammunition, supplies, recruitment, and all other aspects of their program for making war."

"Would you say they have a monopoly in the Afghan poppy-smuggling scene?" Joplin asked.

"Damn near," Watson answered. "It's only a matter of time before they'll be pulling in millions of dollars each and every month of the year."

The President leaned forward in his chair. "I'm going to save a lot of time for everybody this evening. I am issuing a vocal executive order at this very moment; are you ready? Attack that route and put an end to the smuggling. Any questions? No? Good! Do those things that you do the best to bring this intolerable situation under control." He stood up. "I'm off to Camp David."

After the Chief Executive left, Turnbull got to his feet. "I'm going to have to go to my office to get the President's mandate into effect." He nodded to Watson. "Do you have the maps, satellite photos, and other stuff I need to kick through the system?"

"It's all right here in my briefcase," Watson replied.

"Then you and I better get over to the Pentagon," Turnbull said. "It looks like we'll have to drive. I came over here in my POV." He looked at Entienne. "I was just about to sit down to dinner when you called, so I didn't have time to arrange for transportation."

"You can put in a travel voucher, John," Entienne said.

"Will you sign it?"

"Probably not," she replied.

Watson laughed, showing uncharacteristic humor. "Hell! I *did* come over from my office. I have an Agency car outside." He glanced at Turnbull. "You lead, I'll follow. And don't worry. The CIA has parking spaces at the Pentagon. So in case you have to park out at the curb somewhere, I can take you in."

"I have my own personal spot," Turnbull said, determined to top the other guy.

Joplin watched them leave, then turned to Entienne. "Can you believe that we're in the middle of a situation that threatens world peace, and there're two guys involved in this complicated process who are trying to top each other over where they're going to park their cars?"

"Fun and games among the alpha males," Entienne said. "Let's go down to my office, Carl. You and I have our own chores in this Persian Empire shit."

"Tsk! Tsk!" Joplin said. "That's no way for a lady to talk."

"If I were a lady, I wouldn't be in this job. C'mon!"

OPERATIONAL AREA
SOUTHWESTERN AFGHANISTAN DESERT
15 MAY
1045 HOURS

OPERATION Rolling Thunder had ground down to a dull routine of predictable repetition, useless effort, and a mind-set of unending boredom. It seemed to Brannigan's Brigands that they had gone from the tedium of shipboard life aboard the USS *Dan Daly* to a short spate of excitement, then had been tossed into a stagnant period filled with dreary terrain and small foreign people who did not like them very much.

The principal duty now assigned them was to take the DPVs out on patrols across the desert, for no other apparent reason than to burn fuel between stopping at villages to make fruitless searches for hidden weapons caches. A reason for this grind was hinted at from the USS *Combs* after Lieutenant Wild Bill Brannigan sent a scathing transmission to Commander Tom Carey, bitching about how Operation Rolling Thunder had evolved into a "make-work" situation. Carey replied that the former warlord in the OA might have been neutralized almost a year earlier, but it was still necessary to continually check up on him and his followers. Carey's message ended with a strong hint for the Brigands—and Brannigan in particular—to follow orders even if they flew out a window.

Now, after two solid hours of travel, all six vehicles pulled into a small Tajic village they had visited a half-dozen times.

Another procedure they followed was having the Alpha Two vehicle with Connie Concord, Mike Assad, and Dave Leibowitz scope out the area before the detachment actually drove into the vicinity. Afghanistan was a place of nasty surprises where a population friendly one day might turn vicious the next. It only took the Odd Couple five minutes to determine no danger lurked among the huts.

The SEALs had made calls on that community and other similar ones so many times that they had managed to pick up a bit of the Dari language. Their accents elicited polite laughter from the natives, but the Brigands spoke loudly and boldly, feeling as if the less than dozen words they knew made them bi- or multilingual.

As the DPVs came to a stop, all the village kids came running and yelling in anticipation of goodies. Bruno Puglisi had a box of candy purchased at the Shelor Field BX. He stepped down to the ground from the vehicle, shouting at the top of his voice. "Hey, you *atfal*!" he yelled out. "Get over here damn *zut shodan*! Chop! Chop! I got *zyad* candy for you." He began tossing the sweets up into the air, and the kids started a mini-riot of energetic bumping and shoving as they scrambled for the goodies. The adult males, as usual, were the only grownups outside, and they grinned at the sight, each hoping his own children would get plenty to share with the household.

The village chief, an old guy the Brigands had nicknamed "Captain," walked onto the scene. He displayed a wide smile and salaamed to Brannigan. "Hello, Boss. How are you?"

"I'm fine, Captain," Brannigan replied.

"Me too," the old man said. "I am being very fine. Excellent. That is how I am being." His real name was Mohammed Ghani, and his age appeared to be anywhere between forty and ninety-nine. He spoke a strange brand of English, having picked it up in Pakistan, where it is a quasi-official language. Captain had left the village as a young man, snuck across the Pakistani border, and made his way to the capital city of Islamabad. He found low-paying, dirty work at first, toiling as a common laborer until a Pakistani friend steered him to a job in a rather excellent hotel called the Diplomat. He began as a bellboy, but after a few years of loyal and efficient service was named the bell captain. This was where the SEALs got their nickname for him.

Brannigan shook Captain's hand. "Have you and your people been good? You don't have guns or anything like that since we were here last."

"Oh, no, Boss," Captain said. "We are good people here. Yes, sir!"

"The warlord hasn't brought you anything to hide for him, has he?"

Captain shook his head. "I am not seeing him for many months now. You are too strong for him, Boss. Ha! Ha! Maybe you are scaring him."

The Brigands had made a couple of rough searches of the village houses in the past, finding a couple of AK-47s and ammunition. Since there wasn't a large cache of arms, it was obvious the inhabitants weren't dealing in weapons or hiding any for Taliban insurgents, so Brannigan did no more than confiscate the arms. He left the single-shot rifles—mostly tooled for the British Enfield .303-caliber—since the men needed them for hunting.

"You stay good, Captain," Brannigan said. He nodded a good-bye to the headman, then turned to walk back to the detachment. He gestured to Senior Chief Dawkins, and the old salt left where he was standing by the Charlie One vehicle and strolled over to Captain. "Hello, Cap'n. You listen to me *dihyan*, eh? Boss Brannigan he tells us no search your *ghar* too much this time because we no find much. I tell him that's not a good idea. I tell him I think you hide weapons—*bohut* weapons—so we should make another search. But he said no."

"Boss Brannigan is a good man," Captain said. "He is knowing we do not make lies here. We are good people—*bohut* good people!"

"Don't bullshit me, Cap'n!" Dawkins said. He always played the bad guy during visits, to keep the locals off balance. His normal expression was a scowl, and he was good in the part.

"Oh, I am not bullshitting," Captain insisted.

"We have machines that can find weapons," Dawkins said. "We move the machine across the ground or the floor in a house. If there are weapons, the machines tell us. They say beep, beep, beep!"

Captain laughed. "You are *pagal* in the head, Buford. Machines cannot speak."

"These can," Dawkins insisted. "Maybe we'll bring some back with us the next time."

"Oh, you are not having to do that," Captain said. "We are good people."

"Well, we'll see about that," Dawkins said. He heard Brannigan call out his name, and he turned to see the Skipper motioning him to return to Charlie One. He turned his gaze back to Captain, giving the Tajic a warning glare. "You're gonna remember what I told you, *sahi*?"

"Of course, Buford," Captain said, already waving. *"Xuda hafiz!"*

"Xudafiz," Dawkins replied, corrupting the Dari words for good-bye.

Within minutes, the SEALs were in their vehicles and speeding away from the village into the desert. They headed in a generally northwestern direction at a gas-saving thirty-five miles per hour toward the next village on their patrol. After they went about ten miles, Frank Gomez's voice came over the LASH headset. "Skipper, I just got a transmission over the Shadowfire. We're supposed to return to Shelor Field by the quickest route. Carey and Berringer are waiting for us there."

"Good deal!" interjected Lieutenant Junior Grade Jim Cruiser. "As Sherlock Holmes would say, 'The game's afoot!' "

Brannigan turned the wheel, whipping the DPV toward a southeastern route as his men followed.

THE OPIUM TRAIL
AFGHANISTAN
16 MAY
NOON

THE farmers who cultivated and harvested the opium poppies did so for very good economic reasons. If they planted the usual crops—wheat, barley, and corn—each family would earn the equivalent of approximately 150 American dollars per year. But the plants from which heroin is made afforded the cultivators 64,500 afghani annually, which translated into 1500 American dollars per year for the average family. It was not surprising that this tenfold advantage in cash encouraged them to cultivate and process the poppies. The growers drew the juice from the unripe seeds of the plants, and air-dried it until it formed into a thick gum. Further drying of this gum resulted in a powder for the final product that was sold.

The farmers' customers were the smugglers who paid them cash for the illicit crops. They took care of the transport to the rendezvous site, to be loaded onto trucks for delivery to the Iranian-Turkish border, to be sold yet again. This time, the transfer of the product was to other illicit entrepreneurs who would see the powder got to the right people. These gangsters were from the criminal organizations who had the means to process it into heroin for the markets of the West.

The cultivators loved this arrangement, and were deeply grateful for the opportunity to make so much money. It was easy, fast work without the backbreaking struggle of plowing and harvesting grain crops. These planters considered opiates a blessing from Allah. And if the stuff trapped infidels in the hell of addiction, so much the better. That was what the Non-believers of Western civilization deserved.

SURPRISE and astonishment registered on the expressive face of Archibald Sikes Pasha when the donkey train from the stronghold reached its destination. He, Naser Khadid, Malyar Lodhi, Jandol Kakar, and a couple of dozen mujahideen came down from the Gharawdara Highlands onto the plains after several grueling hours of foot travel under the direction of Husay Bangash. Within a quarter of an hour of trekking across the desert, the travelers reached the rendezvous point. This was where the caravans formed up to take opium shipments out of Afghanistan, across Iran, and into Turkey.

In Sikes' mind he had pictured a crude bivouac with more donkeys or maybe camels gathered around an oasis of some sort. Instead, he saw a small cluster of buildings around which were parked six modern military trucks and a dozen civilian pickups that had machine guns mounted on top of the cabs.

Khadid glanced at his English companion, grinning in delight. "This is not what you were expecting, was it, Sikes Pasha?"

"Not by a bluddy long shot," Sikes remarked. He glanced at some more military vehicles on the other side of the buildings. "Who're them blokes over there then?"

"Afghan Army officers," Khadid explained. "Their units bring the stuff this far, then we'll put it on those trucks—which belong to the Iranian Army, by the way—and take it the rest of the way to Turkey."

"Now that makes me nervous," Sikes said. "I ambushed an Afghan motor patrol, remember?"

"The multiple conspiracies going on in modern Afghanistan create a bewildering pattern of inconsistencies," Khadid explained. "These Afghan soldiers are not concerned about what you've done or where you've been."

"That's a relief," Sikes said. "Now wot about them civilian trucks?"

"Those are Toyota pickups that have been fixed up with machine guns," Khadid said. "The weapons are most excellent German MG-3 seven-point-six-two-millimeters that have proven very dependable in the past."

"I wouldn't think those would be necessary," Sikes remarked. "It looks like the law is on the smugglers' side in this operation."

Kakar interjected himself into the conversation. "Our opponents are other smugglers. Rivals, actually."

"Who're the brave lads that handle the German machine guns?"

"Iranian soldiers," Khadid replied. "They have already proven themselves in some rather large battles in the past. We have to be prepared for the worst. By the way, we'll be riding in the cabs of the pickups during the journey. The mujahideen will be in the Iranian vehicles."

"I see," Sikes said. "Do Turkish soldiers take over when we cross into that country?"

Bangash, who had been listening to the conversation, shook his head. "They're the bad guys, dude. The last people we want to see is a column of motorized Turkish infantry roaring our way. That's when the law is against us. But we don't have to sweat that shit till we get close to Turkey. Sometimes, it's best for us to stay on the Iranian side of the border." He strode ahead, motioning the others to follow him. "Those other guys will take care of the donkeys. They'll stay penned up here till we get back from the run with all our goodies. Then we load them up and trek back to the stronghold, where everyone is happy as pigs in shit to see us and the stuff we bring."

The four followed the head smuggler over to the buildings, where a group of military officers stood waiting. Sikes noticed both Iranian and Afghan uniforms among the Army men. When they arrived, Khadid greeted them as old friends. There were some customary Islamic hugs, kissing motions, and backslapping. The Iranian pointed to Sikes. "This is Orakzai's new field commander. He's going on this run to familiarize himself with this part of our operations." Quick introductions were made, but the names went right by Sikes. He really didn't give a damn who they were anyway. What he did make note of was the fact that they didn't seem too surprised to see him. That told him all the military men had already been fully briefed on his background.

As the group stood in conversation, another officer over by the Iranian trucks called out something in Farsi that caught Khadid's attention. He took Sikes' arm and led him over to the man. After an exchange of salutes, a large envelope was handed to Khadid. He immediately passed it on to Sikes. The Englishman frowned in puzzlement. "Wot's this then?"

"Open it, Sikes Pasha," Khadid said.

Sikes took his knife and ran it along the top edge of the envelope. He opened it and pulled out what appeared to be a legal paper. A diploma of sorts was with it. Khadid watched Sikes look at the unfamiliar script of the Farsi wording on the documents. "That's for you, Sikes Pasha," he said. "It is your appointment as *sargord*. You are now officially a major in the Iranian Army. Thus, as it is said in the language of my people, *tabrik!* Congratulations!"

Sikes grinned to himself. After all the strife and trouble, he had finally ended up a proper officer. Maybe the commission wasn't in the Royal Regiment of Dragoons, but it was of field-grade rank. He wouldn't be surprised if he went all the way to the top of the Iranian General Staff. "Say, Cap'n Khadid, how d'you say 'field marshal' in Farsi?"

"Our equivalent is called an *arteshbod*," the Iranian replied.

Motor sounds from a distance caught everyone's attention. They turned to see a convoy of four large military transport trucks coming across the desert toward them. As they drew closer, Sikes noticed they were UK TM 6-6 models. The sight of vehicles used by the British Army caused him a flash of nervousness. But when he saw the green-white-black stripes of the Afghan flag on the bumpers, the new major relaxed.

Khadid noticed him gazing at the trucks. "Sikes Pasha, those vehicles bring us the preprocessed opium poppy powder. The loads are not so much, because there are no modern facilities available for the final production of the powder into heroin; thus, the amount available is limited. But the quantity is sufficient to make each caravan a very profitable operation."

"So wot's gonna happen now then?" Sikes asked.

"The bales will be transferred from the Afghan trucks to the Iranian ones," Khadid explained. "When that it is done, we will begin our journey out of Afghanistan. We are going to spend tomorrow traveling across Iran, and the day after, Allah willing, our caravan will be in Turkey or at the border."

"I'm starting to see a lot o' this part o' the world, hey?"

"Yes," Khadid said. "By the way. Do you wish to be addressed by your military rank or the title you have chosen?"

"I'll stay Sikes Pasha."

CHAPTER 19

COMMANDER Thomas Carey and Lieutenant Commander Ernest Berringer were in a magnanimous mood when the SEALs arrived back at Shelor Field after their hurry-up return from patrol. The two staff officers actually allowed them time to take showers, then go to early chow at the base mess hall, before having them settle down in the hangar for the new briefing.

Clean and belching, the Brigands sat in the folding chairs with pens and notebooks held at the ready as Carey stepped to the front of the group. "It looks like it's déjà vu all over again, gentlemen. You've gone from cold to hot to cold, and you're about to go back to hot again."

Lieutenant Bill Brannigan, glad to see that things were picking up from the slow going of the previous weeks, asked, "Is this a continuation of earlier actions, sir?"

"Negative," Carey replied. "This is a brand-new mission that's being thrust into Operation Rolling Thunder. And it's a damn critical one. The mission statement is as follows: You will make an attack or attacks on an opium-smuggling trail to neutralize the activity."

"Jesus!" Bruno Puglisi exclaimed. "Who the fuck do they think we are? The DEA?"

"There's more than that to it," Carey said. "Now here's the situation. Iran's bid for power now goes beyond WMD programs. They have organized an extensive Special Operations branch in their Army to take over all Shiite insurgencies in the Middle East."

The commander quickly but fully informed the SEALs of Operation Persian Empire with all its implications and ramifications. The potential dangers resulting from Iranian success in the operation were immediately appreciated by the audience.

The N-3 continued. "This program is being financed by their participation in opium poppy-smuggling from Afghanistan to Turkey. Obviously, this operation must be destroyed—not curtailed—but *destroyed*!"

Lieutenant Junior Grade Jim Cruiser raised his hand. "Why not turn it over to the flyboys? Couldn't they bomb the hell out of that route?"

"That won't work," Carey said. "Unfortunately, the way from Afghanistan through Iran and into Turkey could run through hundreds of mountain passes. Aerial bombardment would just slow the bad guys down temporarily. Then they'd pick up the pace along another direction."

"What the hell?" Chief Matt Gunnarson said. "If Afghanistan isn't the best place to hit them, then cream the bastards in Iran."

"That is not even under consideration," Carey said. "So we can forget that little tactic. Politics, diplomacy, and old-fashion chickenshit will allow us to make our attacks only in Afghanistan. As I mentioned, the flyboys won't be able to handle it, so somebody has to go in there and get down and dirty. That means DPVs. The smugglers are using trucks for hauling and machine gun–mounted Toyota pickups for protection.

They've already had some attacks from rival smugglers and even Turkish Army units, but they've shown they can handle any adversity quite effectively. You'll find your enemy consists of professional soldiers. Be on your toes!"

The Skipper was thoughtful. "Mmm. We know the mission and the situation. And I have to tell you, sir, I'm real curious about the execution phase of this operation."

"You are going to be flown by C-One-Thirty from Shelor Field to an area we're calling the Opium Trail," Carey said. "You'll be facing a dozen of those Toyotas, but you'll have six DPVs with two machine guns on each and you can go eighty miles per. It looks like you'll be involved in the same-type combat you had against the armored cars. But it should be easier."

"Excuse me, sir," Senior Chief Dawkins said, "but we're outnumbered two to one, and them Toyotas can go a hell of a lot faster than eighty miles an hour. And as an Alabama farm boy, I do know my pickups."

"The Toyotas don't have run-flat tires," Carey said. "And keep in mind that they are not armored."

"Well, shit!" Puglisi exclaimed. "Neither are we!"

Carey showed an apologetic grin. "What's the name of that old song? 'I Never Promised You a Rose Garden.' "

"Oh, well," Puglisi said with a shrug. "There's also another old song: 'You Always Hurt the One You Love.' "

Carey's grin turned from apologetic to wry. "Yeah. And I do love you guys."

"If you're both through discussing American music, let's get back to the situation at hand," the Skipper said with a frown. "There is one small potential being overlooked. You mentioned rival smugglers. Don't you think if we laid enough hurt on the main bad guys, all the smugglers are going to get together to resist us?"

"We don't know that for a fact," Carey said.

Now Chad Murchison joined in the conversation. "I can foresee yet another situation arising, sir. Could it be that our hegemony would be willing to allow this narcotic smuggling to continue if it could be removed from the Iranian sphere of influence?"

"I take it that, by 'hegemony,' you are referring to our

command structure, Petty Officer Murchison," Carey said. "Let me answer that by saying there is no way that anybody in authority, whether it be political, military, or diplomatic, is going to condone the smuggling of narcotics to the West under any circumstances. The reason this job has been handed to you is that the situation has global implications. If Operation Persian Empire isn't completely obliterated, the domino effect will be catastrophic. It would be a disaster destined to plague the civilized world for decades."

Garth Redhawk brought up another angle. "But if we take out these bad guys, what's to stop the Iranians from working with those rival smugglers?"

"Right," Doc Bradley chimed in. "The Iranians could change outlaw organizations as fast as we could knock them off."

"We'd be shoveling shit against the tide," Joe Miskoski added.

"The answer to that is simple," Carey said. "You have to get rid of the Iranians involved. When they are gone, then things will get back to normal after a while. The rival smugglers will shoot it out, then the winner will control everything. They'll keep all the money, meaning the Iranians get nothing for their Persian Empire." He gestured to Lieutenant Commander Berringer. "Pass out the maps and photos, Ernie."

Berringer had arranged packets of satellite photographs and maps of the smuggling area for the SEALs' use. As he distributed them among the Brigands, the Skipper spoke up again. "What about assets? Surely, there must be one available from among all those miscreants."

Berringer walked back up to the front of the room. "We do have an asset. His code name is Aladdin."

"Are we going to get a chance to meet with him and ask him some questions?"

"Unfortunately," Berringer said, "we have never met him. He transmits his intelligence from an unknown location somewhere in western Afghanistan."

"Well, hell!" Brannigan said. "Give us his frequency and I can have Gomez contact him."

"We have never had a reply when we tried to raise him," Berringer said.

"Jesus Christ!" Brannigan sputtered. "Isn't he working with one of our intelligence agencies?"

"No," Berringer admitted. "He just popped up out of the blue."

"What the hell!" Brannigan barked. "Then how in God's name do you know he's reliable?"

"We have been assured by the CIA that the information he gives us is accurate," Carey interjected.

"Shit!" Brannigan said, standing up. "This Aladdin son of a bitch could be setting us up for a big fall."

"All I can tell you is that it has been determined that he is trustworthy."

Brannigan was really pissed off now. "That isn't good enough for me, goddamn it, sir!"

Now Carey lost his temper. "It's going to have to be good enough for you, Lieutenant! An OPLAN has been drawn up based on Aladdin's transmissions, and you are going to turn that into an OPORD and obey any other orders you are given! Understand?"

"Aye, sir," Brannigan said, sitting down but still seething.

Carey checked his watch. "I will expect a briefback from you at 1600 hours tomorrow. As far as assets go, you will have Lieutenant Commander Berringer and me. That's it! If you have any questions for us, we will be here to help. If we can't answer a specific inquiry, we'll contact the SPECOPS Center on the *Combs*. If the SF staff on board can't get an answer for you, there's nothing else we can do. Let that be enough motivation for you to be prepared for any contingency." He paused and looked at the eighteen frowns directed at him. "Turn to!"

The SEALs did not have time to spring to positions of attention as the two staff officers quickly exited the briefing area.

THE OPIUM TRAIL
16 MAY

THE attaching of the German MG-3 machine guns to the roofs of the pickup trucks fascinated Arsalaan Sikes Pasha.

The mounts had been expertly manufactured and securely attached to the vehicles with six heavy-duty fifty-millimeter bolts per weapon. The arrangement allowed an arc of fire through 140 degrees. Although the MG-3s were belt-fed, there was no problem with belts of ammo dangling off the side. These weapons had belt drums, each holding 150 rounds, that could quickly be changed when reloading was necessary. However, with a firing rate of 1100 rounds a minute, it would take only a little less than eight seconds to empty the weapons with a continual pull on the trigger. For that reason, the gunners had spent time practicing until all could manage four- and five-round fire bursts.

The gunners were professional soldiers of the Iranian Army, and they went to a great deal of trouble to keep their weapons clean and operable. Even in the dusty atmosphere of the Afghanistan high desert, the machine guns looked as if they were ready to stand a full field inspection by a regimental sergeant major. Canvas covers were kept over the MG-3s at all times, except when dismounted for preventive maintenance or during firing exercises. At any time they were exposed to the elements, the Iranians continually wiped and brushed them to make sure no foreign debris worked down into the mechanisms.

The Toyota pickup trucks were just as well maintained. The drivers were also career military, justly proud of their status as driver/mechanics. They came from a society where such skills, while not rare, were still beyond the comprehension of the average person, and their jobs gave these soldiers a prestige that did not exist in Western society. They even received extra proficiency pay.

All in all, even in comparison with the Royal Regiment of Dragoons, Sikes Pasha felt he was in excellent company.

1400 HOURS

THE ride across the firm desert was not too uncomfortable. The ground was firm and fairly flat, making traveling fast and easy. Sikes sat on the passenger side of the Toyota cab, dozing a bit as the journey toward Iran continued. The Iranian soldier driving the vehicle had little to say since he knew no English and Sikes had hardly any knowledge of Farsi.

The monotony of the trip lulled Sikes into his private world of fantasy. He settled back and closed his eyes as images of his glorious future floated through his mind. He could picture the lounge of the Royal Regiment of Dragoons' officers' mess:

THE large-screen TV is tuned to the BBC evening news, in Sikes' imagination, and the rankers sit around in the easy chairs and sofas, their eyes worriedly glued to the images being presented to them as they sip their after-dinner brandies and whiskeys.

"The Middle East is lost!" the announcer declares in his upper-class accent. "The Iranian Army under the command of Field Marshal Sikes has struck its final blow in defeating coalition troops and consolidating the countries of Saudi Arabia, Iraq, Kuwait, Qatar, Yemen, Oman, Afghanistan, and Pakistan under the control of Iran. Western influence has been effectively tossed out of the most oil-rich area of the entire world! What a calamity for the West! The question is, what will be Field Marshal Sikes' next action? The Prime Minister fears this great commander Sikes will turn his military ambitions toward the oil fields of the Russian Federation!"

At this point a major declares, "Sikes? By Jove, chaps! That name is familiar to me for some reason."

"And to me," says a captain nervously, his brandy snifter shaking in his trembling hand.

The dragoon regiment's commander, a crusty brigadier, speaks up. "Now why the devil does the name Sikes mean anything to you chaps?"

Before they can answer, the image of Field Marshal Arsalaan Sikes—with his name on the screen—is seen. He is wearing a field uniform with medals pinned across the front, while epaulets bearing the Iranian national eagle over a wreath

*with crossed batons show his rank. As he begins speaking,
every officer in the room suddenly realizes who the man is.*

*"I say!" the brigadier exclaims. "Wasn't that chap a ser-
geant in this regiment at one time?"*

*"Yes, sir," replies a nearby subaltern. "I believe he went
before some of our officers for approval of his application for
a commission and to become a member of this very mess. I
believe his request was disapproved."*

*"And who were the bloody fools who turned him down?"
the brigadier roars. "My God! The man is a military genius!
There's probably been no one like him since Wellington at
Waterloo!"*

*The major and captain quietly get to their feet and slip out
of the room.*

SIKES was close to falling asleep in the cab of the
pickup truck, a slight smile on his lips.

SHELOR FIELD
SEALS HANGAR
16 MAY
1600 HOURS

TWENTY-FOUR hours had passed since Commander
Thomas Carey's presentation of the OPLAN directing Brannigan's Brigands to take on the opium smugglers in northwestern Afghanistan. Now, after long hours of work and little
sleep, the detachment was ready to present their briefback to
Carey and his fellow staff officer, Lieutenant Commander
Ernest Berringer. Carey and Berringer were seated in the front
row of chairs, their own pens and notebooks ready for use during the presentation.

Brannigan was the first up. He went to the podium at the
front of the room. "We're going to conduct this antismuggling
operation in three phases. The first is the transportation from
Shelor Field to the OA." He turned to the blown-up satellite

photo mounted on the wall behind him, flashing his laser
pointer on a location. "That will be our LZ. We'll need two
C-One-Thirties to transport the six DPVs, personnel, weapons,
and gear. Vehicles Alpha One, Alpha Two, and Charlie Two
will be in the first aircraft. Bravo One, Bravo Two, and Charlie
One will be in the second aircraft. Upon landing, we will
quickly unass the aircraft to allow the two Hercules to remain
on the ground with engines running for the minimum amount
of time. As you can see from the map, the LZ is long enough
that the airplanes will not have to turn around. They'll be able
to make a straight run and get back up in the air as soon as we
and our vehicles are disembarked. They will be back to Shelor
less than forty-five minutes after leaving."

"That should go smoothly enough," Carey said. "Now let's
get into Phase Two."

"Right," Brannigan said. "Phase Two will be the elimina-
tion of the smuggler rendezvous point." Once more he used
his laser pointer. "As you can see, it consists of three mud-
wall buildings. We are going to assume the worst-case sce-
nario and act as if they are well defended and have perhaps a
dozen fighting men quartered there."

"Great!" Berringer said. "And you're probably right. I am
positive they have experienced attacks on the facility from
smuggling rivals."

"Exactly," Brannigan agreed. "We are not going to make
this raid in our DPVs because of the noise factor. We want this
to be a surprise attack, so we will leave the vehicles here"—
once more, he used the pointer—"and go on foot to the objective. I am planning a three-pronged attack, leaving an opening
for escape."

"Good God, Brannigan!" Carey exclaimed. "Are you going to let some of them get away?"

"No, sir. Puglisi and Miskoski will be in position with their
AS-Fifty sniper rifles to knock down anyone who breaks out
of the compound."

Berringer wasn't sure about that one. "Don't you think
Puglisi and Miskoski might have trouble if they have to shoot
a half-dozen or so individuals making a run for it?"

Brannigan shook his head. "No, sir. Our two snipers are

going to be close enough to have easy targets. I estimate the range to be no more than seventy-five meters at the most. Also, the AS-Fifties are semiautomatic."

"Great," Carey said. "Now you're on the ground, you've begun your operation, and knocked out the meeting site. What's next on your agenda?"

"We'll take down the main column of smugglers during their return from their run, but before they're within sight of the rendezvous point," Brannigan said. "They'll be out in the open and roll into our ambush. Things will be simple. We'll be fully mounted and will engage them in a running battle. It will be a repeat of our fight with the armored cars, except these will be Toyota pickups and unarmed transport trucks."

"You say things will be 'simple,'" Carey remarked. "Just what degree of simplicity are you going to employ? I'm referring to your basic tactics."

"We'll kill them, sir," Brannigan replied. "One thing I've learned on Operation Rolling Thunder is that these vehicle battles have to be played by ear. It's impossible to know how the fighting will evolve. So, we'll primarily concentrate on simply killing the sons of bitches, then adapt to any situation that arises."

"Mmm," Carey said. "Yeah. That ought to do it. Okay, Lieutenant, your basic plan is approved."

The next SEAL up was Senior Chief Petty Officer Buford Dawkins. "We're planning on a three-day mission, sir. So we'll have enough MREs for five, just in case things don't go as planned."

"They never do in warfare, Senior Chief," Berringer said. "Your CO just said so."

"Exactly," Dawkins agreed. "Everyone will carry their basic load. These are all big boys with lots of experience, so each man will determine what he'll need, applying the two-day pad I already mentioned. We estimate we'll be putting about three hundred miles on each vehicle. I know that's a lot, but again, I'm employing a pad here. Anyhow, each DPV will burn every drop of fuel going two hundred and ten miles. That leaves ninety more to go, and that will require an extra nine gallons per vehicle, or a total of fifty-four for all six. That makes a grand total of one hundred and eighty gallons. That's already been taken care of with the Army transportation comp'ny here at Shelor Field. Since the jerry cans hold five gallons each, the DPVs will carry two for an extra ten gallons instead of nine, so we'll have an additional six gallons. This is all applied to my built-in pad."

"Yeah, okay," said Carey getting a bit confused by the presentation. "I'm sure you've worked this out to the last drop. Now let's get into ammo."

"Yes, sir," Dawkins said. "We'll have a total of three thousand, six hundred rounds of five-point-fifty-six for the M-Sixteens; there'll also be three thousand, six hundred rounds of seven-point-six-two for the M-Sixties and three thousand for the M-Twos."

"Why the six-hundred-round difference between the two machine guns?" Carey asked.

"The M-Sixties shoot more rounds per minute, sir," Dawkins answered. "And both sniper rifles will be supplied with six magazines each of five-rounds. That'll give Puglisi and Miskoski a grand total of sixty rounds between them. Also, each M-Sixty gunner will have an M-Two-Zero-Three grenade launcher. These are for the attack on the rendezvous."

Carey turned to Brannigan. "By the way, Lieutenant, there are some people who are a bit miffed that you turned in those HK-Four-Sixteen carbines for M-Sixteens. They were hoping for some test results and evaluation from you."

"Piss on that," Brannigan said candidly. "We're going into combat. I didn't want the guys stuck with some new brand of shooting irons."

"Okay," Carey said wearily. "I see your point." He turned his attention to Dawkins. "What about the Javelins, Senior Chief? You haven't mentioned them."

"We won't be able to employ them effectively in this situation, sir," Dawkins said. "You have to stop, dismount, and sight 'em in. Too much trouble."

"That's your call," Carey said. "Thank you for your briefing, Senior Chief."

After Dawkins was dismissed, Doc Bradley covered the medical side of the mission, such as medevac through the Marine choppers at Shelor Field, and Frank Gomez announced that the call signs of Operation Rolling Thunder would stay the same. The last presenter was Lieutenant Junior Grade Jim Cruiser. His briefback was given quickly and efficiently. "We do not expect to require resupply. However, we have made arrangements with Randy Tooley to have such services available through the Air Force."

"Who the hell is Randy Tooley?" Carey asked.

"He's the Shelor Field coordinator of all things important, necessary, and of great consequence to keep things rolling," Cruiser replied.

Carey frowned. "Is he that weird kid driving the Air Force-blue DPV?"

"Yes, sir," Brannigan interjected.

"I want to talk to you about that," Carey said. "This missing DPV you reported leaves many unanswered questions."

"I'd appreciate it if you would wait until after this operation, sir," Brannigan said. "I really have a lot on my mind right now."

"Uh, I suppose I could," Carey said hesitantly. "But you're going to have to give an explanation sooner or later. At any rate, your briefback is approved, so it is now an OPORD etched in stone. Go to it, guys!"

"Aye, aye, sir!" Brannigan's Brigands answered in unison.

CHAPTER 20

THE two C-130s bearing Brannigan's Brigands and the six DPVs made an early morning landing in the reddish illumination of dawn, their props stirring up a miniature but violent dust storm off the hard-packed desert terrain. The unyielding ground provided a perfect landing and short-taxi platform as the pair of large aircraft came in side by side. The Air Force loadmasters immediately turned to lowering the rear ramps as the pilots kept the engines running.

As soon as everything was ready, the SEAL driver/ commanders with their gunners rolled off the airplanes onto terra firma and sped eastward toward the rising sun under Lieutenant Bill Brannigan's leadership. By that time, the pilots had their aircraft running across the desert, quickly picking up speed for the liftoff and return to Shelor Field. Frank Gomez, the M-2 gunner in Charlie Two, impetuously turned and waved at the departing C-130s in an unseen gesture of farewell.

Brannigan would have preferred making the landings at night, or at least late the previous evening, but the Air Force had balked at this. They did not want to risk lives and aircraft by touching down during hours of poor visibility. Since that part of the OA was unpopulated and the enemy had no flyover capabilities, the SPECOPS Center on the USS *Combs* could not talk the USAF out of the landing-time restrictions that forbade operations in the dark.

Now, as the SEALs mentally prepared for the upcoming battle, the DPVs sped across the desert. Everyone's face showed a grim demeanor as the Brigands instinctively gripped steering wheels and machine-gun handles, unaware of the tightness of their fists. The detachment rolled along in column formation toward their jump-off point. That would be the coordinates from which they would launch the attack against the opium rendezvous site. This was another portion of the mission that the Skipper preferred to do at night, but no one was sure when the smugglers would be returning from their run. Thus, it was determined that the quicker the attack, the less the risk of running into Murphy's Law.

Guy Devereaux, sitting beside Brannigan, who was driving Alpha One, had his GPS out, constantly monitoring their exact grid locations. Now and then, he would announce a slight change of direction over the LASH headset, and Brannigan would respond to the instructions that went, "Starboard three degrees . . . starboard five degrees . . . port four degrees." It was not an exercise in exactness, but the Skipper could estimate the proper bearing reasonably well by sighting across the vertical spoke of his steering wheel. Within forty-five minutes of leaving the aircraft, Devereaux announced, "This is it, sir!"

Brannigan braked to a stop, and the other DPVs did the same. Immediately, everyone was off the vehicles and standing with weaponry in hand. Brannigan spoke softly out of habit even though they were still out of sound range of the objective. "Assad! Leibowitz! Front and center!"

"Aye, sir!" came the simultaneous responses. The two scouts left their assigned Alpha Two vehicle and reported to the Skipper. After a quick consultation over the map laid out on the hood of Alpha One, the correct azimuth toward the rendezvous was established.

"You'll have to be quick since we don't know the bad guys' schedule," Brannigan said. "Just give the place a looking-over and figure out what we're facing there. We need to know if they have a heavy-weapons capability."

"Aye, sir," Leibowitz said.

The Odd Couple moved out on foot across the desert, with Assad on alert while his buddy referred to the magnetic compass in his hand. It took only twenty minutes to reach the objective, and the scout team's transmission from Assad was a welcome one: "It's kick-ass time, Skipper."

0710 HOURS

THE detachment had left the DPVs back at their jumping-off point and was now in position to begin the assault. They observed vehicle assignment integrity, lying flat on their bellies as they gazed across the flat terrain toward the objective. Bruno Puglisi and Joe Miskoski, toting their AS-50 sniper rifles, had reported that they were ready for the show to begin on the opposite side. Both SEALs were mentally set to deal with any potential runners who might try to flee the scene of the coming battle. This would consist of close-range, deliberate taking of human life. Back at the DPVs, the M-60 gunners had M-203 grenade launchers on their M-16s, and each carried a load of six additional rounds apiece to put into the tubes.

Frank Gomez's startled voice came over the LASH systems. *"Oigan! Hay unos burros allí en un corral!"* He quickly recovered and spoke again in English. "Hey, guys, there's a bunch of donkeys in a pen over there."

Next came the sound of Mike Assad chuckling. "Let's send 'em to OCS."

"Knock it off, Assad!" the Skipper said.

"Aye, sir!"

"You better keep in mind that we're on an objective, and there're nasty people over there," Brannigan snarled. He was flanked by Guy Devereaux and Andy Malachenko, and spoke again into his LASH. "Vehicle commanders, report!"

"Alpha Two," Connie Concord replied. "Ready!" The others—Jim Cruiser, Gutsy Olson, Senior Chief Dawkins, and Chief Matt Gunnarson—all answered in proper order.

"Very well," Brannigan said calmly. He had been studying the mud huts through his binoculars and had seen no one stirring in the area. It was obvious that the inhabitants took advantage of being able to sleep in late while the main caravan was gone. This was also a sign that their smuggler rivals were no longer a threat, having undoubtedly learned a couple of hard lessons in the past when they tried to raid the place.

The Skipper estimated the range to the objective to be approximately 100 meters, well within the limits of the M-203's 1,500-meter capability. "Okay. The first maneuver element will be Bravo Two, Charlie One, and Charlie Two. The covering element will be Alpha One, Alpha Two, and Bravo One. On my command, the grenadiers will fire one round at the huts. That will be the signal for the maneuver element to move out and the cover element to go to the deck and lay down fire. Get ready. Execute!"

The six weapons were fired at almost the same time, making what seemed like one loud detonation. The projectiles arched upward and the trajectory continued until they hit in a scattered pattern within the site. The wall of one of the huts was blown in and the roof collapsed, crashing down on the men inside.

The maneuver element, responding to the bellowed commands of the senior chief, was already rushing forward under the protection of the covering fusillades that splattered into the target area from the covering element. One individual appeared in a window and began to return fire. Doc Bradley, the only man with a grenade launcher in the maneuvering group, slowed down enough to quickly aim and shoot off a projectile. The round missed the window, but struck the building just below it, sending chunks of dry hard mud inward, cutting down the would-be resister in a whirling shower of loose but lethal earthen clods.

Dawkins' group had reached the edge of the enemy camp,

and the senior chief ordered his men to hit the dirt. Now they became the covering element while Brannigan led his group in a rush toward the huts. The return fire was steadily building up, but the SEALs replied in kind, sweeping the area with three-round automatic fire bursts from their M-16s. The mud construction of the buildings was pocked by multiple strikes of slugs as hunks of the material flew off in all directions. Brannigan's bunch took cover in the collapsed structure, putting down a heavy fire on the other two.

Dawkins led his men into the compound, taking cover near the donkey pen. Both groups of SEALs were now positioned to inflict a heavy cross fire into the other buildings. The fiery fusillades struck windows and blew holes in the walls from two directions. Most of the resisters were down within a half minute, their sprawled corpses badly torn up by multiple hits from the 5.56 rounds. A half-dozen defenders toward the rear couldn't take it anymore. They pulled away from their fighting positions and made a run out the rear where there was no incoming fire.

Bruno Puglisi and Joe Miskoski saw the six people running toward them. The two SEALs lay on the ground, their sniper rifles supported by bipods. They began aiming through the telescopic sights, their trigger fingers working methodically and rhythmically. Every round was a head shot, and the fleeing men's craniums began bursting open like hot ripe watermelons being struck by hard blows from a baseball bat. A couple were flipped over on their backs, three spun around before collapsing to the ground, and the sixth continued running for an astounding half-dozen paces without a head before he stumbled and fell.

The battle was over.

Back among the buildings, most of the SEALs glanced over at the donkeys. They were glad to see that none had been injured during the short, blazing firefight. Senior Chief Dawkins bellowed, "What the hell are you standing around for? Check the area out! There might be some crazy ragheads playing dead."

The men moved through the debris, noting the corpses of

the defenders. All had died in the heavy hail of bullets from the attackers. Pete Dawson announced, "These guys ain't ragheads. They're military. See? Ever'one of 'em is wearing some sort of uniform."

Chad Murchison, who collected military insignia as a hobby, knelt down beside one dead man for a closer look. "Hey! This isn't the Afghan Army. They're Iranians."

Brannigan walked up. "Are you sure, Murchison?"

"Yes, sir," Chad replied. "Those are Iranian insignia without a doubt."

Brannigan looked around. "Where the hell is Leibowitz?"

"Here, sir!"

"Get out that digital camera and take pictures of these guys," the Skipper said. "Commander Berringer will be interested in this."

As Leibowitz went to work recording the unexpected evidence, the rest of the detachment began searching for more intelligence. By that time, Puglisi and Miskoski had rejoined the group. "Nobody got away," Miskoski announced.

Puglisi gave his AS-50 a fond look. "I wish the Godfather in my old neighborhood hadn't been ratted out. If he was still running the family, I could use this baby to make a lot of money whacking guys he didn't like."

"You fucking gangster," Miskoski remarked dryly.

"Hey, it's a living," Puglisi protested.

Dawkins reported to the Skipper, informing him the search was finished without any significant results. "These dead Iranians got nothing that would interest Commander Berringer."

"Okay," Brannigan announced. "Let's get back to the DPVs. We've still got the main smuggler group to deal with."

"Sir," Gomez said. "There ain't anybody to feed them donkeys. Let me put some fodder out in the troughs and make sure they got enough water for at least a few days, okay?"

"Sure," Brannigan acquiesced. "But hurry up!"

Gutsy Olson, Garth Redhawk, and Pech Pecheur joined him to take care of the animals, who were badly shook up from the noise of the gunfight. It only took ten minutes to make sure the beasts of burdens could get by comfortably for a little while.

"Form up!" Dawkins yelled.

The SEALs quickly fell into a column formation and headed back toward their vehicles with Assad and Leibowitz in the lead.

OPIUM DELIVERY SITE
IRANIAN SIDE OF THE BORDER
1100 HOURS

THE sale of the opium poppy powder was not made in Turkey. Instead, the transaction occurred a short distance away on the Iranian side of the border. This temporary arrangement had been necessary due to the increased activity of Turkish Army and police units. These groups had been showing a growing propensity to search out poppy smugglers, even if the Turks could not legally cross over the international border to make arrests. This increased activity had also stymied the arms dealer Harry Turpin; he was unable to bring in an anticipated load of ammunition.

To make sure the restless Turks stayed in their own country, strong armored units of the Iranian Army had scheduled maneuvers in the immediate area. They were well prepared to deal with any incursions into their own native land. The armed Toyota pickup trucks were arranged in such away as to provide an effective defense in case the Turkish authorities decided to use harassing fire to break up the confab.

No money was exchanged at the site. Those individuals involved in the commerce conducted the financial end of the business through banks in Switzerland. Dummy corporations in Asia were used to launder the dollars, euros, pounds, francs, and marks that filtered through the elaborate system. Even agencies of the United Nations were involved, as shady agents of the international organization gave priority to the narcotics trade over humanitarian efforts when there was a great deal of money to be made.

Arsalaan Sikes Pasha stood to the side as the bundles were transferred from the trucks to the smugglers' vehicles. These intrepid Turkish criminals had already worked out alternative routes for getting the goods through their nation's law enforcement nets. While the dealing was going on, Husay Bangash and a couple of other Pashtuns made purchases on credit from peddlers who offered tools, housewares, food, clothing, and other items from the West. These were the goodies loaded on the donkey train that would be taken from the rendezvous point back up to the stronghold in the Gharawdara Highlands. The debt would be paid out of the shares due Yama Orakzai and his people from the poppy sales.

Captain Naser Khadid stood beside Sikes as the exchanges went on. "Well, Sikes Pasha," the Iranian SF officer said, "now you can see why the Pashtun people appreciate all that Pepsi and potato chips and the other items that Bangash brings back with him from these journeys."

"I was looking over there," Sikes said. "I noticed some boxes of chocolate biscuits. Those should be popular."

"And this time there are also canned fruit juices that had not been available before," Khadid said. "Peach and apple flavors will make a nice change. It is unfortunate there is no ice to make them taste better."

"Them Pashtos don't know the difference, hey?" Sikes remarked. "If you'd never tasted icing, you wouldn't mind just plain cake, would you?" He turned his glance over to the bundles still being off-loaded and on-loaded in the exchange. "It wouldn't seem there'd be enough money in these runs to pay for a war."

"This exchange is just part of it," Khadid explained. "Our government is also involved in the sale of the finished product. Every time a Western drug addict or some rich person using the narcotics for recreation makes a purchase, they are financing not only our operation, but other similar ones all over the world."

"Yeah," Sikes said. "And there ain't no bluddy way the Western world can put a stop to it, is there, hey?"

Khadid shrugged. "Only if they made the drugs legal. Then the prices would drop to a point where it would be only as profitable as the buying and selling of candy bars."

"That ain't likely to happen, is it? Wot about all them coppers and others who get payoffs by letting the stuff slip through their systems, hey? They'd be out a pretty penny or two, you can bet on that."

"I must admit we depend on the greed and immorality of the authorities," Khadid said.

The two slipped into silence as they watched the activity continue while the sun rose toward its daily zenith.

BOSTON
19 MAY
1600 HOURS

PENNY Brubaker's packing was almost done. The two maids with her in the boudoir were placing the last things in her trunks after carefully leaving her traveling wardrobe out for the next day's flight to California. The luggage would be shipped by UPS Air within a week.

Her cousin, Stephanie Gilwright, came into the bedroom, glancing at the work going on. "I see you're about ready as well."

"Are all your things packed, Stephie?" Penny asked.

"All ready except for Harrington," Stephie said. She and Penny looked so much alike, strangers thought them sisters. The only real difference in their physical appearances was the fact that Stephie had raven-black hair. "He's still balking at the whole undertaking."

"Then you'd better keep an eye on him," Penny warned her.

"Not to worry. He's downstairs sulking."

"We need to fetch him up here," Penny said. "I think I should give a rather stern warning to my cousin-in-law."

Stephie laughed. "I was hoping you would say so. He's always had a crush on you. Even if he puts up an argument, he'll do exactly as you tell him."

"I always felt a little awkward about his feelings toward me," Penny said. "I was afraid you might resent it."

"Not a bit," Stephie said with a slight giggle. "He married me because I look so much like you. And I married him because his family is so rich. Even richer than my own. Harrington doesn't have to work and as long as I don't interfere with his drinking, he pretty much lets me have my way. It's really quite convenient, and I'm given a generous allowance. Between him and my trust fund, I have some seventy-five thousand a year to fritter away."

"And as your most loyal shopping companion," Penny said, "I bear witness to your extravagant frittering."

"The let's get Harrington up here."

"Mildred," Penny said to one of the maids. "Go downstairs and tell Mr. Gilwright to come up here."

"He'll be the half-drunk little sot in the library," Stephie said. The maid stopped her packing chores and left the room.

"Don't worry, Stephie. He's just being stubborn."

The maid returned within a couple of minutes with Harrington Gilwright behind her. He joined his wife and her cousin. He was an incredibly slim young man with thinning hair and a weak chin. His face was flushed from a couple of quick cocktails and his thick eyebrows were knitted into a frown. "What d'you two want?"

"What we want," Penny said, "is for you to stop being such an asshole."

"Well, why shouldn't I be?" he said defensively. "I'm not at all sure I want to live in California."

"You'll absolutely love Coronado," Stephie said. "The winters are very mild. You can sit out on the veranda in the sun even in January and drink yourself into glorious stupefaction."

"They have patios, not verandas, in California," Penny said. "Anyway, I've already leased us a very nice house on San Diego Bay."

Harrington's frown increased. "The only reason you're taking the place is to be close to Chadwick. I don't see why you don't just go out there alone, and leave Stephie and me in peace."

"I cannot go by myself because my grandmamá will not permit it," Penny said. "Although I'm of age, she is an old-fashioned woman."

"Tell her to mind her own business, why don't you?" Harrington said.

"She still has control over my trusts," Penny said.

Harrington had a perfect understanding of that situation since it was trusts that kept him from having to be gainfully employed. But he wasn't through arguing. "Well, she let you go to the United Nations, didn't she?"

"Grandmamá is a staunch limousine liberal from Massachusetts who believes in the UN," Penny said. "But all that is beside the point. She would only give in if Stephie came with me. And Stephie can't go unless you go without creating trouble on *your* side of the family. So you are going, Harrington. Give in and avoid a lot of trouble."

"We'll be there too long!" Harrington snapped. "I don't like being away from the New England social scene any more than I have to."

"I won't need you and Stephie to be there for very much time," Penny said.

"Yes, you will! Your whole idea of going there is to trap Chadwick into marriage," Harrington pointed out. "That could be, like, never ever. I really don't think he wants to marry you since he's become a seal or a walrus or whatever those brutes call themselves."

"Ha!" Penny laughed. "Men don't know *what* to think when it comes to getting married."

"That's right," Stephie agreed. "That's one subject we women have dominated since time began."

"And another thing," Harrington said, "you have no idea when he's coming back from the Middle East. He might be over there for another year or two."

"Then I'm sure you'll have learned to really love California by then," Penny said.

"Well, we must go," Stephie said, grabbing Harrington's arm. "There's still a lot we have to attend to before tomorrow's flight."

"Let's stop for a drink on the way home," Harrington begged as he was dragged from the room.

Penny turned her attention back to the maids and her trunks.

NORTHERN OA
20 MAY
0700 HOURS

THE SEALs were in position to hit the smuggling column when it returned from its delivery. The Bravo DPVs were a half-dozen kilometers to the west, well concealed in a stand of boulders. Their assignment, under the command of Lieutenant Junior Grade Jim Cruiser, was to report when the bad guys passed their position, then discreetly follow them, remaining out of sight. Senior Chief Buford Dawkins had his Charlies to the east, lying in wait.

The action would begin when the smugglers reached a point directly in front of the Alphas. That was when the Skipper and Petty Officer Connie Concord would take their vehicles into a direct attack on the enemy. The action would be the signal for the Bravos and Charlies to launch their own assaults. Because of the rugged high country to the south, the smugglers would have no choice but to go directly toward one of the SEAL sections if they decided to fight back. That would leave the other two the leeway to play the game in the best way possible, depending on how the battle developed.

But at that particular moment, there was nothing to do. The Skipper sat on the hood of Alpha One sipping a cup of MRE instant coffee. He glanced around at his men in the vicinity. Mike Assad and Dave Leibowitz were playing a brand of pinochle they called "Cutthroat"; Malachenko was using a notebook and pen to explain the pronunciation of the Cyrillic alphabet to Connie Concord; and Guy Devereaux lay on his poncho, reading a paperback adventure novel.

Hurry up and wait.

CHAPTER 21

THE Iranian Army trucks that hauled the opium powder during the trip to Turkey were now empty of the narcotic cargo. The mujahideen who had endured the first leg of the voyage on top of the bundles could now stretch out comfortably in the backs, enjoying intermittent naps interrupted from time to time as the convoy bounced and rolled across the desert on its way back to the rendezvous site.

Two of the vehicles were filled with food and comfort items that were destined for delivery to the people at the stronghold. These would be packed into containers and placed on the backs of the donkeys that the smugglers thought were waiting patiently back at the rendezvous site.

Some new items were among the goods, such as Oreo cookies, butterscotch candy, and small packages of cheese and crackers. These would make welcome supplements to the usual load of potato chips and Pepsi. Bolts of cotton and woolen cloth, sewing kits, kitchen butcher knives, and miscellaneous items of clothing were also among the things purchased by Husay Bangash from the itinerate Turkish peddlers who had accompanied the buyers of the poppy powders.

These sellers' collective profits soared near 1000 percent, but the isolated Pashtuns, without access to legal markets, had no choice but to meet the outrageous prices. The Turkish merchants had a monopoly that afforded them the advantageous position of not having to bargain with their bucolic customers.

The crews on the Toyota pickups could relax their vigilance a bit during the return journey since their valuable cargo was sold and no cash had been given them. The tremendous amount of money paid for the narcotics delivery was still in Swiss banks, but would soon be transferred through international financial institutions until arriving in Tehran. From there, the profit would go to military disbursement centers to meet the expenses of the Jihad Abadi, the scheme that American intelligence had dubbed Operation Persian Empire. Part of the payout would go to the coffers of Warlord Yama Orakzai for his personal profit and expenses. Orakzai Messer would have been angered if he knew what a small percentage of the overall profits he actually received.

Arsalaan Sikes Pasha was in the cab of the same pickup truck he had ridden from the rendezvous site. But his garb was decidedly different for the trip back. The English turncoat was clothed in the proper battle dress of an Iranian combat arms officer. The epaulets bore the subdued—black on olive drab—insignia of an eight-pointed star that designated his rank of *sargord* in the Iranian Army. He had also put away his *puhtee* Afghan cap and replaced it with his old keffiyeh and its *aka*. Sikes thought the headdress in combination with a Western-style army uniform made him better fit the proper image of a true pasha.

He also decided that those of his Arabs waiting for him back at the stronghold would also return to wearing their own keffiyehs. He had noticed that several of his men had adapted the *puhtee* as he did, since it served better than the Arab head coverings in the cooler climate of the Afghan mountains.

Sikes, during the hours of riding in the truck, had turned his daydreaming from fantasies of martial glory to the more practical matters of what he was going to do with his twenty-man force that was the remnant of the former armored car company. The Iranian Special Forces showed every intention of allowing them to remain under his personal intimate command, and Sikes wanted to take advantage of the situation. He had every intention of using them as the cadre of an elite strike force.

The first thing to do, of course, was to make it obvious they belonged to him. The outfit needed an impressive name, and Sikes now knew enough Arabic to come up with something. At first he considered Rafir-min-Sharaf (Guard of Honor), but that seemed too plain and commonplace. Any bunch of soldiers marching at the head of a parade as a color party could be referred to as an honor guard. He needed something that would translate into the English language in a most impressive way; after all, his twenty men would eventually be increased in size to at least a brigade-size unit. That meant it would be reported about in tones of awe by television commentators all over the world for decades to come.

Sikes was completely lost in thought as the Toyota bounced across the desert. After nearly an hour of staring blankly and unseeing out the windshield while his creative mind whirled with ideas, he finally came up with the name he was looking for; and it was simple, direct and impressive: al-Askerin-Zaubi—the Storm Troopers. He was ignorant of the fact that Adolf Hitler used that name for his Nazi street thugs during his rise to power in pre–World War II Germany.

Sikes' countenance assumed a smug grin as his imagination once more created the sound of a frightened BBC news commentator beginning the evening news that would be heard all over the UK. The upper-class, cultured voice began dancing through his mind as he sat in the passenger seat: *The fanatical and elite al-Askerin-Zaubi, the Storm Troopers of Field Marshal Arsalaan Sikes Pasha, struck today at . . .*

There was naught but glory and fame ahead for Archie Sikes of Manchester, England.

NORTHERN OA
0815 HOURS

PETTY Officer Second Class Garth Redhawk leaned across the boulder with his binoculars up tight against his eyes. The field glasses were in perfect focus, providing a clear image of the desert out to the front of his position. The young Kiowa-Comanche from Oklahoma was doing what sailors did better than anyone else, keeping watch on an assigned area of responsibility. For Redhawk, this would be the expanse of terrain across which the returning smuggling convoy would travel on their way to their rendezvous site. He grinned to himself, wondering what they would think or do if they knew their destination was a pile of smashed mud structures filled with the battered corpses of their buddies.

Pech Pecheur, sitting down beside Redhawk, leaned against the boulder. He yawned and stretched. "Cain't you see nothing yet, Garth?"

"Just a few dust devils spinning and hopping around."

Pecheur spit. "I hate this place. Man! I come from the swamps where things is wet. Hell's fire! Even the air you breathe is wet. And it's hot, y'know what I mean? Like folks has got boiling pots all around."

"Well, it ain't like Oklahoma either," Redhawk said. "It gets right warm back home, but if that prairie wind is blowing hot and dry on a summer's day, you feel like you're in a furnace."

"In the summer in Louisiana, folks say that it ain't the temperature, it's the humidity that's uncomfortable," Pecheur commented.

"In the wintertime back home, they say it ain't the temperature that makes it cold as hell, it's the wind," Redhawk pointed out. He pulled the binoculars from his eyes just long enough to blink a couple of times to get some tears flowing for moisture. "Anyhow, I don't like mountains no matter what the weather is like. You can't see far 'cause the terrain gets in the way. Out on the prairie, you have almost an unlimited view all the way to the natural horizon."

Gutsy Olson, trying to snatch a morning's nap nearby,

angrily sat up. "Will you two guys shut the fuck up? It's bad enough sitting out here in the middle of nothing without having to listen to a couple of dickheads carrying on a boring conversation. I wish to hell you'd—"

"Target in sight!" Redhawk interrupted.

Both Olson and Pecheur jumped up and pulled out their own binoculars. They peered out over the desert as Lieutenant Junior Grade Jim Cruiser and Doc Bradley joined them. By the time Pete Dawson came up, the sight of the convoy could easily be discerned in the distance.

"Alpha One, this is Bravo One," Cruiser said into his LASH. "The enemy is in sight. I can't get an accurate count on 'em because of their formation. But they're five hundred meters distance, traveling due east at approximately thirty to forty miles per. Over."

"Roger," came back the Skipper's voice. "Charlie One, did you monitor that transmission? Over."

"Affirmative," Senior Chief Dawkins replied. His section was to the east, directly in the path of the approaching convoy. "We're ready. Out."

SMUGGLER CONVOY

THE dozen vehicles, consisting of six transports and six armed pickups, moved at fifty kilometers an hour at a slight east-by-south course across the firm terrain. The layer of fine dirt was thin in the area, and they kicked up a minimum of dust clouds as they rolled toward their objective. The Iranian drivers were thinking about the cold fruit juices and hot food awaiting them, and the Pashtun mujahideens' thoughts were of getting back up into the Gharawdara Highlands and how happy their families would be with the delicacies and other items on the donkeys' backs.

The transports were in the middle of the formation, while one pickup traveled on point at the head of the group. Two other of the small vehicles were on each side of the convoy, while one "Tail-end Charlie" brought up the rear. Military discipline was being observed in a haphazard manner, and while the gunners were in proper positions by their weapons, most had their minds on other things besides security. They stood up in the backs of the smaller trucks, keeping an inconstant vigilance in their areas of responsibility. Some were close to falling asleep, but having to stand in the swaying vehicles prevented even short naps.

Arsalaan Sikes Pasha, the commander of the fierce al-Askerin-Zaubi Storm Troopers, still sat in a contented frame of mind as he fantasized about his coming fame back in Blighty after the Iranian Army's conquest of the entire Middle East.

BRAVO SECTION

JIM Cruiser had gotten his two vehicles moving as soon as practical. He kept the Skipper informed of his progress as he tailed after the smugglers, remaining out of sight to their rear. The lieutenant junior grade drove the DPV carefully, making sure he followed the tire tracks left by the bad guys. Pech Pecheur, up above at the M-2 .50-caliber, cautioned him when they drew too close to their quarry. His weapon, like those of his gunner partner, Dawson, along with Doc Bradley and Garth Redhawk in Bravo Two, was locked and loaded, ready to spit out the armor-piercing tracer ammo when the confrontation began.

CHARLIE SECTION

CHARLIE One and Charlie Two, fully manned and ready, were parked side by side on the east side. They faced due west on the guesstimated azimuth of the approaching enemy. Senior Chief Buford Dawkins, the section leader, listened through his LASH at the conversation between Cruiser and the Skipper, ready to order his two DPVs into action as soon as they were needed.

SMUGGLER CONVOY

CAPTAIN Naser Khadid sat in the cab of the front Toyota, gazing through the windshield as they rolled across the desert. His thoughts were of his wife and children back in the city of Shiraz in Iran. He missed them, but was consoled a great amount by his Pashtun bride Mahzala. She had become more than a source of sexual relief as she evolved into an agreeable little companion, her skills at cooking and other aspects of housekeeping increasing rapidly. The best thing, of course, was how she had also begun responding enthusiastically to his lovemaking; in fact, his experience with his Iranian wife had convinced him that women did not enjoy sex particularly, but the youthful nymph of the *muta* marriage was teaching him an entirely difference aspect of the matrimonial bed.

The Iranian Special Forces captain began to feel a strong urge to get back up into the highlands for a coupling with Mahzala. He felt a flush of desire as he glanced at the passenger-side rearview mirror. He could plainly see the lead transport truck to the direct rear. He watched it in an absent-minded way for a few moments; then suddenly an explosion erupted from its gas tank beneath the cab.

The large vehicle veered both left and right, then turned over and was completely engulfed in flames. A couple of Pashtun mujahideen emerged from the inferno, running blindly in circles with their clothing on fire.

Now the machine gun mounted on the cab above his head began firing, its expended cartridges bouncing off the right front fender.

THE BATTLE

ANDY Malachenko in Alpha One, after hosing the lead transport with his M-2 heavy machine gun, swung the barrel toward the truck to its immediate rear. Even before he squeezed the trigger, his M-60 partner Guy Devereaux was already splattering the new target with well-aimed bursts of full-auto 7.62-millimeter slugs. When the heavy .50-calibers of the M-2 joined the fusillade, the target vehicle exploded in a fiery burst of ignited gasoline, bouncing completely off the ground. The two Iranians in the cab were enveloped in flames, but several Pashtun mujahideen managed to get out the back. They turned and ran south for the sanctuary of the foothills.

Connie Concord swung Alpha Two over to a more diagonal route toward the enemy column, allowing the Odd Couple to turn their own individual weapons onto the third truck. It came to an abrupt halt an instant before a loud swoosh announced its fuel tank turning into an impromptu bomb. The men in the cab managed to get out as the mujahideen in the rear bailed over the tailgate.

"*GASHTEE junub!*" Captain Naser Khadid shouted at the Iranian driver next to him. "Turn south!"

The man whipped the wheel to the right, almost rolling the Toyota. The machine gunner in the back, who had just started firing at the attackers to their direct front, almost fell out. He grabbed the weapon mount on the cab and held on with all his strength as the centrifugal force of the violent maneuver threatened to throw him off the pickup truck. As soon as the vehicle was on a southerly route, the pressure faded and the guy slid to the bed of the truck. He had no reason to use the machine gun now. The attackers were to his rear, well out of his arc of fire.

Over to the left of the smuggler formation, Arsalaan Sikes had already made his own tactical decision as rounds from four enemy machine guns swept up and down the convoy. He pointed to the south and slapped the driver across the side of the head. The soldier was not angered by the blow that shook him out of shock and instantly obeyed his passenger's frantic gestures. Sikes turned and looked out the back window, sighting the dead machine gunner sprawled and shaking on the deck as the vehicle bounced across the ground in its wild run.

Now the other three Toyotas, carrying Husay Bangash, Malyar Lodhi, and Jandol Kakar, also headed away from the attack. The drivers sighted Sikes' and Khadid's trucks, and hit the accelerators to catch up with the two officers. The sixth pickup had been riddled and sent rolling a couple of minutes before when DPVs appeared from the east and cut loose with sweeping volleys of machine-gun fire.

THE Bravo Section, after disposing of the rear pickup, closed in on the scene of the burning transports. All six were now dead hulks, spewing out obscene orange flames and black, oily smoke. Corpses with smoking clothing were scattered around the vehicles. Jim Cruiser's section immediately began receiving fire from mujahideen on the ground. These were the lucky Pashtuns who had managed to escape the infernos of the big trucks. They were skilled fighters, and had assumed kneeling and prone positions, squeezing off well-aimed bursts from their AK-47s.

Cruiser spotted one group of almost a dozen who had gathered from two of the destroyed transports. "Gunners! Turn your weapons on those ragheads at ten o'clock!" The quartet of SEAL gunners responded immediately, cutting down the resistance with a close-packed combined volley of 7.62 and .50 slugs. The Pashtuns were kicked down into undignified positions of death in the short space of three beats.

The Alphas came to a stop. From their vantage point, they had clear fields of fire into the area of the burning trucks where scattered groups of mujahideen still offered resistance. Brannigan did not have to give any orders as Devereaux, Malachenko, Assad, and Leibowitz did what had to be done with their weapons. Now the Charlies closed in and added their firepower to the scene. The men on the ground died fast in the hail of fire bursts.

"Alpha One, this is Bravo One!" Cruiser transmitted through his lash. "There're five pickups heading south for the foothills."

"Let's go!" Brannigan said, being economic with words since everyone was able to quickly figure out what was going on.

The commander/drivers turned toward the fleeing Toyotas, pressing down hard on the accelerators.

BOTH Sikes and Khadid had sighted the chase vehicles. Although unable to communicate, they both issued the same orders for their respective drivers to kick up to the fastest speed the vehicles could possibly attain. The other three quickly caught on and joined in the run for safety. The pickups were much faster than the DPVs, easily increasing the distance between themselves and their pursuers.

The quintet, now out of range of the SEALs after three full minutes of flight, continued to speed crazily toward the Gharawdara Highlands. After they went some five kilometers, the ground grew rougher as the terrain evolved from the sandy soil of the desert to the rocky expanse that led to the hills. Another few minutes and they had reached the first stands of boulders. The drivers hit the brakes and all ten occupants unassed the trucks, running toward the natural cover with their AK-47s and bandoliers of ammunition in hand.

All the Iranian machine gunners lay dead in the back of the Toyotas, with one exception; that vehicle was empty because the gunner had fallen out due to the violent maneuvering of the driver.

ALPHA One was in the lead of the close-packed formation of DPVs. All twelve gunners impatiently waited to get within range of the parked pickups, and when the distance was right for the M-2s, the gunners sent tracers streaking toward the vehicles. The Toyotas bounced from the heavy slams of armor-piercing rounds.

"Never mind the fucking trucks!" the Skipper said over his LASH. "There isn't anybody there except the dead. Start laying down fusillades up higher in the hills. That's where the survivors went."

Now the M-60s were also within range, and everyone became involved in reconnaissance by fire as they attempted to find where the fugitives had taken cover. The only reward they got for their efforts was the sight of tracer rounds bouncing off rocks and boulders to streak off into the distance.

"Cease fire!" Brannigan ordered.

UP in the rocks, Sikes was at the head of the group as they scrambled toward higher ground. Everyone, including the Iranian drivers, was in super physical condition and had no problem negotiating the rugged terrain. Sikes came across some boulders the size of Volkswagen Beetles, and he scrambled up on them. When he reached the top, he discovered a natural fort. He stopped and turned to the others.

"Right! Here's where we make a stand," he announced. "I counted them Yanks. They got six o' them little fucking buggies and there's three each riding in 'em, hey? That's eighteen of the wankers. There's ten of us and we got concealment and cover here, right? So we'll stand fast and let the bastards come up here after us."

Khadid quickly translated into Farsi for the drivers, then issued orders. Everyone found good firing positions and settled down to wait.

THE SEALs had parked the DPVs and were now some twenty-five meters up the rocky slope that led to the highlands. Lieutenant Bill Brannigan spent a few moments with his binoculars, scanning the boulder-strewn area above, hoping to find some clue as to what the enemy was doing. But he could detect absolutely nothing. "Assad! Leibowitz!"

The Odd Couple left their place in the impromptu skirmish line and went over to report to the CO. They squatted down beside him, and Dave Leibowitz asked, "What's up, sir?"

"Right," Mike Assad said with a grin. "As if we didn't know."

"Did you know I'm about to put your asses deep into some real hairy shit?" the Skipper asked.

They looked at each other, then back at him, and shrugged.

"The bad guys had a good lead on us," Brannigan explained. "They could be hauling ass toward the ridges up there to get out of the area, or they're holed up and ready to fight back." He pointed upward. "Go find out."

"Aye, sir!" came the simultaneous response.

Assad led the way with Leibowitz behind, ready to cover him in case of trouble. They began a zigzag course, working their way carefully through the boulders and sparse brush. Mike's eyes went from looking upward for a sight of the bad guys to looking down to the ground to check for tracks the enemy might have left to reveal the direction they were traveling. After ten minutes of climbing, the Skipper's voice came over the LASH. "If you reach a point where the hair on your necks is raising with apprehension, you're free to break off and return."

"Roger, sir," Dave replied.

They knew exactly what Wild Bill meant. Sometimes, in dangerous situations, there is a certain unpleasant feeling that comes over a combat veteran. It's not fear. The best way to describe the sensation is as an instinctive sureness that something real bad is about to happen. That is one reason why experienced fighting men sometimes are able to survive in situations where rookies are gunned down.

Mike continued the upward trek, unable to spot as much as a single speck of evidence of where the bad guys had gone. Dave, with his M-16 held ready, stayed in his protective mode, ready to put out covering fire if Mike suddenly came under attack. The higher they went, the more nervous they became.

Suddenly both stopped, then squatted down.

A volley of fire swept over them, ricocheting off nearby boulders with sparks and whines. Once more, Brannigan made contact with the Odd Couple. "What's the situation?"

"We're under fire, sir," Mike replied. "Every time we raise our heads to see where it's coming from, it increases."

"Okay," Brannigan said. "That means they know exactly where you are. Can you break off or are you pinned down?"

"We can back down to a better spot," Dave explained, "then we should be able to withdraw okay."

"Do it."

"Aye, sir."

The Odd Couple, the bores of their weapons pointing upward, stumbled downward in deep crouches. It was slow going for about ten minutes, then they were able to get behind a large stand of boulders.

"All right, sir," Mike said. "We'll be back pretty quick now."

"Right," Brannigan said. He knew it was useless to try to catch the fugitives. Everything—cover, concealment, firing positions, and knowledge of the terrain—was in their favor.

"Okay, Section Leaders," Brannigan said. "As soon as the Odd Couple gets back, we'll mount up on the DPVs and go back to the battle site. There may be survivors among those smugglers or whatever they are."

Everyone monitored the orders over the LASH systems and stared upward to catch sight of Mike Assad and Dave Leibowitz. They were perturbed about the escapees, but they had accomplished their mission. The smugglers had been destroyed. A few EPWs would be icing on the cake of victory.

CHAPTER 22

WHEN Sikes Pasha, Captain Naser Khadid, and Husay Bangash came down the path leading the five Iranian soldiers into the stronghold, they were met by a somber, wailing crowd of Pashtun people. The young translator Malyar Lodhi and Sikes's adjutant Jandol Kakar had been sent ahead to bring the bad news of the devastating defeat out on the desert. They had gone straight to Yama Orakzai to tell him of the terrible battle with the fierce American warriors who spewed death from their little cars sent to them from hell by Satan.

Now Orakzai stood in front of the people as the small group of survivors walked up to him. Warrant Officer Shafaqat Hashiri and the nineteen Arabs were in a proper formation off to one side, giving their leader a studied look as he approached. They were glad to see their commanding officer was unhurt.

Khadid held back in deference to Sikes' rank as the field commander, and the Brit greeted the warlord with an embrace. "We were ambushed, Orakzai Mesher," Sikes said. "We had delivered the opium powder and were on our way back to the rendezvous to retrieve the donkeys when the Americans struck."

"Malyar and Jandol have told me about it," Orakzai said. "We must retire to my quarters to discuss this situation. It is a shock that sends my heart and mind reeling. Did none of my mujahideen survive?"

"If they did, they're bleeding prisoners," Sikes said. "They was trapped in the backs o' the transport trucks. I'm afraid most of 'em was blown up." He nodded to the five Iranian drivers. "These were the only Iranians who got away. All the gunners in the back of the Toyotas was killed."

Orakzai could not hide his grief. "*Tsenga haybatnak!* This is a catastrophe! Everything we have worked for is lost!" He looked over to Khadid. "You must tell your superiors about this, Captain Khadid. We joined the Iranians in good faith, yet somehow we are facing a disaster from which we might not recover."

Khadid went into his Special Forces mode. "It is not an insurmountable calamity, Orakzai Mesher. I admit it is an unexpected blow for which I know of no explanation. There must have been treachery, no doubt, but the Iranian Army is more than capable of dealing with it. If we have indeed been betrayed—and I strongly believe that is the case—the culprits shall be eventually found out no matter how much care they take to remain undiscovered. We shall have our vengeance and, ultimately, a great victory not only for Iran but for the Pashtun people. Let us keep in mind that your main goal is to establish an independent nation."

"That seems out of reach now," Orakzai said, close to weeping. "Let us go to my quarters."

The Pashtuns, particularly the women, picked up on their leader's distress. This set off more wailing and loud moans as they watched him turn and walk toward his cave in the company of the Englishman and Iranian.

Khadid leaned close to Sikes and whispered, "These Pashtuns will quickly develop a keen resentment toward us foreigners because of this calamity. Somehow, they will place all the blame on us. I suggest you keep your Arabs close by."

"Bluddy good idea," Sikes agreed in a soft voice.

He gestured to Warrant Officer Shafaqat, who obviously had been having the same thoughts. The Arabs, all armed, formed up into a column of threes and began to follow their leader at a slow pace. Every man of them sensed the tenseness and sensitivity of the situation. The Pashtuns glowered at Sikes' men, but took no overt hostile action against them.

SHELOR FIELD
NOON

THE three EPWs brought back from the battle by the Brigands were being kept in a jury-rigged jail set up in the corner of the hangar. A barbed-wire barrier had been hastily erected to hold them, and a port-a-potty donated by Randy Tooley served their sanitary needs. Senior Chief Buford Dawkins set up a watch bill to make sure they were kept under constant guard. All had been wounded and had received treatment at the base infirmary. Now properly medicated and bandaged, they were under the skilled care of Doc Bradley.

None had life-threatening injuries, but one was suffering from a broken leg. This was the only Iranian. His companions in captivity were Pashtun mujahideen. The oldest, a fellow with a gray beard, had second-degree burns on his chest and arms. His buddy, a young guy who looked to be in his twenties, had taken a grazing hit in the side that tore across his body without damaging any vital organs. The massiveness of the injury came from an M-2's heavy .50-caliber slug.

The Iranian soldier, a machine gunner, had been discovered out in the open, lying helpless with a compound fracture of the fibula just above the ankle. He was also badly bruised from the fall off the back of the speeding pickup truck where he manned his weapon. The SEALs spotted him at the battle site when they returned from the excursion into the foothills. The injured soldier expected them to shoot him straight off. He knew no English, so there was a marked lack of conversation between him and his captors. He tried to be as brave about it as possible, but a very obvious trembling, paleness, and continuing struggle to keep from crying showed he was badly frightened. Later, when he received first aid prior to the trip back to Shelor Field, the Iranian relaxed a bit. An offer of food further calmed him, and by the time they brought him to the Shelor Field infirmary for treatment under a doctor's supervision, the soldier was in a very relieved state of mind. It was obvious no summary execution loomed in his future.

When the Pashtuns were picked up, the pair was sitting cross-legged among their dead brethren in the midst of burned transport hulks. Unlike the Iranian, they were ready to die, though not exactly pleased about the prospect. Once more, the application of care to their wounds brought about a relaxation of inner tension. When they were handed hot rations warmed in an FRH, they realized they would be treated with dignity and a degree of kindness. The old man, who had worked with an American CIA agent during the war against the Soviets, showed a gap-toothed grin as he slurped up a spoonful of spaghetti. "T'ank you," he said.

Before returning to Shelor Field with the EPWs, Brannigan allowed Frank Gomez and the Charlie Two team to make a quick trip to the smugglers' rendezvous site to put out additional feed for the donkeys. When they arrived, they saw that local villagers had looted the place and led the animals away. "The guys will be glad to hear about this," Frank remarked. "They were worried about those little *burros* starving to death."

"Are you kidding?" Chief Matt Gunnarson remarked. "If they hadn't been stole, the wolves would have got them long before they died from hunger. You can bet a prowling pack had already sniffed 'em out."

THE first thing Brannigan did after returning to their hangar at the airfield was to have Frank Gomez send a transmission to the USS *Combs* to inform them of the prisoners. The encoded message gave all the available information about them, but that wasn't much. All that was determined was that one was an Iranian soldier in the uniform of his army. This seemed incongruous since he was on a clandestine, illegal mission, but nobody ever accused the Iranian Government or military of operating in a logical or smart manner. After all, the Iraqis had kicked their asses in a drawn-out war back in the 1980s.

The other two prisoners were described as mountain Pashtuns who appeared to be illiterate, but with an innate self-reliance and a natural ability to endure hardship and discomfort. This last bit of info wasn't included to compliment the two EPWs, but to make it clear they were not operatives in disguise. The pair of stoic men were genuine Pashtun mujahideen.

The S-2 aboard the *Combs* radioed back, instructing the SEALs to continue to take care of the prisoners' wounds, feed them well, and see that they were comfortable at all times. When the senior chief informed the detachment of the orders, Bruno Puglisi gave a snort, saying, "Hell! I wish they'd see that *we* got the same treatment."

Senior Chief Dawkins showed a sardonic leer, saying, "That ain't never gonna happen on my watch, Puglisi."

"Jeez!" Puglisi exclaimed under his breath to Joe Miskoski. "Even them donkeys is luckier'n us."

"Yeah," Miskoski agreed. "You never hear about a donkey going through Hell Week."

"They wouldn't allow nobody to be that cruel to animals," Puglisi pointed out. "The Humane Society wouldn't permit it."

The intelligence officer also forbade any attempts at interrogation. This was to be handled by persons unnamed who would arrive to tend to that most important matter. The Brigands could read between the lines of that latter instruction. There was something above and beyond the ordinary that had been thrust into Operation Rolling Thunder.

PASHTUN STRONGHOLD
GHARAWDARA HIGHLANDS
26 MAY
0615 HOURS

SIKES Pasha's Arab unit and Captain Naser Khadid of the Iranian Special Forces were formed up to leave both the stronghold and Afghanistan. Yama Orakzai Mesher had seen that a donkey was provided for them to make the journey a little easier. Although the Arabs had no need of the pack animals since they had arrived carrying everything they owned on their own backs, Khadid had his radio transmitter, field desk, and other items that were too bulky or heavy for human beings to tote through mountainous terrain.

This exodus was not a voluntary one. Orakzai had made a decision the day before that the best thing he could to for his people was to get rid of the foreigners, then make peace with the Afghan government in Kabul. Khadid, secretly upset about the Iranian mission being ended, had given a subtle warning that this would displease another government, that of the Islamic Republic of Iran, and there would no doubt be a reaction from Tehran. This was his understated way of saying that the Iranian Army would be given full rein to either get the Pashtun group back into their operation or destroy them. Khadid had learned much during his time with Orakzai's people, and knew that a full-blown threat to a Pashtun would be answered by him and Sikes getting decapitated and their heads sent back to Iran in cardboard boxes. Thus, even the subtle warning was given with a friendly smile, along with assurances that the Pashtuns and Iranians would always be brothers.

The *mutas* between Sikes and Banafsha, along with that involving Khadid and Mahzala, was dissolved. It was determined by a couple of old Pashtun women that neither wife was pregnant; thus, the marriage contracts were ended simply and rapidly to accommodate the situation. The two girls returned to their families and, although their fathers were not required to return the bridal gifts, they would have to pay hefty dowries for their daughters to be married again. They were no longer virgins, and even though their innocence had been lost honorably under Islamic law, they were second-hand property. If either father wanted to marry off his daughter, it would cost so much as to be prohibitive. Both consoled themselves with the knowledge they would have daughters at home to look after them in their old age.

When the Arabs and the Iranian officer leading the donkey began their trek from the stronghold, the population watched them impassively. There was some minor grumbling among those who thought the foreigners should be held responsible for the loss of their men on the smuggler run, but since Yama Orakzai Mesher had made no accusations and showed no inclination to punish them, the Pashtuns accepted what appeared to be a peaceful parting of the ways.

WASHINGTON, D.C.
THE STATE DEPARTMENT
28 MAY
2300 HOURS

EDGAR Watson of the CIA's Iranian desk showed the obvious distress of severe jet lag as he sat at the table where a meeting of the Lamp Committee had just been called to order by Arlene Entienne. The other members of the group—Carl Joplin and Colonel John Turnbull—immediately forgot the discomfiture of the late hour when they noticed Watson's condition.

Entienne, as the chairperson, gave the CIA man a few extra moments to make himself comfortable before she addressed the small group. "As I'm sure you all have guessed, some extraordinary circumstances have developed in Operation Persian Empire."

"Excuse me," Turnbull interjected. "I keep hearing about two operations. One is called Rolling Thunder and the other is Persian Empire. I'm confused as to how the two are tied together."

"Then let me make that clear once and for all," Entienne said. "Operation Rolling Thunder refers to a SEAL operation in that OA. Persian Empire identifies the Iranian project of combining all Islamic Shiite insurgencies into one big army under their command. The SEALs, sent on a completely different mission, have now been pulled into that big picture. They are not locked into any one set of activities, but presently are under the President's direct command."

Joplin, thinking of Brannigan's Brigands, asked, "Are they aware of this big picture?"

Entienne shook her head. "No, Carl. But it appears they soon will be. And that includes receiving reinforcements."

"Mmm," Turnbull mused. "It sounds like the shit is about to hit the fan."

"It is," Entienne assured him. "Big-time." She glanced at Watson. "Edgar has just returned from a quick trip to Afghanistan. He had to endure a heavy schedule and a quick turnaround." She gave him look of deep sympathy. "How are you doing?"

He grinned weakly. "I'm holding on, Arlene. And I'm ready to address this august assemblage." After one deep, steadying breath, he began his oral report to the committee. "I am happy to let you know the mission to neutralize that one particular smuggling group has been accomplished by those intrepid SEALs Arlene mentioned. This does not mean that the smuggling of opium poppies has come to an end. Others will take up the slack in that profitable enterprise, but not the Iranians. At least, not for the time being. They have lost the advantageous edge that was financing Operation Persian Empire."

"Then you can bet your ass they'll want it back," Turnbull commented dryly.

"Exactly," Watson agreed. "And they'll not waste a minute of time getting that project rolling. Now! The SEALs managed to take three enemy prisoners of war. Two were rather unremarkable Pashtun mujahideen who were part of the rebel group up in the Gharawdara Highlands. The third was an Iranian soldier who was actually wearing a proper uniform on this secret mission. During the interrogation, I asked him why he wasn't disguised, and he informed me that no other clothing had been issued him. He and his pals had been assigned to the smuggling enterprise from their regular units. They had showed up in uniform and performed their jobs in uniform."

Turnbull laughed. "And got captured in uniform."

"Right," Watson said. "This fellow didn't know much about the big picture and was not actually a member of the Iranian Special Forces. His normal assignment is that of a machine gunner in a regular infantry unit. To put it bluntly, he didn't know shit."

"Then how do we know the Iranians are going to try to recover from this defeat?" Joplin asked.

"We received a final transmission from Aladdin," Watson said. "He informed us that some crack Iranian Special Forces would be making a concerted effort to regain all they've lost. And that will include the destruction of their former Pashtun allies. They are planning on occupying the area. That at least lets us know where future clashes will be happening."

Turnbull was a bit miffed. "We haven't heard one goddamn word about this at SOLS."

"All planning is being done by SOCOM through the USS *Combs*," Watson said. "The staging area will be Shelor Field in southwest Afghanistan. Everyone involved is already pretty much on site."

"Okay," Turnbull said. "Now what about that Pashtun bunch? They had their own goals of establishing an independent nation in the area, right?"

"Right," Watson replied. "However, after seeing the Iranians getting a good ass-kicking by the SEALs, their leader Orakzai is seeing things in a new light. He has made peace overtures to the Afghan government. They are even now hammering out an agreement in which he will turn his war-making efforts eastward to do battle with the Taliban. Orakzai has even consented to evacuate his stronghold in the Gharawdara Highlands."

Entienne, who had been taking notes, looked up from her writing. "Did Aladdin actually say his latest transmission would be his last?"

"Yes, Arlene," Watson said. "At least for the time being. It would appear this intrepid person is going to be unable to contact us."

"Interesting," Turnbull commented. "That could mean he's right in the middle of things over there."

"Who knows?" Watson said.

"What else can you tell us?" Joplin asked.

"Just a summary," Watson replied. "This coming battle in those Afghan hills is going to determine the fate of Operation Persian Empire. If the Iranians are stopped there, they'll be completely stymied."

Joplin's thoughts turned to Lieutenant Bill Brannigan and his men. "And that will be up to a single SEAL detachment?"

"A single *reinforced* SEAL detachment," Watson said. "Additional personnel will be assigned to them."

Turnbull emitted a low whistle. "I don't care how many reinforcements they get. Those guys are in for the fight of their lives."

CHAPTER 23

IRANIAN SFOB
IRANIAN-AFGHANISTAN BORDER

THE newly organized unit had been officially designated as Zur Jamle Entegham—Strike Force Vengeance—and was referred to by its Farsi acronym of Zaheya. It numbered four officers, who commanded sixty noncommissioned officers and enlisted men, for a total strength of sixty-four. Although it was extremely short of being brigade size, the overall commander was Brigadier Shahruz Khohollah. An officer of his rank had been chosen to lead the Zaheya not because of its size, but because of the far-reaching consequences of the mission assigned it.

Neither the civilians in the government nor the General Staff of the Iranian Army wanted to create an attention-grabbing incident along the Afghanistan border. At this point, political and diplomatic events that they hoped were only temporary limited their grandiose scheme for the Middle East. Thus, an all-out war of fully equipped division-size units would do more to impede those ambitions than advance them.

Such a massive campaign would include the thundering presence of armor and heavy artillery, and would bring about a massive international response.

Thus, Brigadier Khohollah suggested that a smaller group of elite troops could make very effective probing attacks into Afghanistan to eventually gain control over a large isolated area in the mountains. These tactics would not attract undue attention, and the territory gained would provide a central base of operations from which a larger invasion could be launched in the future.

The Zaheya consisted of Arsalaan Sikes Pasha's al-Askerin-Zaubi's twenty Arabs, Captain Naser Khadid's handpicked twenty Iranian Special Forces troopers, and a fire-support element under the direct command of Brigadier Khohollah. He had chosen his newly appointed adjutant, Captain Jamshid Komard, as the actual field commander of the heavy-weapons organization. They were set up for rapid deployment to specific areas when needed. The brigadier had chosen two types of support weapons that would be excellent in the confinement of mountain warfare. They were German MG-3 7.62-millimeter machine guns and a particularly nasty Spanish grenade launcher designated the LAG-40. This crew-served, bipod-mounted weapon was belt-fed from detachable twenty-four- or thirty-two-round ammo boxes that could be fed into the breech from either side. It fired the 40-millimeter projectiles at a rate of 215 rounds a minute with a maximum range of 1500 meters, offering a potential of small but deadly detonations of HE that could be concentrated in a small area or spread across a space up to 100 meters wide. This could be accomplished by well-trained crews employing accurately timed two- and three-second pulls on the trigger.

Khohollah could also expect infusions of Arab insurgents from time to time. These would be graduates of the Iranian Special Forces Training Center set up to prepare the mujahideen for unconventional warfare. After the tough eight-week course, the volunteers were destined to be funneled into Sikes Pasha's unit. The Brit enjoyed the very real possibility that he might end up with a hundred or so fully equipped and well-trained assault riflemen under his direct command.

But for the time being, both Sikes Pasha and Captain Naser Khadid's commands were divided into small combat teams of riflemen armed with French FA-MAS 5.56-millimeter rifles. These weapons had selective firing, including burst capabilities, and their worth had already been proven countless times by French armed forces—particularly the Foreign Legion—in operations as widespread as Lebanon and Bosnia. All twenty of the Iranian SF personnel were graduates of the Iranian Army's tough twelve-week mountain survival and combat course, and were capable of splitting up and grouping as the tactical situation dictated.

However, the most colorful unit in the Iranian force was Sikes Pasha's Arabs, the al-Askerin-Zaubi. They had been issued the latest Iranian camouflage uniforms that were patterned after the type used by the Russian Army. Sikes Pasha had his corporals and sergeants retain their British chevrons, although he wore the device of an Iranian major. Also, Warrant Officer Shafaqat had changed the crown insignia of the British for the single bar of an *ostvar*, the Iranian equivalent of his rank. Each member of the unit was back in his keffiyeh headdress with the *akal* to hold it in place. Everyone, from Brigadier Shahruz Khohollah down to the lowest-ranking rifleman in Khadid's rifle teams, now referred to the egotistical Brit as Sikes Pasha. A special order from the Iranian High Command mandated the courtesy. It was not as much to commend Sikes as it was to attract additional Shiite Arabs to the cause.

The Iranian government spared no expense for this elite fighting force. Every officer and man was supplied with modern night-vision capabilities, communications that included LASH headsets, the latest in field rations, first-aid kits, and comfort items such as ponchos and small camp stoves.

The fortified position occupied by the Zaheya along the Afghan border had been constructed a year and a half before by Iranian Army personnel under the supervision of Russian military engineers. They and their construction equipment and machines had been flown in undetected by a small fleet of Mi-10 flying crane helicopters at a time when the area was largely ignored. A high mountain field with an empty flat terrain offered a perfect landing spot.

The Russian job bosses took advantage of a series of caves in the area, connecting them with deep trenches and well-fortified fighting positions that faced eastward toward Afghanistan. Wells were also sunk to bring up pure cold artesian water. No doubt, any veterans of the Soviet-Afghan War among the supervisors were delighted to be constructing a project that had the fantastic potential of contributing to a future defeat of the Afghan fighters who had made their lives so miserable back in the 1980s.

The Iranian officers coordinating the effort emphasized the need for protection against aerial attack since the chance of Western air forces being engaged against the site was almost a certainty. The Russians complied by reinforcing the fortifications with tiers of heavy logs and packed earth. The caves required no additional construction or alterations.

1 JUNE
0700 HOURS

BRIGADIER Shahruz Khohollah stood in front of his assembled force in the field that once served construction helicopters. To his left, he saw Sikes Pasha and his twenty-man force of al-Askerin-Zaubi. The Storm Troopers looked magnificent and nearly exotic with their keffiyehs as they stood at a strict position of attention. They seemed like a unit from the old British colonial days when white officers, often from working-class backgrounds, turned to the dangers and uncertainties of isolated areas in Queen Victoria's far-flung empire as their only chance for military fame and glory. The old tradition was now being carried out by Archibald Sikes, an English lad from working-class Manchester.

The middle formation of the brigadier's force was made up of Captain Naser Khadid and the twenty Iranian Special Forces troopers. They had adopted the name Shiraane Saltanat: the Imperial Lions. The Shiraane—as they were referred to within the Zaheya—were clad in camouflage battle dress, sporting the black berets of Special Forces. These were modern empire-builders, drawn into an impending do-or-die war by an overly ambitious government.

And over to the brigadier's right was the fire-support group led by Captain Jamshid Komard. They were dressed in the same uniforms as the Special Forces, except their headgear consisted of small black turbans styled in the manner of those widely worn in northern Iran. This detachment was divided into three two-man crews for the LAG-40 grenade launchers and seven two-man crews for the MG-3 machine guns. These were pragmatic, determined men who had taken no special name for themselves. It was enough knowing that the riflemen would depend on them for covering fire to accomplish assigned missions whether attacking or defending.

Now Brigadier Khohollah called them to stand at ease. "Soldiers!" he addressed them. "You have been brought here as a vanguard. This is a great honor for a small fighting group such as us. There are great plans that will result in our nation and religion avenging the past injustices and encroachments of the West. These are humiliations that have been forced on us for over ninety years. The people of the Middle East will revere you, the people of Europe and America will fear you, and Allah will reward you."

He had chosen his words carefully to placate Sikes Pasha's men. They would be needed, like all their brethren, to advance Iran's ambitions. Later, when that area of the globe was completely dominated by Iranians, the Arabs' native countries would be ruled by military governors sent out from Tehran. This was the colonial modus operandi of the ancient Persian Empire.

Now Khohollah began pacing up and down as he continued. "There have been setbacks, as we all know. But such unfortunate instances were expected, and we do not reel from these small defeats. The big attack will begin from here and by you. Are you ready?"

Cries of "*Bale, Satrip*" and "*Aiwa, Zaim*" came from the Zaheya troops as they made affirmative replies in Farsi and Arabic.

"Detachment commanders!" Khohollah bellowed. "Take

charge of your commands and move them into their fighting positions."

Sikes Pasha, Captain Khadid, and Captain Komard called their separate units to attention, then faced them to the west to begin marching to what was to become their front lines.

CORONADO, CALIFORNIA
3 JUNE
1400 HOURS

PENNY Brubaker came downstairs from the expansive two-story home she had leased as a residence for her and her cousin Stephanie and hubby Harrington Gilwright during the wait for Chad Murchison's return. They had one full-time maid for cooking, laundry, and light housekeeping, and an agreement with a maid service that sent over a team of women to clean the large house a couple of times a week. The luxury domicile was located in a gated community on the east side of Coronado looking out over San Diego Bay.

Penny walked across the dining area and out onto the patio, where Stephanie and Harrington sat at the canopied table. When Penny joined them, she could see that Harrington was already well into his cups. A shaker of martinis was by his elbow, along with a bowl of olives already spitted on picks for the many drinks he planned on consuming. He held the long-stemmed glass in his hands, sipping lightly from it. Penny sat down, frowning at her cousin's husband. "It must be nice to have a hobby."

Harrington raised the glass. "It does make the time go by faster. As a matter of fact, Penny darling, I think it's turned out that I enjoy California better than you or Stephie."

Stephie snorted. "I'm surprised you remember we're in California. You've been potted every day since we got out here."

"I can't wait for winter," Harrington said. "They tell me it doesn't snow in Southern California. It's quite warm, actually, even in January and February."

"You haven't been out of the house more than three or four

times," Penny said. "Who did you meet that told you they have mild winters?"

"Mercedes told me," he said, referring to their full-time Mexican maid.

"Speaking of Mercedes, where is she?" Penny asked. "I want a sandwich."

Harrington replied, "She went on a liquor store run for me."

"Why don't you give her your liquor wants on regular shopping days?" Stephie asked. "They sell the stuff in the grocery stores here. That way, she wouldn't have to go out three or four times a week. The poor girl could pick up your weekly liquor needs in one trip."

"I don't like to plan ahead," Harrington said. "And variety is the lice of spife. Ha! I mean, spice of life."

"God!" Penny exclaimed. "Whatever she buys for you will have the same effect. You'll get drunk on your ass. What difference does it make what you drink? Just tell her to pick up a half-dozen bottles each of vodka and vermouth."

Harrington took another sip of his martini, then pulled out the pick and stripped an olive off between his teeth. "I shall require much more vodka than vermouth, darling Penny."

"You'll be dead before you're thirty-five," Stephie said.

"And you'll be the rich Widow Gilwright," Harrington responded. "Think of all the money you'll have."

"I can't wait," Stephie said, grinning at Penny.

"But even if I die at thirty-five, I'll still live longer than Chad," Harrington said. "If he has a death wish, he should find a more pleasant way of getting killed than in some horrible war somewhere. Why pick such an uncomfortable and possibly painful way to leave this mortal coil, as Shakespeare referred to this miserable world? There is an abundance of alcohol and drugs to do the job in a nice, peaceful, civilized manner."

"You wouldn't understand," Penny said, "so I'm not going to even discuss Chad with you."

"I'm having a little trouble understanding him too," Stephie said.

Harrington was curious. "Now what could Chad Murchison have done that has confused and disturbed you so?"

"The other day Penny and I were out at the beach," Stephie said. "We saw a mob of military guys running around in groups. Each bunch was holding a big rubber boat over their heads. God! They must have weighed a ton!"

Harrington raised his eyebrows. "How odd!"

Penny interjected, "And they were just about exhausted. They would run into the surf, jump in the boat, and row out. Then turn around and come back. They must have done it a dozen times. All this time, some other guys were yelling very angrily at them. Each time those miserable boaters returned to the beach, the ones who must have broken some rule or something had to do push-ups."

"And the water is cold here!" Stephie exclaimed. "They were wearing jackets and pants and boots, but the poor guys were shivering like a blizzard was blowing. They looked like they were about to die!"

"I'm about to die from just hearing about it," Harrington said with a smirk. "Who were they? A bunch of apes from the San Diego Zoo?"

"We asked a couple of women who were next to us on the beach," Penny said. "They told us those guys were volunteers for the SEALs. That was part of their training."

"God!" Stephie exclaimed. "It really blew my mind when I thought of Chad doing that."

"One of the women told us her husband had been in SEAL training but quit," Penny said. "She said he was in the middle of something they called Hell Week. Evidently, those guys do all sorts of hard training with very little sleep and no mercy shown to them. She said her husband just decided it wasn't worth it. Evidently, most of the guys volunteering for the SEALs don't make the grade."

Harrington was silent for a moment before speaking again. "I'm having a problem picturing skinny Chadwick Murchison not only going through such torment, but actually successfully completing the awful program."

"He's not skinny anymore, Harrington," Penny said. "Whatever the SEALs did to him was beneficial. I mean, like, spiritually as much as physically."

Harrington drained the glass, then refilled it from the shaker.

"And you want to marry him? They must have turned him into an animal!"

"He is," Penny said with a smile. "A *hunky* animal!"

"Yeah!" Stephie exclaimed. "Show me his picture again, Penny!"

"I wish I had known that was what it took to win your heart, Penny dearest," Harrington said, miffed by his wife's admiring remarks about Chad. "I would have become a SEAL myself. It would have been worth the pain and agony to have your heart as Chad has it."

"I don't think you appreciate what we've just told you, Harrington," Stephie said. "You would have lasted about a minute and a half out there."

"If that long," Penny added. "You should have seen those guys."

Harrington looked around. "How long is it going to take Mercedes to fetch my liquor?"

UNREO CAMP
WEST-CENTRAL AFGHANISTAN

DR. Pierre Bouchier and his relief and education organization were back in business. After going to Kabul, they went through a complete refitting and received a half-dozen new personnel to replace those who had departed. With the reorganization taken care of, the UNREO team had been dispatched to the high desert to set up a camp to serve a new set of Pashtuns.

These people were from the Gharawdara Highlands stronghold. After the defeat suffered by the Iranian SF and smugglers, the Pashtun leader Yama Orakzai could see the handwriting on the wall. Whoever kicked the Iranians' arses would soon be kicking his. Orakzai's big plan for establishing a Pashtun nation in western Afghanistan was not going to happen anytime soon. And if he kept up alliances with a bunch of losers like the Iranians, his dreams of independence would be squashed forever. After kicking out Sikes Pasha, Captain Naser Khadid, and the Arabs, Orakzai turned to a Pashtun custom known as *nanwatai*.

This is an act of abject submission to a conquering enemy. The loser approaches the victor in unreserved humility, begging for forgiveness and mercy. The vanquisher is expected to be more than merciful because of this humble act; he is expected to be nothing short of magnanimous, restoring the loser's dignity and making no attempts to punish or debase him.

It was in the spirit of *nanwatai* that Yama Orakzai sent out peace feelers to the Afghan authorities. He wanted to take his people back to their original home site and reestablish their former lives.

The government in Kabul was relieved to react in accordance with the gesture, not so much in kindness as happiness at having this thorn in their sides removed under amicable and honorable circumstances. However, they bent the basic rules of *nanwatai* a bit by insisting that Orakzai make his clan an open society. He must accept the aid and teachings of UNREO, cooperate with them, and see that his people obtained all the advantages of what the foreigners had to offer. The Pashtun leader agreed to the terms with a great show of gratitude. He was even willing to turn over all heavy weaponry to the local army commander. Some rusty Soviet Dashika machine guns and 82-millimeter mortars were presented to the soldiers. This act was even filmed for local TV consumption to set an example for other warlords. Of course, the authorities were unaware of a vast arsenal hidden deep within the weatherproof caves of the former stronghold.

The government agent who monitored Orakzai's "acquiescence"—the word "surrender" was never used—was a veteran of relations with warlords. His name was Zaid Aburrani, and he was well known by Brannigan's Brigands. It was Aburrani who oversaw the taming of the former powerful warlords Ayuub Durtami and Hassan Khamami after the SEALs had dealt them a proverbial "ass-kicking" on their first mission. Now he was having an easier time of it.

Orakzai was very happy to deal with Aburrani, whom he knew very well. They had been involved in the opium poppy industry for several years before Orakzai took his people to the Gharawdara Highlands. Now that the Pashtun mujahideen would cease their fighting activities and get back to farming, they would return to poppy cultivation up in the hidden meadows of the mountains above their village. Zaid Aburrani would see that they were not molested and would have easy access to the old smugglers, who had now taken back the opium trail the Iranians could no longer use.

It was like that old song with the refrain: *Boy does the money come in!*

**THE WHITE HOUSE
THE OVAL OFFICE
WASHINGTON, D.C.
5 JUNE
1015 HOURS**

A rapping at the door caught the President's attention. He looked up from the press briefing he was preparing and called out, "Come in."

Arlene Entienne entered the office. She was elegant and beautiful as always, but it was obvious she was tired. "Good morning, Mr. President."

"Hello, Arlene," he replied to the greeting. "I heard you came in at four A.M. today."

"Yes, sir," she replied. "I received a call from Edgar Watson at the CIA a little after three. Operation Persian Empire has kicked up into high gear."

The President got up and walked over to the side of the room where a coffeepot was plugged in. He poured a cup of the brew, then brought it over to Entienne. "Here, Arlene. You need this."

"I sure do!"

"Did we hear from Aladdin again?" the President asked, sitting back down.

"Edgar said it was a quick transmission," Entienne answered. "Evidently, he is in a particularly dangerous area. At any rate, he informed us that a compact group of Iranians and Arabs are occupying a fortified area in the far west of the Gharawdara Highlands. When the time is right, they'll make their move. Their objective, of course, is to gain control of the Gharawdara Highlands in western Afghanistan."

"A 'compact' group, hey?" the President remarked. "They evidently don't want to make a big fuss. That's good. We don't want to either."

"Mr. President," Entienne said, "you gave me authorization to put your special executive order into effect. I did so at a little past five this morning."

"Alright," he said. "It's amazing when one considers the fact that this sensitive international crisis is going to be settled by dozens rather than thousands of troops."

"It's a mind-boggler, alright," Entienne stated.

"And now our own so-called compact group will answer the challenge. They will go into harm's way." The President sighed. "The worst part of this job is having to put the lives of our finest young people at risk." He stood up and walked to the window, gazing out pensively. "I cannot describe how much it distresses me."

Entienne got to her feet and went over to him, standing close to the Chief Executive. "Would it make you feel better if I reminded you they were all volunteers?"

"Not really."

EPILOGUE

TWENTY-THREE men arrived on the latest flight from Kuwait to be added to the roster of Brannigan's Brigands. However, one was not exactly a reinforcement. Petty Officer Second Class Arnie Bernardi was a Brigand reporting back from Kuwait, where he had been TDy on a training mission. Bernardi's initial joy at being reunited with his old outfit was dashed when he learned of Milly Mills' death. His mood spiraled rapidly down as he experienced a combination of sadness and guilt at not being with the detachment during the battles out on the desert. He truly felt he had let his buddies down, and nothing they said eased his feelings of regret.

Bernardi's fellow passengers had been dispatched into the OA for this one specific operation, of which they knew absolutely nothing. They would have been surprised to learn that their new commander was as uninformed as they. This new mission had evolved out of an earlier one titled Operation

Rolling Thunder, and was renamed Operation Battleline by the powers-that-be who ran Special Operations in the Middle East. The Skipper found it irritating to be moved laterally from one tactical situation to another without feeling the first had been satisfactorily wrapped up as an undeniable victory. The ever verbose Bruno Puglisi felt the same, and was not bashful about expressing his disenchantment: "The whole thing is too fucking half-ass to suit me," he stated candidly and loudly. "It's like changing opponents at halftime in a football game."

The C-130 that brought the personnel to Shelor was one of a quartet that had been arriving since the day before. The earlier trio was crammed with ammunition, equipment, rations, and other war-making material. Randy Tooley had been going crazy coordinating unloading, storing, quartering transit personnel, and all the other headaches that go with the preparatory activities for a campaign in the mountains.

Randy's basic attitudes remained unchanged; the senior airman still found it inconvenient to wear a uniform, salute, use the title "sir" or "ma'am" when speaking to commissioned officers, or observe any military protocol whatsoever. Because of this new set of circumstances that had evolved into a problematic turmoil, Colonel Watkins, the base commander, became even more tolerant of Randy's unconventional behavior. The kid was fast, efficient, keeping the operations of the facility going along smoothly and in a timely manner through his totally dedicated efforts. Packing him off to the stockade for insubordination would not only accomplish nothing in reforming the young guy, but would create a loss to the Air Force during his incarceration. Things ground to a standstill badly enough when Randy became upset by a dressing-down from some chickenshit NCO or officer and went off by himself to sulk for a day or two. There was an unofficial standing order that he was never to be carried AWOL on base personnel reports.

Randy continued to use the misappropriated desert patrol vehicle that a grateful Lieutenant Brannigan had given him for past services rendered. The young airman, knowing well when guile and subterfuge were necessary, immediately had it

painted Air Force blue and stenciled with some phony registration numbers across the hood. He happily zipped around in
the purloined conveyance as he tended to his duties.

The new SEAL arrivals, after disembarking from the
C-130, were ushered quickly to the hangar Brannigan's Brigands used as a headquarters, living quarters, and warehouse.
The newcomers found bunks and mattresses waiting for them,
but no blankets or sheets. That meant they would be slumber-
ing in sleeping bags and/or poncho liners. Senior Chief Petty
Officer Buford Dawkins had chow passes for them through the
efforts of Randy Tooley, which meant the newcomers could
get hot food in the base mess hall rather than have to consume
MREs in the hangar. All the facilities at Shelor Field were
open to them: BX, base theater, NCO and enlisted men's clubs,
and the swimming pool. The only downside to their stay was
being confined to the base. For reasons of the tightest security,
no one was permitted to wander off the Air Force property unless on official duty.

As soon as things were down to a dull roar, the senior chief
called a formation. He and Chief Petty Officer Matt Gunnarson formed up the thirty-six enlisted men for a roll call to
make sure that everyone assigned to Operation Battleline was
all present and accounted for. The two chiefs were relieved to
find that each man listed on either the manifests from the aircraft or the original roster for Operation Rolling Thunder was
exactly where he was supposed to be. Nobody was AWOL,
lost, or wandering aimlessly in a haze of ignorance and uncer-
tainty. The detachment, now with three officers and two chief
petty officers, numbered a grand total of forty-one romping,
stomping Navy SEALs who were available for the coming
combat.

While the enlisted men were being checked in after the
arrival of the last C-130, a new officer, Ensign Orlando Taylor,
went inside the hangar to find the detachment officers. Brannigan and Lieutenant Junior Grade Jim Cruiser were in the corner
cubicle used as a headquarters of sorts, going over the roster
and beginning to organize the assault sections for the coming
operation. Ensign Taylor dropped his gear by the door and
knocked. The Skipper looked up and noted the somber young

African-American. "You must be our newly assigned Ensign Taylor. Come in."

Taylor stepped inside the office and rendered a faultless salute. "Sir! Ensign Taylor reporting to the commanding officer as ordered."

"Welcome, Taylor," Brannigan said, offering his hand. "This is Lieutenant (JG) Jim Cruiser. Take a seat and join the party."

"Thank you, sir," Taylor said. He took a chair as invited, sitting stiffly and formally.

Cruiser gave him a friendly smile. "How was the trip over?"

"Everything moved on schedule," Taylor said. "I am anxious get into the program. When will I be able to meet my men?"

"Right now, Ensign," Brannigan said, "you don't have any men. Jim and I have been mulling over how to reorganize the detachment for the new operation. We went from a total strength of eighteen men to forty-one. Besides the increase in personnel, we also have some added weaponry. All that has to be married together into an effective fighting team. I know that sounds melodramatic, but it's fact." He pushed the rosters and other papers aside. "Well, now, tell us a little about yourself."

"Sir," Taylor said. "I received my commission through NROTC at college. I attended a mostly African-American institution of learning in Georgia. I have only recently completed BUD/S, and this is my first assignment."

Cruiser smiled. "Well, I guess you really don't have too much to tell us."

"No, sir," Taylor said. "But I look forward to this auspicious beginning of my Naval career. Although I hold a reserve commission, I plan to make a career of the U.S. Navy."

"Fine," Brannigan said, reaching back for his papers. "I've got a couple of ideas to discuss. Jump in any time you feel froggy."

"Yes, sir," Taylor said. "Thank you, sir."

"Okay," Brannigan said. "The first thing I want to do is organize a patrol team."

"I take it you'll start with the Odd Couple," Cruiser said. "And don't forget Redhawk. He's a natural."

"Right. And I think I'll put Connie Concord in charge of it.

He's a first class and about ready for chief. It's time to start grooming him, don't you think?"

"Yes, sir," Cruiser said. "And I noted that there's a Petty Officer Matsuno on the roster. I know him. He'd make a good addition."

Brannigan wrote down some notes. "Done! And I'll leave Gomez and Bradley in headquarters with me." He sank back into thought for a moment. "Another thought has just this instant occurred to me. This coming operation will be perfect for a sniper team."

"Puglisi and Miskoski," Cruiser said. "That goes without a second thought."

"It shall be done, sayeth the gods of war," Brannigan said, writing down their names. "Okay. I can see we'll be able to have three assault sections with two fire teams each."

"Don't forget a SAW gunner for each one," Cruiser urged him.

"Right, Jim. You take the First Section," he said, writing down the assignment. He glanced over at Taylor. "The Second Section is yours, Ensign."

"Aye, sir," the young man said.

"And, of course, the Third will be honchoed by the intrepid Senior Chief Petty Officer Buford Dawkins, the pride of Alabama."

"You have some guys left over," Cruiser pointed out.

"It's all part of my cunning master plan," the Skipper said with a wink. "That will be our support section of machine guns. Seven-point-six-twos, as a matter of fact. I'll let Chief Gunnarson run that particular show." He gave Taylor another look. "Any suggestions, Ensign?"

"Negative, sir."

"Have you been in combat before, Ensign?" Cruiser asked.

"Negative, sir."

"In that case, I have some advice for you," Brannigan said. "You'll be the leader of an assault section, understand? You *are* the commander, but you listen to the advice of the senior petty officers. Developing that habit will be invaluable to you not only in the beginning of your career, but even after you're a salty old dog yourself."

"Yes, sir."

When Brannigan slid the diagram of the organization over to Cruiser, the impassive Ensign Orlando Taylor gazed steadily at the two veteran officers. The one thing he wanted to conceal from them was his fear; not the fear of death or injury, but the fear of failure. He had been raised in a family headed by a capable, ambitious father. The outcome of this paternal supervision was a fierce rivalry among the four Taylor brothers, who had been taught that anything short of success was not an option.

Cruiser handed the quickly sketched manning chart to Brannigan. "I'd say it's good to go."

"Fine," the Skipper said. "So let's put it into reality, shall we, gentlemen?"

"Lead on, sir," Cruiser said.

The three officers got up to go outside. Taylor followed the two seniors, his apprehension growing.

GLOSSARY

2IC: Second in Command
2-Shop: Intelligence Section of the staff
3-Shop: Operations and Training Section of the staff
4-Shop: Logistics Section of the staff
AA: Anti-Aircraft
AAR: After-Action Report
ACV: Air Cushion Vehicle (hovercraft)
AFSOC: Air Force Special Operations Command
AGL: Above Ground Level
AKA: Also Known As
Angel: A thousand feet above ground level, i.e., Angels Two is two thousand feet.
APC: Armored Personnel Carrier
ARG: Amphibious Ready Group
AS-50: .50 caliber, semiautomatic sniper rifle with scope
ASAP: As Soon As Possible
ASL: Above Sea Level
AT-4: Antiarmor rocket launchers
Attack Board (also Compass Board): A board with a compass, watch, and depth gauge used by subsurface swimmers

AT: Anti-Tank

ATV: All-Terrain Vehicle

AWOL: Away Without Leave, i.e., absent from one's unit without permission. AKA French leave.

BBC: British Broadcasting Corporation

BOQ: Bachelor Officers' Quarters

Briefback: A briefing given to staff by a SEAL platoon regarding their assigned mission. This must be approved before it is implemented.

BDU: Battle Dress Uniform

BUD/S: Basic Underwater Demolition SEAL training course

BX: Base Exchange, a military store with good prices for service people. AKA **PX** in the Army, for Post Exchange.

C4: Plastic explosive

CAR-15: Compact model of the M-16 rifle

CATF: Commander, Amphibious Task Force

CDC: Combat Direction Center aboard a ship

Chickenshit: An adjective that describes a person or a situation as being particularly draconian, overly strict, unfair, or malicious

CHP: California Highway Patrol

CLU: Command Launch Unit for the Javelin AT missile

CNO: Chief of Naval Operations

CO: Commanding Officer

Cover: Hat, headgear

CP: Command Post

CPU: Computer Processing Unit

CPX: Command Post Exercise

CRRC: Combat Rubber Raiding Craft

CRT: Cathode Ray Tube

CS: Tear gas

CSAR: Combat Search and Rescue

CVBG: Carrier Battle Group

Dashika: Slang name for the Soviet DShK 12.7-millimeter heavy machine gun

DDG: Guided Missile Destroyer

DEA: Drug Enforcement Agency

DPV: Desert Patrol Vehicle

Det Cord: Detonating Cord

DJMS: Defense Joint Military Pay System

Draeger Mk V: Underwater air supply equipment

DZ: Drop Zone

E&E: Escape and Evasion

EPW: Enemy Prisoner of War

ER: Emergency Room (hospital)

ESP: Extra-Sensory Perception

ETS: End of Term of Service

FLIR: Forward-Looking Infrared Radar

Four-Shop: Logistics Section of the staff

French Leave: See AWOL

FRH: Flameless Ration Heater

FTX: Field Training Exercise

G-3: The training and operations staff section of a unit commanded by a general officer

GPS: Global Positioning System

Gunny: Marine Corps slang for the rank of Gunnery Sergeant E-7

H&K MP-5: Heckler & Koch MP-5 submachine gun

HAHO: High-Altitude, High-Opening parachute jump

HALO: High-Altitude, Low-Opening parachute jump

HE: High Explosive

Head: Navy and Marine Corps term for toilet; called a latrine in the Army

HEAT: High Explosive Anti-Tank

Hell Week: The fifth week of BUD/S that is five-plus days of continuous activity and training with little or no sleep

Hors de combat: Out of the battle (expression in French)

HSB: High-Speed Boat

Immediate Action: A quick, sometimes temporary, fix to a mechanical problem

IR: Infra-Red

Island: The superstructure of an aircraft carrier or assault ship

JSOC: Joint Special Operation Command

K-Bar: A brand of knives manufactured for military and camping purposes

KD Range: Known-Distance weapons-firing Range

KIA: Killed In Action

Keffiyeh: Arab headdress (what Yasser Arafat wore)

KISS: Keep It Simple, Stupid—or more politely, Keep It Simple, Sweetheart

LBE: Load-Bearing Equipment

LSSC: Light SEAL Support Craft

Light Sticks: Flexible plastic tubes that illuminate

Limpet Mine: An explosive mine that is attached to the hulls of vessels

Locked Heels: When a serviceman is getting a severe vocal reprimand, it is said he is having his "heels locked," i.e., standing at attention while someone is bellowing in his face.

LSO: Landing Signal Officer

LZ: Landing Zone

M-18 Claymore Mine: A mine fired electrically with a blasting cap

M-60 E3: A compact model of the M-60 machine gun

M-67: An antipersonnel grenade

M-203: A single-shot 40-millimeter grenade launcher

MATC: A fast river support craft

MCPO: Master Chief Petty Officer

Medevac: Medical Evacuation

MI-5: United Kingdom Security Agency

Mk 138 Satchel Charge: Canvas container filled with explosive

Mossad: Israeli Intelligence Agency (ha-Mossad le-Modiin ule-Tafkidim Meyuhadim—Institute for Intelligence and Special Tasks)

MRE: Meal, Ready to Eat

MSSC: Medium SEAL Support Craft

Murphy's Law: An assumption that if something can go wrong, it most certainly will

N2: Intelligence Staff

N3: Operations Staff

NAS: Naval Air Station

NAVSPECWAR: Naval Special Warfare

NCO: Noncommissioned Officers, i.e., corporals and sergeants

NCP: Navy College Program

NFL: National Football League

NROTC: Naval Reserve Officer Training Corps

NVG: Night-Vision Goggles

NVS: Night-Vision Sight

OA: Operational Area

OCONUS: Outside the Continental United States

OCS: Officers Candidate School

OER: Officer's Efficiency Report

OP: Observation Post

OPLAN: Operations Plan. This is the preliminary form of an OPORD.

OPORD: Operations Order. This is the directive derived from the OPLAN of how an operation is to be carried out. It's pretty much etched in stone.

PBL: Patrol Boat, Light

PC: Patrol Coastal vessel

PDQ: Pretty Damn Quick

PLF: Parachute Landing Fall

PM: Preventive Maintenance

PMC: Private Military Company. These are businesses that supply bodyguards, security personnel, and mercenary civilian fighting men to persons or organizations wanting to hire them.

PO: Petty Officer (e.g., PO1C is Petty Officer First Class)

POV: Privately Owned Vehicle

P.P.P.P.: Piss-Poor Prior Planning

PT: Physical Training

Puhtee: An Afghan rolled cap stocking cap that can be worn in many ways

RHIP: Rank Has Its Privileges

RIB: Rigid Inflatable Boat

RIO: Radar Intercept Officer

RPG: Rocket-Propelled Grenade

RPM: Revolutions Per Minute

RTO: Radio Telephone Operator

Run-flat tires: Solid-rubber inserts that allow the vehicle to run even when the tires have been punctured

SAS: Special Air Services—an extremely deadly and super-efficient special operations unit of the British Army

SAW: Squad Automatic Weapon—M-249 5.56-millimeter magazine or clip-fed machine gun

SCPO: Senior Chief Petty Officer

SDV: Seal Delivery Vehicle

SERE: Survival, Escape, Resistance, and Evasion

SF: Special Forces

SFOB: Special Forces Operational Base

Shiites: A branch of Islam; in serious conflict with the Sunnis

SITREP: Situation Report

SNAFU: Situation Normal, All Fucked Up

Snap-to: The act of quickly and sharply assuming the position of attention with chin up, shoulders back, thumbs along the seams of the trousers, and heels locked with toes at a 45-degree angle

SOCOM: Special Operations Command

SOF: Special Operations Force

SOI: Signal Operating Instructions

SOLS: Special Operations Liaison Staff

SOP: Standard Operating Procedures

SPECOPS: Special Operations

Special Boat Squadrons: Units that participate in SEAL missions

SPECWARCOM: Special Warfare Command

Sunnis: A branch of Islam; in serious conflict with the Shiites

T-10 Parachute: Basic static-line-activated personnel parachute of the United States Armed Forces. Primarily designed for mass tactical parachute jumps.

Taliban: Militant, anti-West Muslims with extreme religious views; in serious conflict with Shiites

TDy: Temporary Duty

Three-Shop: Operations and Training Section of the staff

TOA: Table of Allowances

Two-Shop: Intelligence Section of the staff

U.K.: The United Kingdom (England, Wales, Scotland, and Northern Ireland)

UN: United Nations

Unass: To jump out of or off something

UNREO: United Nations Relief and Education Organization

USAF: United States Air Force

USASFC: United States Army Special Forces Command

USSR: Union of Soviet Social Republics—Russia before the fall of Communism

VTOL: Vertical Take-Off and Landing

Watch Bill: A list of personnel and stations for the watch

Waypoint: A location programmed into navigational instrumentation that directs aircraft, vehicles, and/or vessels to a specific spot on the planet

Whaler Boat: Small craft loosely based on the types of boats used in whaling. They are generally carried aboard naval and merchant vessels and are diesel-powered.

WIA: Wounded in Action

WMD: Weapons of Mass Destruction: nuclear, biological, etc.